I0582080

The Snake Handler's Wife

A Vega & Middleton Novel

Sue Hinkin

Literary Wanderlust | Denver, Colorado

The Snake Handler's Wife is a work of fiction. Names, characters, places and incidents are either the product of the author's imagination or are used fictitiously, and any resemblance to actual persons, living or dead, business establishments, event or locales is entirely coincidental.

Copyright © 2025 by Sue Hinkin

All rights reserved. No part of this publication may be reproduced, distributed, stored in a retrieval system, or transmitted in any form or by any means, including photocopying, recording, or other electronic or mechanical methods, without the prior written permission of the publisher, except in the case of brief quotations embodied in critical reviews and certain other noncommercial uses permitted by copyright law.

Published in the United States by Literary Wanderlust LLC, Denver, Colorado. www.LiteraryWanderlust.com

ISBN print: 978-1-956615-54-8
ISBN digital: 978-1-956615-55-5

Other Books by Sue Hinkin

Deadly Focus
Low Country Blood
The Burn Patient
The Mermaid Broker
The Rx For Murder

Dedication

As always, to my mom, the poet, and my dad, the preacher.

Mark 16:18

"They will pick up serpents with their hands, and if they drink the deadly poison, it will not hurt them..."

CHAPTER ONE

I t was beginning.

The Man walked stealthily through the pre-dawn darkness. A single yard light cast tepid shadows along the ranch's outbuildings. The scent of horse flesh and creek willow filled his nostrils, soothing a hint of nervous anticipation as he entered the barn.

The faint rattling sound emanating from the basket he carried calmed him further.

The first step in this divine plan came upon him in a holy vision. Directed by God, like the Israelites in Israel, he would own this land and inhabit it for His glory.

Approaching the stall, the gravel beneath his boots crunched like soft tissue paper. The Paint horse nickered. The Man stroked the equine neck and spoke reassuring words as he slipped inside the enclosure. The brown and white stallion watched him carefully, stomped once, but showed little sign of concern.

The Man opened the basket in the far corner of the stall and watched the serpent slither from its confines into the straw. The rattle's ominous susurration accelerated.

The Man whispered to the horse, "As in the Book of Genesis, *the serpent shall be in your path and bite your heel so the rider will fall...*"

He kissed the animal's warm cheek, reflecting on serpents in the Garden before leaving the barn. The horse snorted and shook his head. *Don't do this*, he seemed to say, but it was prophesied.

Shutting the stall door, The Man further reflected on the next step toward fulfillment of his sacred ambition. It was in the hands of an unsure blonde girl who loved him with an addict's compulsion. The snakes etched on his body stirred. He had to have her, now.

The Man disappeared into the darkness just as the sky began to lighten in the East.

—

Pulling at a loose strand of her dark, wavy hair in anticipation, Lucy Vega gazed over her laptop screen to the slate gray Pacific less than a mile away. The annual "June Gloom" had cast its dreary marine pale across the landscape. She was waiting to Zoom chat with Michael Burleson, her lover, life partner, and father to their four-year-old son, Henry. Michael was a network war correspondent for TV news who almost lost everything from the curse of alcohol abuse. With Lucy's support, he was back on track, five years sober.

The zoom link kicked in and he was on the screen. Eyes like sea glass, messy brown curls, he wore his usual utilitarian black T-shirt. A smile warmed her heart.

"Hey, beautiful," he said, rubbing his neck. "I miss you."

"Then get that cute butt of yours out here." After two years in New York, Lucy was thrilled at the thought of being together as a family this week at her ranch in the mountains above Malibu, where she'd grown up after her parents and younger brother died in a car accident. The last several promises

Michael had made to join her and Henry at this place, her spiritual home on Earth, he hadn't kept. But this time it would be different.

She continued, ignoring niggles of fear and disappointment. "Our son has a long list of to-dos with daddy. Starts with the Santa Barbara Zoo and ends with a new bike without training wheels." Lucy laughed. "My list is short. I just want you in my bed every night, at my complete beck and call."

His smile seemed forced. "Sweetheart, we have to talk. Something's come up."

Her chest tightened with a disturbing old feeling. "What is it, Michael? Are you okay? Are your, uh, plans changing?" Not again. It couldn't be.

A long-time news photographer, Lucy's well-trained eye quickly scanned the digital scene before her. His context would tell the story. The setting was not Michael's office in Manhattan or their dining room table in Brooklyn. Thick, peeling layers of paint—military green, bone gray, and umber the color of faded blood—provided a grim backdrop. The edge of a chipped Cyrillic-inscribed sign hung in a dark top corner of the frame.

Michael Burleson was not in New York.

He was not on this continent.

He was not coming to the ranch.

"Where the hell are you?" she demanded. "Obviously not packing for your trip to Southern California to see your family. As promised!"

Michael took a deep breath. Lucy knew this was hard for him. She hoped to make it hell.

"Okay, let me explain. Out of nowhere, Jay Levinson, you know, the Bureau Chief—"

"Give me a break. I know who he is. Our kids go to pre-school together."

"Of course, sorry. This opportunity came up literarily overnight. You know how things move in this business. Boom. They're opening a Fallujah office."

Lucy was momentarily dumbfounded. She cleared her throat. "Did you actually say Fallujah? Like in Iraq?"

"Yes, well, we're trying it out for six months. Just six months, a year max. They offered me the start-up, along with two staffers I can choose. It's a chance of a lifetime, babe. The network trusts me again. I have to take it, Luce. If this goes well, there may be an opening in Rome coming up. Until then, you, Henry, and I—we'll live in the Middle East—just for a short stint. Would be an adventure."

Lucy pressed her palms against her eyes. The network loved him again. His dark days and subsequent recovery from addiction added to his appeal. We journalists were vultures at our core.

She raised her head. "A decade and a half ago, before we met, I spent two weeks on assignment in Al Ambar province, stationed in Fallujah at the end of the war."

"I know. I remember you telling me about it. I thought you might enjoy returning to see how it's changed. *Fallujah: Then and Now*. Great subject for a photog."

"Don't patronize me." Lucy shook her head. "We'd probably be living in the same walled compound I stayed in back then. Probably the same mortar rounds and bullet holes, plus some new ones pocking the damn walls. Am I right?"

"Well, maybe, yeah. But it's not so bad anymore. It's a different time. That's why the network's coming back in. There's a great city market and even a new mall. Lots of American goods."

Lucy's laugh was scornful. "Despite the Islamic Republic's PR machine, women are still treated like crap. And every other person on the street in that city is probably still suffering from PTSD. Henry can play in fields where IEDs are left over from the last incursion."

"Lucy, I'm so sorry to drop this on you." He twitched in his chair. "But things are way better here now. Truly. Six months will go by in no time."

"The Iraqis, apart from their politicians, are an incredibly kind and hospitable people. But things can go south there in the blink of an eye." She stood and began to pace, wanting to run away, then gritted her teeth and sat back down. "But it's not about Iraq. It could be anywhere. It's about something more fundamental." She pressed her fingers to her temples. "I can't trust any kind of commitment from you, can I?" His inability to show up for her and their son told the whole story. "All we wanted was two weeks of your precious time. Two! Life is short. God only knows what we have left." Lucy turned away. Her thoughts skittered to a dark corner of her experience—to the accident, and to her uncle's murder.

"Honey, this is just a one-off thing." His face said he wasn't sure at all that was true. A young man in military garb interrupted to hand Michael a stack of papers.

Lucy shook her head again, dismayed. "I gave up everything and moved to the East Coast so we could have a chance at being a normal family. Hurting me is awful, but lying to your son is inexcusable." Her hand slapped the table; the laptop bounced. She was tempted to throw it across the room.

"Things between us have been so good," Michael said. "We can make this work, Luce. Give it a chance."

"I'm not your news groupie. I thought you finally had your priorities right. That family was first. You promised that. What a fool I've been. People never change." Why couldn't she just say *I'm done.*

"Lucy, I..."

She heard the screen door slam and the pounding of little feet on the Saltillo-tiled kitchen floor. Henry, their beautiful boy with the same translucent eyes and brown curls as his dad, burst onto the porch. Her broken heart ached in her chest.

"Mommy, mommy! Odin's sick. Bit by a snake. In the leg. Needs a shot."

"What are you talking about, honey?"

The screen door slammed again and in came Alyssa, Lucy's

teenage goddaughter who sometimes helped with childcare. "Your horse was bitten by a rattler," she said, out of breath. "Cody's on the phone with the vet right now."

Odin, a twenty-three-year-old brown and white American Paint horse, had been Lucy's beloved companion since she was fifteen. Over the years, he'd saved her life in so many ways. She couldn't lose him, too. Lucy's chest tightened with dread.

"Alyssa, can you stay with Henry while he talks to his dad?"

"Of course." The girl slid onto the chair next to Henry, who was already chatting away with his father.

Terrified and upset, Lucy raced to the paddock.

CHAPTER TWO

At the edge of the corral under a gnarled olive tree, Odin stood rigid, as if he'd been electrocuted. The area above his fetlock was a swollen melon ready to explode.

Lucy didn't bother unlocking the gate, but clambered through the fence rails and ran to her stallion's side.

"Odin, Ody boy, it's gonna be all right." She stroked his neck.

His eyes were glazed, and foam drooled from his mouth. As Lucy pressed her face against his muzzle, he nickered softly. Warm to the touch and his breathing was labored. Abject fear ripped at Lucy's throat.

Cody Hitchcock, her twenty-one-year-old neighbor and a talented equestrian stunt man, held up his phone to indicate he'd made a call. "Doc Sinclair's on his way. He's fifteen minutes out. Over at Donnelly Farms giving tetanus boosters to the goat herd."

"Thank God he's close." Lucy pushed back her hair and wiped her wet, storm cloud eyes. "Doc's on his way, Ody," she crooned. "You love, 'ol Doc. He gives you carrots."

The horse let out a whoosh of breath and staggered, as if ready to collapse. Lucy and Cody steadied him. "Is he having trouble breathing?" Lucy asked, her own breathing coming hard. She was trying not to hyperventilate. "You think he's going into shock? That can happen. Vital organs shut down. Oh, my God."

"Keep him calm." Cody said. "Channel peaceful energy to him, Luce. He's gonna be okay." Cody checked his phone. "Ten more minutes."

Lucy nodded, struggling to keep her heart from exploding.

In less than ten, a cloud of dust rose from the road leading up to the barn. The Santa Monica Mountains Veterinary Clinic's green Ford 250 truck rumbled to a stop at the paddock. Cody opened the gate.

The man who stepped from the vehicle was not old Doc Sinclair. "Hey, Cody, nice to see you again," the man said.

Lucy winced. A new, unknown person on the scene was disturbing. Where was old Doc?

Cody nodded at the vet, then said to Lucy, "This is Doc Sinclair's son. We met at a movie shoot over at Paramount Ranch a month ago. He was the on-scene veterinarian. Heath, this is Lucy Vega. Odin's hers."

The vet grabbed his medical bag and stepped through the gate toward Lucy, extending his hand. "Good to meet you, ma'am. Let's see to that horse."

The new Dr. Sinclair was tall and broad-shouldered, with reddish hair and a neatly trimmed beard. "Where's your dad?" she asked. "He's known Odin since he was a colt when I first got him."

"My Dad and Mom are traveling in Europe. When they get back, he's going half-time—sent a letter to all his clients a couple months ago. I just moved back here from upstate New York— I'm taking over the large animal part of the practice."

"I guess I missed the letter, but welcome." Lucy turned and he followed her to into the paddock.

"So, what happened here?" Heath Sinclair's focus shifted completely to the horse. He listened to Odin's heart, took vitals, and inspected the swollen leg.

Cody explained. "Looks like a rattler got into his stall last night and nailed him. I found it stomped to death early this morning. It's over there at the edge of the barn. Didn't want Odin to see it again and freak out."

"Good thinking," Sinclair said.

Lucy saw the long black rope of a snake with pale gray markings laying in the dirt.

Dr. Sinclair drew a vial from his bag. "I'm going to give him anti-venin. Should begin to see some relief for Odin in about thirty minutes. His breathing is rough, but I don't think we'll need to intubate. The snake didn't get him in the nose. Lucky on that one." He measured the dosage from a vial, then plunged the needle into the horse's shoulder.

Feeling like the injection had been rammed into her very guts, Lucy took a couple of deep breaths. Odin barely reacted to the shot.

"He's going to be okay, Lucy," Sinclair said. "That leg'll take a while to heal, but he's going to be fine. I'll stay here for the next hour or so to monitor him. Will also treat him with an anti-inflammatory, antibiotics, and something for pain. Sound good?"

"Yes, please stay until he starts to come around." Despite the antidote, she was wracked with fear of losing him, of some sudden setback threatening recovery.

"Sure, no problem." After a few minutes, the vet checked Odin's vitals again. "Heart's already not racing as fast. A good sign."

He hung the stethoscope around his neck, carefully observing the equine patient. Next, he kneeled down and pulled out bandaging supplies. With gentle hands, he inspected the snake bite again, cleaned and covered the damaged area with an antibiotic cream, then wrapped the leg.

Sinclair stood back from the horse to observe his job, then turned to Lucy and gave her shoulder a quick, reassuring pat. "He's going to make it. So are you. I promise your buddy here will be up and causing double trouble again soon."

Before she realized what she was doing, Lucy threw herself into Doctor Sinclair's arms and began to sob.

CHAPTER THREE

Moments later, shocked at her outburst, Lucy pulled away from the unflustered veterinarian. He smelled of earth, horses, and coffee. Scents that were solid and grounded. But what was she doing? Completely losing it.

"I'm so sorry. Totally embarrassing myself." She drew a tissue from her pocket and blew her nose. "My husband, well, we're not technically married, but we're seriously together. Were." The dam was weak, and the story gushed out. "He's the father of my son, and well, he was supposed to come to the ranch for two weeks beginning this Friday, and instead, he went to Fallujah for, like, probably a year." She blew her nose again. "I agreed to move to New York so he could work on his career, but he won't even spend a couple weeks here with me and Henry. Hell, I'd take a couple of days. Everything feels like it's falling apart." She sniffed hard to keep from sobbing again. "And then Odin." She stroked the Paint's brown and white cheek. "Anyway, you saved this fabulous being. Thank you." She put her lips to Odin's muzzle and kissed his soft nose. "He means everything to me. Been one of the only constants in my life since I was a teen." She stifled a wail of grief.

"Glad I could help." Sinclair smiled. It was a nice one.

Lucy chastised herself for being so desperate for a man to put his arms around her that she found herself in this ridiculous display. How totally pathetic. "Sorry about my little crying scene." She had to settle down and not further humiliate herself. "Although I did cry in your dad's arms a few times when I was a kid, and we had to put down various dogs and a guinea pig."

"We love our critters like family, sometimes more," he said.

"Yeah, so true." Lucy blew her nose again. Her hands were still shaking.

"And your husband, your significant other that you're not married to—I hope he has a good excuse for choosing Iraq over Malibu. I was stationed in the Middle East as a medic. Complicated place." He shook his head.

"Definitely complicated." It took all Lucy had to stop herself from another round of stupid crying and blabbering her life story to a stranger. This was not her usual behavior. She didn't fall apart.

Cody approached Lucy and the vet with the rattlesnake at the bottom of a pail. "Here's the perpetrator."

Sinclair took a close look; his brows drew together. "That's not a species from this part of California. You see these guys way up north where it's much colder. Mind if I take it with me?"

"Be our guest," Lucy said. "Why do you think it's down in this part of the state?"

Sinclair let out a long sigh. "Who knows? Global climate change has seen crazier things."

"Mommy, mommy!" Henry came tearing across the yard with Alyssa at his heels and the two dogs, Maddie the Golden Lab mix, and Bugle the Beagle, alongside. "Did Odin get a shot?" He climbed the fence rails and took a hard look at the vet.

"Yes, honey. This is Doctor Sinclair. He gave Odin medicine to make him feel better."

Henry eyed the medical bag at the vet's feet.

"Would you like to see the medicine bottle and the syringe that I gave Odin the shot with?"

Henry climbed down from the railing and rushed through the corral gate toward the doctor and the sick horse. Lucy caught him before he could get in Odin's range.

"Come on over to my truck, young man," Sinclair said, picking up his supplies. "Let's look at what's in my doctor's bag, away from Odin so he can rest."

Henry bought into that plan. He and Heath Sinclair spent at least half an hour going through all the doc's medical equipment. They listened to everyone's heart with the stethoscope and checked out the dead snake. No heartbeat. The doc gave the boy a plastic pin that said *Junior Veterinarian.* Henry adored it.

Finally, Sinclair had to take off. "Gotta finish inoculating the goats." He began to pack up his supplies.

"We got goats," Henry declared. He hustled off toward their pen with Alyssa.

"You must have children," Lucy said. She joined Sinclair at the truck. "You're great with my son."

"Got a six-year-old daughter, Gracie."

"Very nice. How're she and her mother taking the move to California?"

"Adjusting okay. But it's just my daughter and me."

Lucy wondered what the story was there, but refrained from asking. "Now I'm remembering," she said, "Doc told us about you. He thought you should've gone to vet school at UC Davis where he graduated from, and you went to Cornell instead. Traitorous."

Sinclair chuckled. "Took him a while to forgive me, but I wanted a change of scenery. Kids need to do their own thing, right?"

Lucy smiled. "For sure." She thought about her many adventures as a news photographer. Her Uncle Henry, who raised her, wanted her to be an accountant and help him in his real estate ventures. No way.

"I sold my partnership in an upstate New York vet practice and found a little farmstead in Old Agoura. It's nice. Anyhow, gotta get back to a previous appointment."

"The goats?"

"Yep." He finished stowing his supplies.

"Thank you for everything," Lucy said. "I can't tell you—"

"No need. I'll be by in a couple of days to check his leg. Looks like his vaccinations are up-to-date but he might need another round of antibiotics. In the meantime, keep Odin calm, hydrated, light food. I'll email you with follow-up instructions. Is Cody going to be around to help with him this week?"

"Actually, he leaves in the morning for a month on a film shoot in Utah. But I'll be fine."

Heath Sinclair nodded, climbed into his truck and, with a quick wave, accelerated down the long driveway to Kanan Road.

Lucy returned to her horse's side. Odin's big chestnut eyes were clearing, and the sun was breaking through the marine layer at last.

CHAPTER FOUR

The next morning as Cody's Uber to LAX pulled away, Odin, his leg bandaged and swollen, nickered at the paddock fence. Lucy pressed her face to his soft muzzle—he was going to miss the kid as much as Lucy was. The relief she felt as the horse began to recover was profound. But so was her growing sense of abandonment. The burden she carried of loss was heavy. With Cody doing stunt work on the TV Western and his grandfather, the ranch handyman, traveling back East with his woman friend, the two Hitchcock men were off the grid. Even her beloved Elsa, the grandma who had helped raise her, was away for the summer visiting cousins in Norway. And finally, Alyssa, who'd been helping with Henry, was going to dance camp for six weeks before starting her senior year in high school. Lucy's ranch family was in the wind.

Soon it would be Lucy and Henry alone on the big property. They'd be fine. After all, she'd survived a fire that had burned the ranch to the ground. And she knew how to use a rifle and her .357. But there was something about that snake in the stall that hit Lucy badly. Was she just being paranoid? For sure.

Her phone rang.

"Hey, girl. Whatcha doin'?" Bea Middleton, Lucy's best friend and Alyssa's mom, sounded annoyingly perky.

"Oh, not much. Just sitting in the garden feeling sorry for myself and watching Alyssa teach Henry some kind of synchronized swimming routine in the pool. Thanks for lending her to me for the week, by the way. I've got forty black and white images to print for my show in Calabasas next month. Thanks to your daughter, I got lots done."

"She loves being with y'all at the ranch. And I'm thrilled you're finally having your own show."

"You've been after me to do it for years."

"Glad you finally listened to 'ol Beatrice. Doesn't happen often." She chuckled. "So hey, I'm on my way to pick up said daughter armed with Cheese Louise pizza bagels, a bottle of freshly squeezed orange juice primed for mimosas, and a couple quarts of that salt caramel chocolate pecan ice cream you like so much. All to be consumed in any order or combination your little heart desires."

"Oh, honey, you do know how to cheer up a friend."

"Always got your back, sweet pea."

Bea was the only person Lucy knew who could make being callously abandoned by your partner and left alone with your kiddo seem like a pajama party.

Bea laughed. "The feast'll put you in a sugar and carb coma so fast you won't even remember what's bothering you."

Lucy sighed. If only it were that easy.

"What *is* bothering you, girlfriend?" Bea asked. "Alyssa said you and Michael had some kind of spat on FaceTime. And Odin was bitten by a rattler? Sweet Jesus, I worry about you out there in that wilderness."

Lucy chuckled. It felt good. "The snake thing was so freaky, but Odin's going to survive. Thank the good Lord. The rest, I'll fill you in when you get here." Lucy dreaded going over the sad acknowledgement that she was second choice to a dicey career move by the supposed love of her life.

Bea continued. "Okay, but guess what? I'm bringing a special friend with me."

"Who? Your brother? Is Luther visiting from Savannah?"

"Well, practically my brother, but hell no, not Luther this time. It's Rio Deakins! And my feelings for that fine dude haven't been brotherly for at least a decade. About to pick him up outside baggage claim right now."

"Rio! What's he doing in town?"

"Speaking at a conference on Social Justice at Loyola Marymount Uni next week. He's coming with Alyssa and me on the ride up to dance camp."

"That sounds fun."

"No kidding. Anyhow, see you in an hour or so with Professor Hotness." Lucy couldn't help but share the excitement in her friend's voice.

"Oh my God, there he is!" Bea shouted. A horn honked. Bea's phone disconnected.

"Alyssa," Lucy called out, "Your Mom's on her way. Better get out of the pool and get your stuff packed."

Alyssa thanked her for the heads-up and dashed off.

Lucy wrapped Henry in the big, fluffy towel and held him close. He smelled like sunshine and swimming pool. She kissed his cool, damp cheek. Michael had no idea what he was missing.

—

As Bea inched along the passenger pick-up lane, the day sweltered and the air smelled of automotive exhaust. Nothing truly registered, however, except the gorgeous, six-foot-four black man who was not only a former athlete but also a brilliant Emory professor with a heart of gold. Oh, and he rode a Harley. Hard not to fall for the guy. His smile alone made Bea almost pile into the back of the small pickup in front of her.

Rio had been informally adopted by Bea's family when he and her brother were in fifth grade and Bea was in third. He was the youngest of seven kids with a single mother who struggled with chronic drug issues. He spent so much time in the Middleton household that they finally just bought bunk beds for the boys and welcomed him in.

The truck pulled away and Bea slid her car into its vacated spot. She jumped out, barely avoiding being clipped by traffic battling for curb space.

"Beazly girl," Rio shouted.

"I've been telling you not to call me that since I was in grade school." She primped her hair and danced his way.

"Bring it in, little sister."

He swept her into his arms, kissed her cheek, and swung her around. Laughing, he set Bea down and stepped back to check her out. "Look at you. You've gone natural on me."

"I have."

"Where's the signature designer dress, Manolo Whatnik's, and long hair?"

"Now that I have my own business, I can be stylin' anyway I want." She hit a chippy pose.

"The new gig looks good on you."

Bea smiled at his approval. "Thanks, darlin'. Can't wait to bore you to death with the deets. We're the number three online news site in the metro and gaining fast on the competition. "Load your stuff in the back and let's hit the road."

They pulled out of the airport, chattering with their usual ease. Except for the fact that Bea wished it could go on forever. Unfortunately, Rio, the man of her dreams, was already spoken for. When she finally realized her feelings for him, he'd just put a ring on the finger of another woman. A woman Bea had introduced him to. Such irony. A romantic relationship while he was married was out of the question. Didn't stop her from fantasizing, however.

CHAPTER FIVE

L ucy was picking up Henry's toys when the doorbell rang. She glanced at her watch and frowned. Who would be up here so early on a Saturday morning? Bea was at least a half hour away.

She checked the ring cam and saw a tall, willowy young woman with long, straight blonde hair and stunning facial features. Shifting nervously from foot-to-foot, she wore blue jeans and a sweetly feminine white eyelet blouse. Didn't look like the type to be selling something. And definitely not a Mormon missionary.

Lucy opened the door.

The woman clasped her hands tightly, almost as if in prayer. "Uh, hello. Lucia Vega?"

"Yes." The girl felt familiar, but Lucy was sure they'd never met. "Can I help you?"

"I'm um, Michael Burleson's youngest daughter, Jaime."

The air whooshed from Lucy's lungs.

The girl's eyes were the same glassy blue as her father's and Henry's. The shape of her face was Michael's, too.

Lucy struggled to snap out of the shock at this person

dropping onto her doorstep like a rock from space. "Oh, my goodness," she said. "We've invited you down from Santa Cruz so many times, but never heard from you. I was afraid we'd never meet." She opened the screen door. "I can't believe you're here. Please, come in."

The young woman stepped into the house, eyes flitting about the entry like she was trying to get her bearings. "I'm sorry I didn't call ahead. It was all so spur-of-the-moment. I had your address, but no other contact info."

Lucy gave her a warm hug. The woman's rigid body softened. "Amazing to finally meet you," Lucy said. "It's just that, uh, your dad..."

Jaime's eyes narrowed to flinty slits. "He's not here, is he?"

"Yes, I mean no, I mean yes, he's not here. He's in Fallujah for six months, maybe more."

"Fallujah?" the young woman looked away, inspecting the living room ahead, and its high beamed ceiling. Then she spoke. "The same old story." She turned back to Lucy. "I'm really sorry. I know what it's like to have him disappoint you."

Lucy pulled at her silver hoop earring. "Well, I guess I knew what I signed on for. He never pretended he wasn't crazy about the job." She didn't know why she felt like she had to defend him. "Come on out to the back porch, honey. Meet your baby brother, half-brother."

Sitting on the wicker couch, four-year-old Henry, in swim trunks, was wrapped in the damp towel with a slice of sticky watermelon in his hand.

Jaime stood at the porch entry, looking at Henry with wonder and confusion. She licked her lips and pulled a small package from her pocket.

Henry was already checking out the newcomer and seemed to like the looks of her. "I'm Henry. What's your name?"

The pretty young woman crossed the room and kneeled at his side. "I'm Jaime. I have a little gift for you, Henry. Do you like trucks?"

"Uh huh." He nodded and his tangled curls jiggled.

She handed him the package. Henry dropped the watermelon rind on the coffee table and tore open the wrapping paper revealing two Matchbox toys—a firetruck and a firefighting helicopter. Although the ranch had burned down before he was born, it was forever a thread in conversations and photos. Maybe because of that, he had a fascination with all things firefighting.

"What do you say, Hen?" Lucy asked.

He thanked Jaime and started to buzz around with the chopper. Jaime looked pleased and relieved that her gift was a hit.

"Can you stay for brunch?" Lucy asked. "A couple of dear people will be joining us. You should meet them. They're like family. Bea Middleton, you'll love her. She's Henry's godmother and my closest friend. We've been in the news business together for years. And her childhood friend from Atlanta; he's a professor at Emory."

Jaime looked unsure. She seemed shy and was likely anxious about meeting new people. Sliding her cell phone from her pocket, she fidgeted with it, then put it away. Lucy noticed her bitten fingernails.

Jaime pressed her hands together in prayer mode again, seeming like she was trying to relax. "Very kind of you to invite me. I'd be honored to meet my little brother's godmother." She glanced at Henry and chewed at her lip. "I should call my husband, let him know I'm going to be late."

"Husband? You'll have to tell me all about him." Lucy was sure Michael had zero knowledge that his youngest was married.

Henry, who never missed a thing, said, "I your brother?"

Lucy's stomach knotted. "Jaime is one of daddy's two grown-up daughters, which makes her your big sister. We've told you about them. Do you remember seeing pictures?" Lucy had rehearsed explaining it all to the Henry so many times, but now couldn't remember anything she'd planned to say.

"Will you take me to get frozen yogurt sometime?" Henry asked. "And to the playground?"

"Of course I will. I'd love to do that." Jaime's response was enthusiastic.

Henry smiled and continued to play with his new toy. For him, a relationship with Jaime was a done deal. Lucy wished she could be as blissfully accepting of surprises.

CHAPTER SIX

Bea and Rio drove down the Incline just past the Santa Monica pier where westbound Ocean and California Avenues spilled from the palisade onto Pacific Coast Highway. The sun silvered the tips of rolling blue waves as the BMW headed toward the long promontory of Point Dume and Lucy's *Rancho de la Vega* in the Santa Monica Mountains just inland from there.

"I love it here," Rio said. Cool salty breeze ruffled fronds of palm trees along the road where surfers peeled out of wet suits and cyclists pedaled precariously along the narrow shoulders.

"Why don't you look for a job in Southern California? You know people at Loyola, USC, UCLA. You and Lindsay would be happy here."

He sighed and rubbed his chin. "Cali's crazy expensive, and I like Georgia. I'm happy at Emory, but we stayed in Atlanta because of Lindsay's job at CNN. He looked at her and smiled. "I sometimes forget she was your intern there."

"Thanks for the reminder. Makes me feel ancient."

Rio chuckled and continued. "But now she's been

reassigned."

With a snap of surprise and confusion, Bea asked, "Your wife reassigned? Where? New York?"

Rio looked at her like he couldn't believe she was asking the question. "To Fallujah. Along with your son."

"What?" The car swerved.

"You didn't know?"

Bea's mouth fell open in shock. "No frickin' clue."

"Yeah, Michael Burleson was okayed to choose two people to take with him to re-open that office."

Burleson? In Iraq? "That's probably what Michael and Lucy were arguing about on Zoom. Alyssa told me about it."

Rio nodded. "All happened really fast. He needed folks to take with him who he could trust and who could leave Atlanta on a dime—my wife, and your son."

"I can't believe Dexter didn't tell me." Bea's twenty-three-year-old had long been mentored by Rio and had the man's same independent streak. And admittedly hers, too.

Shaken by the news, Bea pulled off into the parking lot of a small seafood restaurant where diners sat outdoors at picnic tables and seagulls squawked overhead. She opened the car's center console and rummaged until she'd found an Advil. She swallowed it with a chaser from her water bottle. "He was probably afraid I'd make a scene. He'd be right."

"Lucy knows about Lindsay and Dex being with Michael over there, right?" Rio asked.

"I'm betting she doesn't." Bea drummed her fingers on the steering wheel.

Rio reached out and squeezed her hand. "I know you're worried about Dexter, but the kid can take care of himself. He's smart, ambitious and foreign reporting really excites him. Michael is giving Lindsay and Dex an incredible opportunity to gain international reporting experience."

"Yeah, I guess I should be grateful that the intrepid correspondent Michael Burleson is taking them under his wing."

"As long as he stays sober, he's a brilliant journalist." Rio pressed the overhead button to open the sunroof. It slid back, and the car filled with bracing ocean air. "I think Lindsay idolizes him." He looked away from Bea.

She rolled her neck. "So, you're okay with her being there? That's a shitty place to be a female."

Rio nodded. "You know her. She lives for a challenge." From his body language, Bea didn't need to add out loud that Burleson was one attractive, engaging man. Pulling back onto the highway, she accelerated toward Point Dume and *Rancho de la Vega.*

Rio hesitated, then said, "Lindsay and I are not doing too well these days."

"I'm sorry to hear that." In spite of Bea's feelings for Rio, she'd long ago learned to compartmentalize them into an emotional drawer with a firm lock. And despite believing that Lindsay was far too self-absorbed and recklessly ambitious to care deeply for anyone, Bea never wanted to see a marriage in jeopardy. "Doesn't help when she's on the other side of the world."

"Maybe that's the plan," Rio said. "Distance. Makes the heart grow fonder, yeah?" He scrubbed at his whiskery chin. "Or destroys everything you thought you had."

The lightness of the day had turned into a heavy weight.

CHAPTER SEVEN

Alyssa lugged her hot pink duffle bag onto the porch. Lucy gazed fondly at the head-turning seventeen-year-old with a puff hairdo and cornrow braids. Long gorgeous legs ended at cut-off denim jean shorts. The girl stopped abruptly when she saw Jaime.

"This is Jaime Burleson, Michael's youngest daughter, and Henry's sister," Lucy said with a nonchalance she didn't feel.

Alyssa's eyes widened. "Wow. Nice to meet you, Jaime." She stumbled forward over her gear bag to shake the girl's hand. "I like your dad. He's a lot of fun, and really smart, and hot. Like for an old guy."

Jaime's smile was forced. "That's what people tell me." She turned her attention back to Henry, who preened under her attention.

Alyssa side-eyed Lucy. Lucy was well aware of Jaime's resentment toward her father and wished she could do something to help heal the wounds. Michael had been an absentee father for too much of his daughter's life. And like him, the daughter had struggled with substance abuse. Since Michael turned his life around over the past years, he'd repeatedly reached out to her, but she never responded. Until now, when he was gone. Again.

Jaime said, "I hear you're off to a dance camp. Sounds totally lit."

"Yeah. And this is the first year I'll be a junior counselor. I'm pretty stoked. Are you on break from school? I think your dad mentioned that you're at UC Santa Cruz."

On the floor with Henry as he examined his Hot Wheels, Jaime turned toward Alyssa. "Yep, I'm taking a break, not sure what I want to do with my life. Needed a change." She stroked Henry's cheek. "I'm looking for a job down here. Probably working with children. My boyfriend—new husband, is working at a church camp near Simi Valley."

"Oh, cool. Camp can be such a great experience for kids."

Jaime turned her attention back to her little brother. Alyssa watched her closely.

The sound of gravel popping outside as a car pulled in caught their attention.

"It's Bea and Rio." Lucy ran to the front door to welcome them. She was beyond happy to have good friends, armed with food, libation, and hugs, walk through the door.

Bea Midleton was a stunning, dark-skinned Black woman in her mid-forties, with eyes that sparkled like brown diamonds. Rio was equally wonderful, beautiful, and always engaging. Lucy loved them both. For the next hour-and-a-half, she forgot about everything sad and stressful.

Until Bea said, "So, Luce, my son failed to tell me that he and Lindsay—yes, Rio's wife Lindsay—are the two people your man has taken with him to open the Fallujah office."

Lucy froze for an instant, then belted down what was left of her mimosa. "Are you kidding me?" She grabbed another half of a pizza bagel and took an aggressive bite. "Well, that's a helluva surprise. Why didn't he tell me? I guess we got interrupted with the snake bite fiasco." She stopped chewing for a moment. "At least they're all people we trust to have each other's backs."

Bea nodded and Rio barely responded. He gazed forlornly into middle space.

Jaime's cell phone buzzed. She checked caller ID. "Excuse me for a minute, I have to take this."

"The study is down the hall," Lucy said. "It's quiet in there."

"Okay, thanks." Jaime quickly left the porch.

"And I'm gonna use the bathroom before we head north." Bea rose, following Jaime along the dark hallway until the young woman disappeared into the study. Pausing near the door to eavesdrop on the phone conversation, Bea wanted to know more about Burleson's daughter. Over the years, Michael had shared with she and Lucy a lot about the kid's struggles with self-esteem and addiction issues.

"I did it," Jaime said, excited. Her voice was low and conspiratorial. "I'll call you back later. And the horse is okay. I'm glad about that." Jaime listened to the person on the other end of the call for at least a couple more minutes. There were lots of uh-huh's, then an apologetic goodbye. Bea thought it sounded like the young woman was being scolded for something. The air had definitely been let out of the balloon of her initial excitement.

Hustling down the hall to the bathroom before Jaime emerged from the study, Bea had no idea what was going on with that phone call. She'd ask Lucy more about the girl's situation after taking Alyssa to camp. She glanced at her watch. It was time to go.

CHAPTER EIGHT

Lucy's high spirits waned as her thoughts returned to Michael and his absence. Too soon, it was time for Bea, Rio, and Alyssa to leave for the dance camp near Morro Bay. Goodbyes and safe travels were called out, then Bea motored toward Kanan Dume Road where they'd drive through the canyon to Agoura Hills and the Ventura Freeway.

As they pulled away, Jaime stood next to Lucy in the yard with Henry's hand in hers.

"They're really nice," she said.

"Yeah, they're family. It comes in all different shapes and sizes, right?" Lucy looked at her beautiful son and was again taken by the strong resemblance to his big sister and their dad. At that moment, an impetuous thought popped into her head. She turned to Jaime. "I don't suppose you'd be interested in caring for Henry for a few weeks until you find a better job? I pay pretty well. I have a photography show I'm behind on and could use some help around here." Lucy knew her request was maybe a little bit mimosa-influenced, but Jaime seemed so kind to Henry.

The young woman flushed and said, "I couldn't accept money to be with my brother."

"Oh, yes, you could. I insist. What do you think?"

A smile lit Jaime's pretty face, the first real animation Lucy had seen.

"I'd love to do it." Jaime bent down and gave Henry a warm hug. He giggled and hugged her back.

Lucy wondered what Michael would think when he heard that his Jaime would be caring for their son at the ranch. He might be a tiny bit upset since he didn't completely trust his daughter. But after all, Jaime was here with Lucy and Henry, and Michael wasn't. To Lucy, that spoke volumes.

—

With a heavy heart, Bea watched her daughter skip off with a gaggle of other junior counselors, leaving her mother behind with a quick peck goodbye. A staffer handed out dance camp T-shirts and bunk assignments. Rap music played from a loudspeaker, and kids hurried toward the community building for a big orientation meeting.

Tears filled Bea's eyes. "Do you know that ninety percent of your presence with your children is over by the time they're eighteen? That's so depressing. I have only one more year with her. And Dexter's on the other side of the globe, where he's probably gonna be shot by a sniper."

"Shot by a sniper?" Rio shook his head and put his arms around her. "You know you're a bit of a drama queen, don't you?"

"Well, it could happen."

"Anything could happen. That's the world we live in, darlin'. You've had wonderful times with your kids. You're an awesome mother, and you'll have more wonderful times with Alyssa and Dexter. It's far from over, Beasley. It's just another chapter."

She pulled back and lightly punched his arm. Sniffled, blew her nose. "Why are you so good at talking me off the ledge?"

"We got more than a three-decade history, little Mama. Guess I know you pretty well."

"Rio, if you and Lindsay don't work out, will you marry me? I mean it." The man was so kind and so damn beautiful. "Why aren't we together? I mean, forever." When Bea's emotional lock box occasionally cracked open, the desire for him was always there, only more intense, no matter how much distance she tried to conjure.

"Well, if you recall, you'd just split from your second husband when you finally realized I'd been in love with you since you were eight and I was ten. I'll always be mad for you. But by then, I'd fallen for Lindsay." He removed his aviator sunglasses and rubbed his eyes. Rio took her hand and led her back to the car. "Let's get to the hotel. Okay if I drive? You've put in a lot of time behind the wheel today. Morro Bay Inn, right?"

She nodded and handed him the key fob. Rio didn't seem like himself today. Maybe it was the long trip from Atlanta and his concern about his wife. The car beeped and the doors unlocked.

They said little and listened to an oldies R&B station on the half-hour drive through San Luis Obispo to Morro Bay. Morro Rock, a stunning volcanic outcropping sacred to the Chumash people, welcomed them. Usually, Bea loved the sight of the rock and the seaside village and looked forward to an early evening stroll along the Embarcadero where she conjured images of native American campfires in the growing dusk. Tonight, she felt only anxious and tired.

They checked into adjoining rooms and ordered meals to enjoy on the balcony overlooking the bay. The sun was low behind the rock, giving it a mystical halo. The evening mist gathered in the garden below and the sensuous scent of night blooming jasmine sweetened the salty air. Bea plunked down on the couch when their dinner arrived. She poured them both a glass of garnet-red merlot.

Rio came into the room and leaned against the edge of the

desk. A pall of strangeness crackled in the air. "Can we talk, Beatrice?"

The situation should have been lovely and relaxing, but he'd called her Beatrice. She gulped. "Of course."

He took off his jacket and threw it onto a chair. The form-hugging, creamy T-shirt he wore called attention to how ridiculously fit the guy still was. Looked like he could still play running back for the Georgia Bulldogs. Bea reached to hand him a glass of wine. When he looked away, she set the glass down and crossed the room, gathering him into a tight embrace. "Rio, talk to me. Something's going on. What is it, sweet man? Are things that bad with Lindsay?"

He pulled back from her arms, hesitated for a second, then took her face in his hands. Their kiss was long and deep. She'd been waiting for this her whole life. She was on fire; but he was married. They couldn't do this. This was not who they were.

Rio tore himself away and staggered toward the catering cart, grabbing the bottle of wine.

"I'm losing it," he whispered, almost to himself. "I'm sorry, Bea."

She was not sorry but shamefully knew she should be.

Rio was pretty much a teetotaler, so Bea was surprised when he guzzled down two glasses of merlot. He sunk onto the couch and rubbed his neck again.

"Rio, talk to me."

"Okay, okay. Here's what's happening." He groaned.

Bea sat next to him, not touching him. The air still smoldered between them. "What the hell is going on, baby?"

"So," Rio began, "your father left me a letter that I received from your mother two months ago."

"A letter? What are you talking about?"

"It had been in your dad's safe deposit box. Twenty years after his death, she finally got around to looking at the contents of the box. Her friend Judge Carwell, you know they're dating, he encouraged her."

"Yeah, I try not to think about those lovers getting it on in their late eighties. I guess I'm a perpetrator of ageism." Although she could still see herself being wildly attracted to Rio whatever their year count.

"Well, he's pressuring her to get her estate in shape and she's finally taking it seriously."

Rio stood, walked over to his briefcase and pulled out an envelope. "Your mother said she's long known about the contents of this." He handed it to Bea and sat back down. "It's addressed to me from your father."

"It's from Daddy? To you? What's this about?" She opened the envelope and began to read. A cold sweat rose on her skin. She looked over at Rio, feeling like she was about to throw up or have a heart attack, or both.

"I can't believe this." Tears filled her eyes. The letter dropped to the floor. "You're…"

Rio slumped against the far side of the couch. "I'm your brother."

Bea struggled not to hyperventilate. "This is insane. We could have—" It was a while before she was able to speak again. Finally, she said, "Okay, now it makes sense, how you were so easily welcomed into our family, and everyone who didn't know us assumed you and Luther were siblings."

"Because we were."

"No!" Bea covered her head with her arms. "I'm going to stay in complete denial as long as possible." Dreams of his smooth, dark skin next to hers and the soulful kisses she would never receive again had to be permanently extinguished. It was devastating.

Rio uttered a plaintive sigh. "The summer my mother tried to get clean, she worked as your dad's temporary church secretary while old Mrs. Marsden was on leave with gout or something like that."

"Your mother was beautiful and smart."

"And a narcissistic addict, manipulative as hell," Rio said.

"Your dad admits that they slept together once after a conference at the Coffee Bluff Conference Center on the Savannah River."

"And she named you 'river,' Rio." Bea's heart was breaking. Her father, the man she idolized, had cheated on her mother. But that betrayal created the man she loved with all her heart. The man she could now never have. "Guess I better rescind my marriage proposal."

"More wine?" Rio asked.

"Hell, yes. Ring up for another goddamn bottle."

CHAPTER NINE

After several weeks of a morning marine layer fogging the coast, the new day dawned clear with the horizon sharp and silvery as a razor. It was just 6:30 when Lucy checked on Henry. A growth spurt left him needing extra rest, so he'd be sacked out for at least another hour. Quietly, she shut the door. The pups, Bugle and Maddie, followed her downstairs, their nails clacking on the Saltillo pavers like castanets.

It was time to bring the horses from their stalls into the paddock where she'd feed them. Lucy gathered her messy hair into a ponytail. She padded through the living room in old flannel PJ bottoms and an ancient St. Olaf College T-shirt, a tribute to her Norwegian father. She slipped her feet into well-used Wellies parked just inside the front door. The vet would be stopping by later to check Odin's leg and Lucy wanted all of her creatures taken care of by then.

She stepped onto the sandy flagstones of the front terrace. In the rafters over the door, she heard familiar clucking. Omlette, Lucy's big yellow Buff Orpington hen, roosted alongside Howard the tabby cat, not thrilled to share his usual lookout with an interloper.

Her surprise didn't stop there. Turning to the barnyard ahead, Lucy was shocked to find practically a damn petting zoo. All the animals were out of their enclosures, wandering randomly. How did they get out? What the heck had happened?

Immediately, she counted the animals to be sure none had been carried off by coyotes or hawks. Or big owls. Or the worst-case scenario, evil people. There were eleven chickens, not including Omlette, and five pygmy goats, their heads buried in the flower boxes while decimating the pansies and marigolds. Twin burros named Sonny and Cher, whom she was caring for while neighbors were on vacation, were also among the escapees. She groaned as Sonny relieved himself in the middle of the drive.

Rushing over to the hen house, Lucy spotted the damage. Yellow lab Madison sniffed and growled. Lucy winced at what she saw. The chicken wire had been cut, not pulled apart or damaged by animals. The door frames had been splintered by a hammer or an axe. Vandalism, pure and simple. The same with the goat shelter.

Who would do this? It made no sense. Lucy tried to ignore the cold, painful needles of fear. She'd call the police after she got the animals rounded up. And dammit, it was time to upgrade her security cameras. This could have been worse—at least nobody was burned or bleeding. The thought was unsettling. Scenes of the past arson-sparked brush fire that had decimated the ranch flickered in her head. The images, the smells, would always remain as embers in her mind easily stirred to life.

Refusing to let bad recollections and the petty crime intimidate her, back at the barn Lucy angrily grabbed a pitchfork and loaded flakes of alfalfa into the feeder in the corral. She buckled Odin's bridal and led him out first, followed by Cheyney Hitchcock's two pretty chestnut mares she'd had in residence almost as long as she'd had Odin. She traded handyman work for equine boarding with the former stuntman, who was also Cody's grandpa.

After mucking out the stalls, she grabbed a roll of chicken wire nestled amid the hay bales and dragged it to the henhouse. Stringing this fencing across the damage would work temporarily until she found someone to do a proper fix.

Lucy stopped and kneaded her aching neck.

In his Paw Patrol jammies, Henry emerged from the house and slid onto a rocking chair by the front door, munching on a banana. The dogs pranced over to him, hoping for a handout. They loved fruit. Just then, a vehicle rumbled across the bridge over the arroyo below. Heath Sinclair's truck was coming up the drive from Kanan Road. What time was it? Lucy groaned. She looked like hell. She tried to shake out bits of hay tangled in her hair.

Sinclair pulled the dusty truck into the barnyard and emerged with his medical bag in hand.

"Hey, Lucy." He looked her over and smiled.

"Morning, doc." Lucy felt a flush warm her cheeks. "I swear this is not my usual...okay, yes, it is. But I'm normally changed by now."

"Hi, Doctor Heath," Henry yelled.

"Hiya, Henry," the doc called back. The boy was by his side in seconds.

Bugle was left finishing the banana.

Lucy pulled at her threadbare T-shirt. "Had a little crisis early this morning. Had to reschedule my usual spa treatments."

He smiled again and raised his eyebrows as donkey Cher ambled past with a vining geranium hanging from her mouth.

"Looks like the whole farm's on walkabout."

"Yeah." Lucy shook her head. "Vandalism. During the night."

Sinclair's light attitude darkened. "Did you call the sheriff?"

"Was about to."

"Mind if I take a look?"

"Please do."

He followed Lucy and Henry to the enclosures and inspected the damage carefully. "You need to take photos to document everything. You have security cameras? I heard from my dad that you're a photographer."

"Yeah, well, a negligent one in this case. I have four cameras surveilling the house, the barn and the yard, but they've been out of commission for months. I've been gone for so long I guess I let stuff slip." Lucy berated herself for not staying on top of the maintenance. Whether she was in New York or Malibu, she needed to take better care of things.

"You should get somebody out here immediately," the doc said. "This could have been worse."

Lucy swallowed hard. "Believe me, I know."

He ran his hand over the cut fencing. "Okay, Lucy, let's take a look at Odin."

CHAPTER TEN

Sinclair followed Lucy and her son back to the barn. They opened the corral gate together. Odin actually walked toward the doctor. That horse knew a good guy when he saw one. Lucy smiled and scrubbed her fingers through Henry's silky curls just as Jaime Burleson's old Corolla chugged up the drive and parked beside the vet's truck. It was her first day officially caring for her little brother.

Jumping out of the car, she appeared happy and animated. "Hi, everybody."

Henry ran up to her and gave her a hug, then raced away and followed the doc to the corral.

Jaime's eyes searched the yard, immediately hitting on the wayward animals. "What happened here?"

In a low voice Henry couldn't overhear, Lucy explained about the vandalism. "I'm just telling Henry that the enclosures got broken, trying to avoid any big explanation. I don't want him to be afraid."

"Yeah, good idea." She looked over at Henry, then smiled. "Thank you for hiring me, Lucy. I'm so excited to be here."

"We're excited to have you."

"Maybe I could help with fixing the hen house and stuff," she said.

"What do you mean?"

"My husband is a terrific carpenter. He can fix anything."

The young woman practically glowed with enthusiasm and pride. Nothing like new love. "I thought he worked at a youth camp," Lucy said.

"Yep, on Saturdays, Sundays, and Wednesdays, he's the pastor. The rest of the time he's also the camp's maintenance guy and handyman. Owns the place. He's actually off today. I could call him right now."

Lucy nodded eagerly then paused. "I don't want to interfere with his time off."

"Oh, no problem, he likes to being helpful. And he'd enjoy seeing where I'm working and meeting you all."

"Okay, then, that would be great. I need to get this taken care of as soon as possible. In the meantime, maybe you could talk Henry into going over to the henhouse with you to collect the eggs. I'd like a minute with the vet."

Jaime laughed. "Sure. I've never collected eggs. Henry can show me how."

She practically skipped over to the fence where Lucy did quick introductions with the vet. In seconds, Henry had his sister's hand and was leading her to the coop. Chickens are a curious bunch, so several of them followed.

When Jaime and Henry walked away, Lucy ran into the house and dashed upstairs. She tossed the pajamas into the laundry basket. After slipping on underwear, a pair of jeans and a fresh blue polo shirt, she splashed water on her face, ran a brush through her hair, did a quick hygiene check, then hustled back to the barn—all in about five minutes. She chuckled. Nobody could call her *high maintenance* in the beauty arena.

The doc was in the process of rebandaging Odin's leg. It was still very swollen—down from an oozing watermelon to a grapefruit.

She crouched at the vet's side. "What do you think?"

"I think you did an excellent job of caring for the wound. I just gave him a shot of Novocain, clipped off a bit of necrotic tissue, and put in a couple stitches. Nothing looks infected."

"I'm so glad to hear that. When do you think I can ride him again?"

The doc hesitated. "It's going to be at least a month, Lucy. After these stitches are out early next week, you can walk him around the ring—if he wants to. Don't force it."

"Understood. I'm so grateful he's alive." She wiped watery eyes, then looked at Sinclair and laughed. "Don't worry. I won't cry all over you again."

"Be my guest." He stood and offered her a hand up. With a ridiculous flutter in her chest, she accepted, then went to Odin, whispering words of praise and running her hand over his warm neck and flanks.

Sinclair took a quick look at his watch. "I have an hour before I need to be over in Calabasas. Let me help you round up the runaways. I'm great with goats."

"That would be fabulous," Lucy said. "Have you had breakfast?"

"Had some coffee at home, so I'm not gonna kill anybody."

Lucy laughed again. It felt like warm sunlight as her anxious brain began to relax. "Good to know. Okay, you herd the goats. I'll get the chickens. Got a box of mealy worms they'll do anything for. The burros will follow the goats. Then, I'll make you breakfast. Got a nice fruit salad, can scramble some eggs fresh from the nest, and I made a rhubarb pie last night."

The vet's big hazel eyes lit up. He was a handsome man. "Rhubarb pie? For breakfast? I like your culinary style, Miss Vega. Let's get this roundup going. I'm suddenly starved."

—

Lucy had to smile. Jaime and Henry were proud of their stash of fresh eggs—twelve, in an array of colors—cream, browns, speckled green, and pale blue. Lucy cooked up a terrific batch of scrambled cheesy eggs, Henry's favorite, and doled out fruit salad and pie slices. It was a happy breakfast, and they were all sad to see Dr. Heath Sinclair go on his way.

Lucy cleaned up the kitchen while Jaime, and Henry built a space station with Legos on the porch. She glanced at the clock. A Facetime with Michael was happening in fifteen minutes. It would probably not be an easy conversation. He would not be thrilled about the Jaime situation. In the meantime, she filed an online report with the County Sheriffs. They texted that they'd send someone to check out the situation in the next few days when they had an officer available. Minor vandalism to ranch outbuildings was clearly not a hot issue.

Lucy hung her apron on a hook and joined Jaime and Henry on the porch. Grabbing her laptop, she tucked it under her arm. "Gonna video chat with your dad in just a few minutes. I'll be in my office, and I'll come get you both when it's your turn to talk to him. Sound good?"

Henry clapped his hands. He loved video-chatting with his father.

Jaime made a face. "I don't need to talk to him. We never talk."

Lucy was unwilling to let the bad blood fester. She had to at least try to facilitate communication. "Well, if you're going to work here with us and be part of the family, which I hope you are, then you'll have to start."

The girl scowled, but nodded her head in grudging agreement. She and Henry dove into a book on dinosaurs while Lucy set up for the call in her office.

—

"She's what?" Michael's eyes popped open wide and his voice rose. "She just showed up at the ranch, and now she's taking care of our son?"

"H*er brother,* three days a week, so I can get some work done. You're not the only one with a profession in this family."

"I know, Lucy, and I know I've been the priority for the last year."

"Two-and-a half years we've been in New York."

"Okay, but hear me. Jaime isn't reliable."

"Swears she's clean. No drugs. She looks healthy and seems very motivated to get her life together."

"She's easily led. You can't trust her. She'll say she's taking him for ice cream and go shoplift something from the boutique next door while the kid is waiting on a bench. You don't know her, Lucy."

"Give her a chance, Michael. She's doing great. Everybody needs a chance."

"Not with our child."

Lucy looked up and sucked in a quick breath. Jaime stood at the door, her face burning with disdain.

"He's bad-mouthing me again. That's what he's done my whole life."

"Jaime, that's not true," Michael protested.

"It *is* true. And look at you, gone as usual. It's hard to take a screen image bounced off a satellite thousands of miles above the earth seriously." She flipped her long hair over her shoulder and crossed her arms. "Henry deserves better. I won't let you ruin him." She turned and stomped down the hall.

Lucy felt a flash of concern. Had she taken Jaime on a little too quickly?

CHAPTER ELEVEN

It was Henry's turn to talk to Michael, who unhappily glowered in nighttime Fallujah.

"Daddy!" Henry appeared and dashed to his mom's desk. He crawled onto the chair and pushed his sweet face in front of the laptop screen. Michael's sour expression brightened.

"Daddy, Daddy, my big sister's here. She plays with me. We got eggs and had cheesies with Doc Heath."

"With who?"

"The new vet," Lucy said, ignoring a vague pang of guilt.

"A rattler snake bit Odin, but he's okay. Doc saved him. Showed me stuff in his doctor suitcase. And all the animals got out today, and he helped mommy catch them. He's nice."

As father and son chattered non-stop, Lucy went to the hallway where Jaime leaned against the far wall, talking on her phone. Michael was a man who could have conversations with heads of states and toddlers to equal effect. But not with his daughter.

—

Early afternoon, Jaime's new husband, Mark Wenter, arrived in his pickup. A tall, handsome young man with shaggy brown hair, he was dressed in jeans, a long-sleeved flannel shirt buttoned to the neck, and leather work gloves. In the truck bed he had a big toolbox, high tensile wire fencing, and 2x4s ready to patch up the damage.

Bugle ignored him and hung with Howard the cat on the patio. Maddie, owner of some random watchdog genes, growled. Lucy reprimanded her.

Jaime dropped Henry's hand and ran across the gravel into Mark's arms. He gave her a quick kiss and then, slightly embarrassed, pried her arms from around his neck.

Lucy shook his hand. His grip was confident and firm. "It's so kind of you to run out here on your day off to work on the outbuildings," she said.

"Happy to help." He had a husky drawl that whispered maybe Arkansas or Tennessee. "We'll get everything fixed right up, no worries. And maybe you could try gettin' those cameras Jaime told me about back online while I'm here. I'd feel a lot better about you women and a little boy out here by yourselves if your security's up and runnin'." He smiled. "Not to imply that you can't handle yourselves."

Lucy thought about the .357 and the rifle in her gun safe, about the time she'd had to shoot someone to survive, and about once firing an AK for so many rounds it burned her hands like a hot curling iron. But she didn't have a child back then. She was a different person. It was a different life. Now, she could no longer afford to take such risks. "Good suggestion," she said to Mark. "I'll sort the cameras right now. It's not a hard fix. I'll be in my office reinstalling the software if you need me."

"Sounds good. Jaime sent me photos of the damage, so I think I picked up everything we need at Home Depot."

Lucy liked his calm demeanor and sense of self-assurance. He was a good balance for Jaime's volatility, if the interaction Lucy had seen with her father, was an indicator. The girl and

Henry retired to the family room to watch an episode of *Peppa Pig*. Maddie remained on the porch tracking Wenter's movements.

Three hours later, Mark appeared and took Lucy for a tour of his repairs. Jaime and Henry trailed behind.

"Impressive," Lucy said. "Looks better than the original job. Jaime was right—you're really good."

Mark blushed a little and thanked Lucy. She noticed his wrist was bandaged. He noticed that she noticed.

"Caught it on some barbed wire last week. Always something when you're trying to maintain an old property."

"I can relate. I hear you're the owner."

"Yeah, well, it's been in the family for a long time. Can't let it all fall apart on my watch now, can I?" He shifted his weight from foot-to-foot. "My folks founded the place in '68. Near a hundred acres and some decent buildings—cabins, a chapel, music space, and a big mess hall we use for group activities. They left it to me when they went to the Lord a few years back. COVID."

Lucy touched his arm in shared grief. He winced, and she quickly withdrew her hand. "I lost my parents, too, when I was a kid. Not easy."

He nodded and looked away.

"Where's your camp located?" she asked. "Jaime said you're both living out there."

He peeled off his work gloves. "Camp's east of the Simi Hills. Used to be a real nice spot but it's getting too hot out there. Climate change and all. I'm starting to look for another piece of land that might be closer to the ocean, or up north where it's cooler. Simi's practically a desert."

"Good, affordable property's hard to find in California, as you well know."

Mark nodded. He looked back at the Vega ranch house, then passed it to the ocean. "You have a real nice spot, ma'am."

"I'm very fortunate," Lucy said. "This place has been a

shining star in my life."

"Nice for Henry to be able to grow up here, inherit it someday," he said.

"I'm always trying to teach him early to be a good steward of the property." Images of Henry without her on the ranch at some inevitable point, were too sad to deal with. Her thoughts went again to her lost family. It was a psychic button she could never avoid tripping. It took her years to accept that grief never ends. It just comes in waves that are less catastrophic. She changed the subject. "Okay, anyhow, I got the other four cameras back online."

"Great." Mark had a reassuring smile. He took a quick glance at his watch. "Should I take a peek at the pictures, make sure the cameras don't need repositioning before I go?"

"I'd appreciate that." Lucy brought up the security cam app on her phone. The camera views sat in a grid along with four images from the ranch house perimeter and four aimed at the outbuildings.

"Right on the money," Mark said. He looked at his watch again. "Gotta run, Lucy. Jaime and I have a Monday night supper meeting at camp in an hour and a half. Was really nice to meet you. Whatever you need, just let my wife know. We're grateful for the opportunity to help out. She feels particularly blessed for the chance to connect with her little brother. God is good."

"I can't tell you how much I appreciate those sentiments," Lucy said. She was not an organized religion person herself, but respected the comfort it gave others.

"Oh, one more thing," Mark added. "The latch on the goat shed is sprung. I jimmied it to work for now, but I'll bring a new latch and hinges later in the week. Shouldn't take me more than a half hour to install."

"Thank you so much, Mark. And don't forget to leave me the receipts." Lucy turned to Jaime, "You were right about your honey, Jaime, he's a gem."

The girl's face lit up like she'd seen the Holy Ghost himself. Lucy chuckled.

After goodbyes, Jaime and Mark took off down the drive in their respective vehicles. Henry bounced on his toes and waved. Lucy, hugely relieved that all the critters were safe, noticed a small bumper sticker on Mark's truck as he drove off. It was a cross with a serpent as the upright and a wood beam bisecting the snake draped in the white cloth of redemption. She wondered what kind of belief system the young pastor subscribed to. Lucy'd ask Jaime about it soon.

CHAPTER TWELVE

E arly the next Friday morning, Lucy finally received an email that a police officer would be coming in the afternoon to inspect the damage. She explained that the coops had been fixed and that she'd sent photos of the original destruction to the cops and the insurance agency. It had also rained and whatever prints that might have remained were now history. She got no response.

Then, there was a long phone call with Bea who told Lucy, amid an onslaught of tears and hyperventilation, that her beautiful and adored Rio Deakins was her brother. Her idolized Baptist minister father had cheated on her mother. And to add to the stress, her son Dexter had, along with his network reporter job, taken up playing semi-pro basketball in Iraq and had a crush on a local girl.

Bea groaned. "A crush on a local girl could get the kid murdered. She probably has big, scary, fundamentalist brothers. With AKs. Oh my God, Lucy. Michael promised he'd watch over my baby boy. And look what happened!"

"Okay, girlfriend," Lucy said, feeling her friend's pain but knowing parents have zero control over who their precious children fall in love with. "You cannot spend the weekend at home catastrophizing and on the verge of a panic attack."

"Not on the verge, no verge—totally off the rails! I can't feel my hands," she wailed. "My heart is shutting down!"

"Listen, honey, take a beat and do that box breathing the Navy seals do. That's helped before." Both Lucy and Bea suffered from anxiety issues. Over the years, they'd gotten really good at helping each other cope.

"Yeah, yeah, okay. I'm doing the breathing," she said, voice raspy.

After a few minutes of talking Bea down, Lucy said. "It's no silver bullet, but I've got wine and a nice charcuterie board ready for you here, sweetie. Henry will be asleep by eight and we'll watch *Bridesmaids* for the billionth time and drown our sorrows together. Can you drive?"

"Yeah, I think so. Okay, fine, but forget all that fancy stuff. I'm hitting Mickey D's drive-through for Big Macs, fries, and McFlurries. And apple pies."

"Girl, you're definitely over the edge."

"Uh huh. Lookin' into the abyss."

The plan was agreed upon.

—

Lucy and Henry finished a dip in the pool and were sitting on the porch discussing what they felt like snacking on when there came a knock at the door. The dogs started barking, then quickly quieted. Lucy pulled out her phone and checked the security cam. A smile spread across her face. A handsome, dark-haired man in his early fifties was petting the dogs with gusto.

"Who is it, Mommy?" Henry started to skip toward the door. "Is it Daddy?"

Lucy was practically knocked to the floor. The pain of that dashed expectation felt as physical as emotional. She had explained to her son that his father would be gone for several months, maybe longer. But kids don't have any sense of time. How could Henry possibly understand? He couldn't. Lucy pulled herself together, almost staggering as if she'd been hit.

"It's not daddy, honeybun. It's an old friend of Auntie Bea's and mine, Pete Anthony. He's a police detective, and he's gonna look at the chicken coop and the goat shed." L.A. County Sheriff Pete Anthony was a long-time homicide detective, not a minor property crimes cop. Why was he on the scene? "He hasn't seen you since you were two years old."

"I'm grown up now. Does he want ice cream?"

"He might." Lucy stumbled to the door and threw it open.

"Pete! It is so incredibly good to see your face. What are you doing here? Come in, come in." Her heart hummed with pure glee at seeing this man.

Pete stepped through the doorway as he always had—in a tsunami of high energy, dark hair slicked back, and a John Travolta in *Saturday Night Fever* swagger. They embraced in a warm hug.

"Lucerino! Long time no see, babe. I was down at the Malibu station on something else and overheard the dispatcher assigning some lame dude to your case. I grabbed it before they knew what hit 'em." He laughed. "I needed a few minutes of loose goats and Lucy Vega." He bent down to Henry's level. "And who is this handsome young man tucked behind you?"

"I'm Henry. Do you want some ice cream?" He stepped out of mama's shadow.

"I'd love ice cream, that is, if I'm not disrupting your mom too much."

Lucy grinned. Seeing Pete again was a fabulous blast from the past. One that was complicated and real and good. As Bea's former long-time lover and Lucy's dear friend, he was a piece of her life that she'd been missing since she'd left L.A. for New York. "I'm beyond thrilled to see you, detective. Get your butt in here." He followed her into the kitchen.

Pete had this Italian-Cajun thing going on that could make

a woman feel special. He also had an over-protective streak that had driven Lucy and Bea to distraction more than once. It was among the reasons he and Bea parted ways. But he was all Pete—zero pretense and a heart as big as California. One couldn't help but love him. Unless you were a bad guy, then you'd want anyone else but pit bull Pete Anthony on your tail.

"Ice cream first? Or coop inspection?" he asked Lucy.

"Ice cream!" Henry shouted.

"You heard the boss." Lucy opened the freezer. She knew Bea was on her way and hadn't seen Pete since they'd broken up two years ago. She texted her friend a quick message. *"Get ready for a yummy surprise. See you soon."* Lucy chuckled— Bea was going to kill her, then thank her. These two former lovers needed to at least be friends again.

Lucy pulled out a tub of strawberry frozen yogurt. Henry sidled up next to Pete. Lucy spooned the icy treat into bowls and passed them out.

"Is that a gun under your jacket?" the boy asked.

"Observant little man, aren't you?" Pete ruffled Henry's pool-damp hair. "A good eye— that's an important if you want to be a police officer when you grow up."

Henry licked his sticky, ice creamy lips. "Uh huh. I got a good eye. I saw the man let the chickens out. But I think I want to be a vet-rim-arryam."

Lucy let out a little gasp. "You saw who let the chickens out?"

Henry nodded. Pete and Lucy exchanged stunned glances.

CHAPTER THIRTEEN

Henry crawled onto the padded window seat in his bedroom overlooking the animal enclosures and the barnyard. He clutched a tattered T-Rex dinosaur stuffie, reminiscent of the *Velveteen Rabbit*—one-eyed, grubby, and dearly beloved.

"What were you doing walking around in the middle of the night, young man?" Lucy asked.

"The goats were making noise." He turned to Pete. "Goats bleat." He imitated the sound.

Lucy and Pete couldn't help smiling.

"Okay, so you looked outside," Lucy continued. "What did you see?"

"Snowball and the other goats." He turned to Pete again. "Snowball is white."

Pete said. "Good name for a white goat. Did you see any people near the animals?"

"A man. Maybe it was Cody."

"Cody's our resident equestrian stuntman and ranch hand," Lucy explained to Pete. "Lives above our barn when he's in town, but he's in Idaho on a shoot. I've known him since he was

Henry's age, and I'd trust him with our lives. It wasn't him."

Pete nodded and questioned patiently. "Henry, you remember what the man was wearing?"

Henry shook his head. "It was night."

"Yeah, hard to see in the dark, right? But is there anything at all you can remember about this dude? Silver cape? Light saber?"

The boy laughed and made another goat noise. "Nope." He climbed down from the bench, cuddling his dino.

"Okay, thanks, Henry," Pete said.

The kiddo tossed his stuffed toy into the air then caught it. "Big Bubba butted him, and the man fell down." Henry laughed again.

"He fell—huh." Pete scratched his chin. "Let your mom know if you think of anything else, okay, little man?"

"Okay. Can I go play with my tablet now, mom?"

"Sure, honey." Lucy watched her son dash down the stairs, then she turned to Pete. "Big Bubba's that brown goat over by the water trough." Lucy pointed across the drive to the largest of the pygmy goats.

"Bubba, Snowball. Not much to go on, Luce. Could be just a random act of some bored asshole." Pete squinted, perusing the enclosure. "There anybody you pissed off recently?"

Lucy shrugged. "Anyone I'd have pissed off is either in jail or long gone. The only new people in my life are the veterinarian who saved Odin from a rattlesnake bite and Jaime Burleson, Michael's daughter. She's taking care of Henry a couple days a week so I can get ready for my photo show."

Pete's eyebrows drew together. "As I recall from the distant past, Burleson's girl, the younger one, was having addiction problems. Major self-image issues."

"Good memory, Detective. She's clean now and on the right track. I really like her. You know me, been teaching Filmmaking part-time at Santa Monica High for years. I love that young adult age, even with all their drama and angst. Or maybe because of it."

"As a father of two of the nasty creatures, teaching teens is one of the many things I admire about you, Miss Vega." Sweetly, he patted her hand. "So, how's prep for the big exhibition going?"

"It's coming too fast; I still have a lot of printing to finish." Lucy pushed back her hair. "Show's called *Touch*. Theme's of people connecting. I have forty black and white images from the last fifteen years. Actually, there's a pic of you and Bea in it."

"Huh?" Pete grimaced. "I don't think so, my lovely."

"You both signed the release back then." Lucy smirked. "It's of you in front of a steaming pot of bouillabaisse holding a spoon for Bea. She's about to take a taste. Her eyes are closed and you're watching her like you could eat her. Very sensual."

Pete nodded with a sad face. "Food and sex. Even when we hated each other, we always had those two things going on." He cleared his throat. "But back to the investigation. Show me what you got."

As he snapped overhead photos of the yard with his phone from the window seat, Bea's BMW came tooling over the bridge and rolled up to the ranch house. Gravel crunched as she hit the brakes. Omlette squawked from the rafters. Lucy watched Pete's eyes widen as she stepped out. She had fabulous long, dark legs.

"Whoa. Speak of the devil." Pete cleared his throat. "And she's even wearing a blue dress."

"Mitch Ryder?" Lucy remembered the classic rock tune.

"Uh huh. Shit." Pete licked his lips. "She looks good. But I can tell by that big bag of grub that she's having one of her meltdowns."

"Yup. You might as well pile on. You'll have to help pick her up off the floor when she sees you, though." Lucy grabbed his hand and pulled him down the stairs as Henry let Bea through the front door.

—

Jaime lay amidst the soft sheets of their bed, dressed in a virginal white nightgown, waiting for God's instrument to rejoice in her loins. She rarely missed service, but today she was feeling ill and decided to rest in their cottage. Pastor Mark, her husband in God, was by now mid-meeting, rousing the congregants to religious ecstasy. She had seen it many times before and was always stunned at that man's power and humbled that he had chosen her as his vessel.

The organist would be pounding out the old time spiritual, *King of Glory,* backed up by a portly middle-aged woman on an electric guitar and a pimply drummer, barely a teenager. A crowd of around fifty people would fill the meeting room, clapping their hands, dancing, babbling in tongues and crying out in praise to the Lord. On the front riser, Jaime's handsome lover, his hair sweated to his scalp, his tie loose and shirt buttons open to expose a broad, gleaming, serpent-tattooed chest, would reach into a basket and pull out two writhing rattlesnakes.

"They will pick up serpents with their hands; and if they drink any deadly poison, it will not hurt them..." The verse from Mark 16:18 was etched on the rough wooden cross behind him.

The worshippers always screamed when the snakes were revealed and would raise their hands heavenward. Several women in the front row would begin to quake in orgasmic rapture, but Jaime knew only she would be the recipient of Mark's zealous love.

She saw it all in her mind's eye. The music ramped, building to a fever as Pastor Mark Wenter held up the rattlers and rubbed them across his body. He'd gyrate in a way that would make Elvis look like a Puritan. The pastor's tight trousers called attention to his godly manhood. Women tore at their clothing and had to be led away.

A group of singers in gold choir robes with a snake and cross embroidered on the breast, jived down the center aisle's stained carpet onto the stage to sing out the glory. An elderly man in the back row often fainted and fell from his folding chair. What looked like a rescue team administered water and smelling salts. The guy would soon be up and back at it, shaking his arthritic booty and blinking his rheumy eyes.

Drums banged out the rhythm. The snakes curled and squirmed. Believers fell to their knees before the dais, confessing and proclaiming their repentance and devotion. For another half hour, until the pastor pulled the plug on the mania, worshippers exhausted themselves in religious fervor. Finally, the snakes would be returned to their basket, and the crowd dispersed, drunk on Pentecostal gorge.

After another quarter hour, the young pastor would excuse himself with the basket of snakes secured beneath his arm and turn what remained of the crowd over to the care of two octogenarian ushers. He would leave by the side door and jog across the campground to his cabin, where Jaime readied herself to care for his needs.

She snapped back to the present when she heard the front door open, then slam shut. Jaime's body trembled with anticipation as the holy man, always shedding his clothes as he ran through the living room and across the kitchen, burst into the bedroom arrayed only in black tats of serpents slinking up his legs, across his groin, and slithering around his torso. Their mouths were open, and fangs bared. It was a frightening thing, but all he wanted in return for granting her a sacred place in his life and ministry was for her to sublimate her fear into the ecstasy of surrender and belief.

And to help him get the Vega ranch.

CHAPTER FOURTEEN

In the quiet darkness behind the ranch house, Lucy and Bea languished in the steaming spa, wine glasses empty, bodies floating weightlessly in the womb-warm water. A single candle flickered on a table.

In the night sky overhead, far enough from the ambient light of the city, stars salted the fathomless, black universe. Lucy opened her arms heavenward and stretched. The view was always humbling. Human existence was clearly a mere blink in time. Less than a blink.

"How many of those starry flecks of fire, matter, and mystery dust are now dead?" she wondered out loud. "How many are bursting to life for the first time?"

Her two pups were curled nearby on a beach towel. If only she could stay in the moment like they could.

Bea sighed. "Way too heavy for me to contemplate, sister, 'specially after half a bottle of chardonnay. I'm such a lightweight." She pushed back her curly, damp hair.

"How was it seeing Pete?" Lucy asked. "It's been a long time since you two gave up and walked away from each other."

"Ah, that man. Gorgeous, smart, independent, rough around the edges."

"A lot like you, except for the rough edges part."

Bea kicked her feet, splashing warm water Lucy's way. "Hey, we're going to try again, at least to be friends, taking it super slow. I'm going to join him at his daughter's high school regional volleyball tournament next week. I've known her since she was in grade school. Will be great to see her again."

"Ah, dipping a toe into the Pete Anthony waters. Nice."

Bea smiled and nodded. "His daughter, Gianna, is being courted by several NCAA Division I teams. I went through that with basketball a million years ago. But maybe I can still give her some perspective."

"And your son? You finally figure out that his girlfriend isn't the daughter of some crazy extremist?"

"Yeah. Her parents immigrated from Iraq to Detroit before she was born. She's a University of Michigan grad."

"Great school."

"Uh huh. Has a degree in Public Health. She heads an NGO, a relief agency, that helps impoverished Iraqi mothers and children."

"Sounds like someone Dexter would fall in love with."

"We'll see."

Lucy smiled. "Congratulations."

"For what?

"A few years ago, you'd already be on a plane to Fallujah to drag him home. But you're here. Very good, Beatrice."

"I might be mellowing in my old age." She finished a last sip of wine. "This is the first time I've felt relaxed in weeks." Her voice was a soothing whisper, but Lucy could see her dark eyes pierce the languid steam. "And then there's you."

Lucy's calm body tightened. "Me? What do you mean?"

"You're in *such* a good state of mind these days." Bea rolled her eyes. "I can see you obsessing about what's going to happen with Burleson, and it doesn't look good, if you ask me. And you haven't, but I'll favor you with my two cents, anyway."

Lucy shrugged. Here it comes—the usual unwanted advice that would ring uncomfortably true.

"I know you love each other, Luce, but you love the idea of a *real* family more than anything, and he loves his job more than anything. The twain will not meet."

Lucy blew out a long breath, her throat tight with unexpressed pain. "I had to give Michael and I a chance. He said he'd make it right this time."

"And how'd that go for you, honey?" Bea frowned.

Lucy knew the end was coming. Tears rolled down her cheeks, and she dunked under the water for a moment to wash them away.

"And then there's the photo show," Bea continued. "You act like it's just an exhibit at a local library, but our news outlet is going to be covering it, so is the *L.A. Times*, *Lens World*, *ArtNews*, probably *PhotoDoc* magazine, too, and the Hollywood trades. I'm not the only one who's been waiting for this. You have fans."

"Thanks for reminding me." Lucy groaned and submerged beneath the warm bubbles once more. She came up sputtering. "And I have to fly to the Big Apple next week to pack up our stuff and get it back here. I guess we'll keep the apartment for when Michael is in New York again."

"Moving is such a drag," Bea said.

"No kidding. I'm gonna ask Jaime if she can stay here with Henry on Thursday late morning through Monday evening. What do you think? It would be a tough trip for Henry—a long flight and then hours with a babysitter. All his toys being jammed in boxes."

"Yeah, agreed—he'd be miserable. You trust Jaime enough to let her stay here with your child?"

"I think so. I mean, yes. I've researched both she and Mark on social media—not much presence anywhere on the Net. A few cute pictures of them with kids at the camp he runs.

Certainly nothing concerning. Mark seems like a good guy. Treats Jaime nicely and has been super helpful around the ranch."

"Good to know," Bea said. "I was afraid you might have let her into your life a little too fast." She hoisted herself from the spa onto the edge of the pool. Her wet skin gleamed in the pale glow of the candle. "I still think that might be the case."

"She's clearly crazy about her brother. And it's for just a few days. Jaime can call you if she needs to, right?" Lucy asked.

"Of course. I'll stop by and check on them over the weekend."

"That would be awesome. Thank you. And she's got the vet's number if anything needs care in the animal department."

"Sounds like a plan, Lucia." Bea wrapped herself in a beach towel. "Now, tell me more about the vet. Scottish heritage, you said?"

"Yeah, his dad, our vet since forever, once gave me the rundown on the Sinclair tartan plaid. Old Doc Sinclair's retiring. But as for his son, there's nothing to tell. My life isn't an episode of *Outlander*."

"One can only wish, sweet Sassenach. What's his name? Hagrid or Angus?"

Lucy chuckled. "It's Heath. Just moved here from upstate New York to take over the large animal part of the practice."

"Hot, smart, independent? Loves his family?"

"Maybe."

Bea laughed. "Well, I can see I'm not going to get anything out of you on this dude. Yet." She rubbed her eyes. "Anyhow, girl, I think I'll hit the sack. I'm totally wasted. You coming up?"

"In a few minutes. Go ahead." Lucy rested her head against the edge of the spa and closed her eyes while Bea let herself though the pool gate and into the house. Bugle followed Bea, ready for his comfy cushion upstairs. The screen door to the porch creaked shut behind them.

Soon Lucy was surrounded by nothing but darkness and the

sounds of the night chaparral. Crickets chirped, a night bird called, and the wind picked up, whooshing through the grasses. The song of coyotes in the distance, frightening to some, was a lullaby to Lucy. The salty smell of the ocean mixed with the scents of sagebrush, eucalyptus, and creek willow. She took a deep breath and smiled—this was as close to heaven on earth as it got. When she climbed out of the spa, the cool air caressed her hot skin with icy licks. A high gust rattled the leaves of nearby cottonwoods. The candle guttered and extinguished in a puddle of wax. Lucy doused it in water.

Maddie moved from her beach towel and skulked to the edge of the fence surrounding the pool. She let out a low growl and began to pace.

The wind whipped, pulling Lucy's hair. She huffed, refusing to be intimidated by a spike of silly anxiety. "Mads, it's okay. Just a racoon or something." Worst-case scenario, a skunk. "C'mon girl, let's go inside."

Grabbing Maddie's collar to be sure the dog wouldn't bound into the darkness, Lucy pulled her to the door. Once inside the porch, she peered back through the screen. The wind picked up with even more intensity. A dark figure disappeared down the trail to the creek. Grabbing her cell phone, she brought up the security cam over the pool. Nothing.

Was the shadowy figure just a figment of her imagination? Of course. There was nothing on the camera. But was it wise to leave Jaime alone here with Henry when she headed off to New York? She'd ask if Mark could stay with her.

CHAPTER FIFTEEN

Monday morning, Bea sat at the kitchen island with Henry and Lucy, finishing a second cup of coffee and a scone.

She glanced at her smartwatch. "Guess I'd better get a move on. Almost eight o'clock."

Lucy poured her another splash of coffee. "That's late for you."

Bea stretched. "Pays to be the co-owner and publisher. Small benefits, right? And nothing like a bit of time out of the fray to remind me that we're all just specs in the greater cosmic scheme of things, as you observed looking at the sky last night."

Lucy smiled.

A moment later, the doorbell rang, and Henry went running for the foyer. Lucy's eyes followed him.

"It's Jaime!" He unlocked the door and pulled it open. "No! It's Doc Heath." He bounded out onto the terrace. "Hi, Doctor Heath. Bea and mom are eating scones."

"Be right there, Heath." Lucy jumped from her kitchen stool and headed to the door.

Bea was at her heels. "So, I'm gonna get to meet the

handsome veterinarian."

Lucy slipped her feet into rubber boots and whispered, "I never said he was handsome."

"I can read your body language like a book, my friend." Bea grabbed her overnight bag and followed Lucy outside where the vet, Henry, and a beautiful ginger-haired girl, perhaps six years old, smiled up at Omlette. The *watch-chicken* clucked from the overhead porch rafter. Heath was giving the dogs head rubs. They pranced and fawned over him. Odin snorted from the paddock across the yard.

"Sorry I'm a little early," Heath said. "Just found out I have an urgent case up in Camarillo as soon as we're done here."

"No problem. We're early risers. Heath, this is my friend Beatrice Middleton. She spent the weekend with us."

The two exchanged greetings. He offered Bea his hand to shake but she passed it by in favor of an enthusiastic hug.

"And who is your lovely little friend here?" Lucy asked the doctor.

"This is my daughter, Grace."

"Welcome, Grace." Lucy said.

The child gave a shy nod.

"Can Grace and me go play on the swing?" Henry asked, bouncing excitedly. He was an outgoing munchkin who loved company, unlike his more introverted mother.

"If it's okay with her dad," Lucy said. "We just hung a new saucer swing from the olive tree."

Heath stroked his daughter's shiny curls. "Sure, but I'll only be a few minutes, little one."

The two kids, instant friends, rushed off.

"Is it take-your-daughter-to-work day?" Bea asked, smiling.

"Not exactly. There's no school today, teacher conferences. My mom and dad usually watch her when I have to work, but they're still in Europe. Gracie loves to come with me if we have baby animals to take care of, but this is going to be a long procedure with an old bull who tangled with a mountain lion.

Won't be sweet or pretty." Heath sighed.

Lucy glanced over at the children. "Why don't you leave her with us? They can play, swim, we're going on a hike along the stream later. Henry would love company." Sounds of laughter came from beyond the corral. "They seem to have hit it off."

The vet's forehead creased with concern. "You're very kind but that's too much to ask. She'll be fine."

"Listen, let me walk Bea to her car," Lucy said, trying to ignore her friend's sly smile and slight nod of approval. "She's gotta get to work. You can think about it while you take Odin's stitches out."

Lucy linked Bea's arm in hers and the two walked quickly across the yard where the car was parked next to the barn.

Bea grinned. "Uh-huh. Wish I had a sick animal that needed a vet. Heath Sinclair—so Scottish. I'm thinking of the opening music for *The Outlander*. Hot dude's tartan cape is billowing in the wind along with his short kilt. Those broad shoulders are set for the caber toss or maybe a rugby scrum, or a roll in the heather with a Mexican-Norwegian time-traveler."

Lucy winced. "Oh my gosh, Bea. Stop. You should be a romance writer—pure fiction. You don't understand...I love Michael Burleson. He's my son's father. I'm still committed to him."

"But is he committed to you?" Bea's warm brown eyes studied her with concern. "Michael regularly disappoints you and his baby boy. And as you described it to me, I think maybe you got more out of the five minutes sobbing in that vet's arms the other day than you have from Michael in years."

"What? No." Lucy chewed on her lip. "Michael, Henry and I did fine in New York. We were a family there."

Bea shook her head. "Michael was biding time until he could get a break and go back to an international reporting gig. When the opportunity popped up, he disappeared overnight. Literally. And he'll do it again."

Lucy looked over her shoulder toward the cold gray ocean,

away from Bea's steady gaze.

"My first husband was like that—put everything else before me and Dexter," Bea said. "Thought the sun rose and set on himself and his pro basketball career. Don't settle, sweet pea."

Lucy stopped abruptly, her face twisting into an angry scowl. "Go to work. Leave me alone, Bea. I don't need this negativity." A flicker of hope for the relationship with Michael still taunted Lucy. She couldn't walk away until there was nothing left but smoke in the wind.

"It just hurts me to see you treated badly." Bea hugged her stubborn friend.

Lucy shrugged her off, turned and hurried back to the paddock where Heath was finishing up with Odin. She wrapped her arms around herself to keep the shards of her heartbreak from exploding through her chest.

CHAPTER SIXTEEN

B ea pulled onto Kanan Road, heading toward Agoura Hills and the 101 Freeway. It was a beautiful and relatively quiet commute through the Santa Monica Mountains. She was feeling a tinge of regret for what she had said to Lucy about Burleson. Maybe she wasn't giving them enough credit, maybe they could pull off a 7,500-mile long-distance relationship—if Lucy did all the compromising.

Her SAT phone pinged. She'd bought it the minute she got the word that her son had taken up residence on the other side of the planet. It was him calling now. The time difference was twelve hours, so he had probably just finished dinner. Excitement and love for the kiddo warmed her heart. Then fear. Was something wrong?

She pressed connect. "Dexter, is everything all right?"

"Hey, mom, all is well. Kind of. Just needed to touch bases. I want your advice."

"You never want my advice, hon. What's going on?"

"Well, this one is out of my wheelhouse." There was a pause, and then Dexter said, "I wouldn't get involved at all, except it's

Lucy. We've always been super close. She's like my second mother."

"I know, baby. I just spent the weekend at the ranch with her. What's the deal?"

He seemed to be taking a deep breath. "Well, here's what's goin' down. I think, I mean, I'm sure. Michael and Lindsay are hooking up."

"Oh, no." Bea felt her stomach drop.

"It's a small community here and, well, secrets are hard to keep. I feel terrible not telling Lucy, but I don't know how to, you know, say nicely—your man is fucking another woman."

Bea slowed the car way down as she approached the first of three tunnels through the canyon. There was still a pale scar on the traffic barrier between Kanan and the deep ravine where Lucy's uncle had crashed to his death years ago. She shivered at the recollection. The investigation of what turned out to be his murder was how Lucy and Michael initially connected.

"Mom, are you listening?"

"Oh, sorry, sweet pea. I'm pulling off the road so we can talk. This is all pretty upsetting."

"For sure. So, can you tell her? You're her best friend. I'm totally not comfortable doing it. I mean, I don't want to be a snitch, but it's Lucy and we have to protect her."

"For sure. You know, I had an inkling that this could happen. Lindsay is smart, beautiful, almost divorced from Rio, and she and Michael both want the same thing—high-powered international journalism careers with few strings attached."

"Yeah, they're a lot alike," Dexter said. "I'm learning tons from those two, but I don't actually like either of them."

Bea started to get heated. "Damn Michael Burleson, putting you in this position. You or I shouldn't have to tell her. He should step up and own the truth. If she hears it from someone else through the grapevine, she'll never forgive him and that might have blowback for Henry, even if she doesn't intend it. If Michael levels with her, at least he gets some props for being honest, the duplicitous asshole."

"That makes sense, but I don't think he's gonna be straight-up with Lucy anytime soon."

"Oh, yes, he is." Bea banged on the steering wheel. "Go get the prick. Mama wanna talk to him. Now."

"But—"

"Now, Dexter."

—

Jaime sat on a lounge chair near the arts and crafts area, watching the youngest little camp community members gluing macaroni onto construction paper. A beautiful dark-haired woman a few years older than herself oversaw their efforts. There was one child the woman watched with particular interest.

Jaime winced as a painful cramp twinged. She rubbed at her belly. The pregnancy test was positive, and Mark was thrilled at the news. Jaime, however, was pretty much terrified. She thought she was ready to be a parent, but she was having second thoughts that were obviously too late. Around ten weeks too late.

The dark-haired woman, somebody said her name was Isabella, looked her way. Jaime raised her hand in a little wave. The woman hesitated, but did the same, then turned back to the children.

Jaime had of late been craving the company of other females, but Mark insisted that she, as his Chosen One, not mix with the others. The only woman he gave her permission to talk to was the midwife, May Lou, who'd birthed him along with most of the others here at the camp. Jaime thought she gave off really creepy vibes. Jamie didn't like the way her hands lingered in intimate places during her gynecological examinations. And because Jaime was the Chosen One carrying Mark's child, the exams were frequent.

Jaime was looking forward to sharing the pregnancy news

with Lucy. She and Mark were there to basically entrap Lucy in their web, but she was beginning to feel uncomfortable with that plan. Probably just the hormones making her weepy and soft. She'd have to buck up; she was the favored one, and he had a congregation to expand for the eternal glory of God.

Closing her eyes, she prayed for the strength to do what needed to be done.

A bit later, almost asleep in the sun, Jaime heard a rustle of fabric and whispered words.

"Once I was the Chosen One. Be careful. Say nothing."

Jaime's eyes popped open. The young woman named Isabella turned and limped away.

CHAPTER SEVENTEEN

Henry hung between Mark and Jaime, holding their hands, kicking his feet, swinging and giggling. Lucy swallowed hard. "I've never been away from my son before."

With her heart hammering and palms moist, Lucy tossed her carry-on onto the rear seat of her SUV. She had plenty of clothes and essentials in New York, so she didn't have to pack much for the trip. She'd have lots of extra room to load up Henry's favorite books and stuffies. Lucy wiped nervous hands on her jeans.

"We'll take good care of him," Jaime said. She smiled at Mark, probably imagining what their little family would soon feel like when their own sweet baby arrived.

But Lucy found the morning's news of Jaime's pregnancy both exciting and concerning. Was the young woman ready for the responsibility? Recovering from addiction, she was just getting her life together. And she hadn't told either her mother or father she was going to have a baby, let alone that she was married.

"A few days with Henry will be good training for us," Mark

said.

Reassuring promises weren't registering in Lucy's skittering brain. "Okay, I know you'll be wonderful with him. I mean, you run a kid's camp, after all. I'm so grateful to you both. So," she swallowed hard, "his car seat is already in your truck. The flight information, phone numbers for Bea, the doctor, and the vet are on the fridge. Sometime on Saturday, Bea will stop by to pick up my photographs. She's going to deliver them to the picture framer in Santa Monica." Anxiety propelled Lucy's words fast as an auctioneer. She tried to slow herself down. *Chill, girl*, she admonished. "On Monday, unless I call you, feel free to head on home after you drop Henry at preschool. I'll pick him up after lunch. And, and..."

Was there something she was forgetting? Did the world not have cell phones if there was anything else? She huffed at herself.

Jaime pulled her in for a hug. "We're good, Lucy. Have a great trip."

"Mommy's bringing my toys home," Henry declared. He ran into his mother's open arms and gave her a cinnamon toast-flavored kiss and pressed his baby-soft cheek to hers. Squeezing the little man tight, it took everything she had to keep from shedding tears. What if the plane crashed? What if her baby boy had a terrible accident? She had to stop the crazy catastrophizing. On the other hand, her family members tended to die unexpectedly.

Lucy psychically slapped herself back to reality and, with last goodbyes, hopped into the car. With a honk and a wave, she drove off toward Kanan-Dume Road and PCH. Glancing into the rearview mirror, Henry was happily up on Mark's shoulders. With her son and the ranch receding behind her and a lonely Brooklyn apartment to be packed up looming in front, the tears she'd tried to swallow finally came hard.

—

From the window in Lucy's office, Mark watched Jaime and Henry floating on rafts in the aquamarine pool. Compared to his church camp in the desert east of the Simi Hills, this place was a paradise. Just where he and his ministry deserved to be.

He returned to the filing cabinet where he'd found hard copies of Lucy's Will and Trust. There was enough in these files to provide him the information he needed to create a codicil to the Will granting him and Jaime custody of Henry along with complete oversight of the kid's inheritance. Into perpetuity.

Mark's parents, fools that they were, would have spent their lives, and his, holed up in Eden's Gate, that dusty, run-down cracker camp. Mark was certain that God was guiding him to prosperous heights. With help from the venom, he'd had visions from the Lord. When he was feeling conflicted as a youth about wanting a richer life in every sense of the word, the Lord reminded him that through Mark's ministry, he saved souls by spreading the Gospel. It was clear that abundance—in both rapture and possessions in His name—were blessings for his servant. Pastor Mark Wenter, deserved. And if he had a prayer of ever being taken seriously and rising into the media's stratosphere, he had to have the location, the look, and the trappings of success that gave him credibility with big donors.

And sometimes in pursuit of the greater good, lives had to be sacrificed. He stretched his shoulders and rubbed at his neck, recalling the scripture. Leviticus 24:16 said, *"And whoever blasphemes the name of the Lord shall surely be put to death."* When his parents made their blasphemous choice and killed his first snakes, Mark and his sister cousin, May Lou, took the ministry and the camp into their own hands. And mother and father disappeared into the earth.

Footsteps sounded in the hallway. Mark snapped out of his reverie as Jaime appeared at the study door. She leaned against the jamb, looking sexy in a hot pink bikini.

"Finding what you need, sweetheart?" she asked.

"That and more. It's just a matter of time." His eyes caressed her body appreciatively.

She smiled with a demure lowering of her head. "We promised to take Henry out for frozen yogurt, like now. Remember?"

"Okay, get changed and we'll go." Mark shut the file drawer and pushed the chair back to the desk with a grin. "You drive me crazy, so gorgeous, but I'll keep my snake in the basket for now. There's always tonight."

"Whoa," Jaime gasped and pressed her abdomen. When the pang abated, she said, "Mark, I think there's something wrong. My uterus aches all the time, and the pains are getting sharper. Maybe I'm going to miscarry. I'm really scared. I think I should see a doctor, like a real doctor."

He frowned. "I told you to talk to May Lou about this."

She gritted her teeth at the thought of May Lou—a nasty, bloodless stick of a woman. "I did, but she said it was just nerves, and—"

Mark crossed the study and took her into his arms. "Jaime, beautiful Jaime. May Lou has delivered hundreds of babies for over twenty years as a midwife. She knows women's bodies as well as she knows the Scripture—which is considerable. And whatever happens with this pregnancy, it's God's will. Be brave, Jaime. Serving the Lord is never easy. Trust in Him and all will be well." He looked at her with big, soulful eyes. "Can you do that, my love? For me? For Him?"

She pressed her body to his, as if trying to draw strength from his touch. "Of course I can. I'm sorry. I'll deal with whatever comes."

"That's my girl. Now go get dressed and we'll hit the yogurt shop. Okay, love?"

Jaime gave him a peck on the cheek and scurried down the hall to collect Henry. Returning to the open laptop, Mark finished hacking into Lucy's security system and aligned the cameras so he could over-ride or manipulate content with a quick sequence. His strategy was falling into place.

CHAPTER EIGHTEEN

A hoard of noisy six-year-olds in bright orange, grass-stained uniforms with *Malibu Beach Yogurt Company* stenciled across the backs, swarmed the counter like flies on fresh meat. Beleaguered parents tried to keep the excited kiddos under control, with varying success.

"It's the first game they've ever won," a harried ponytailed mom with a wrist full of sparkly diamond tennis bracelets said to Jaime. "Is your kid on our team?"

"No, just taking care of my little brother this weekend."

Mark stood a few yards behind, looking bored and inching back toward the door.

"Ah, second family, right?" Ponytail Mom blinked tight eyelids. "The adult children have been neglected and then the shiny new little ones arrive with the shiny new wifey. The asshole men tend to do a better job at parenting the second time around."

"Not sure about that," Jaime said. The woman's bitterness and pretention were irritating, as was the truth to her comments. The noise, the heat, the smell of sugary yogurt was making Jaime nauseous. Her belly ached and she wanted to bolt from the shop.

Henry squeezed in front of her. "I want two scoops, please. Chocolate and bubble gum. Is that okay?"

"Sounds fine, bud," she said. "Looks like it'll be a wait though."

Henry pushed forward into the scrum of mini-soccer players.

"Hilliard, Osbourne, get over here," Ponytail Mom yelled. "Let's go." The boys came whizzing by her with smoothies as big as they were. "Take care," she said to Jaime.

"You, too."

"Gracie!" Just in front of Jaime, Henry was suddenly hugging the vet's daughter. Orange-uniformed, the girl was on the team.

"Hi Grace," Jaime said, happy for a change of focus. "So nice to see you, sweetheart. Congratulations on the big win."

"Thank you." The girl licked her double-scoop cone.

As Jaime stood on tiptoes to see if Dr. Sinclair was nearby, that's when it happened. Ponytail Mom's twin boys, swiping at each other like feral cats, fell into Mark, drenching him with light blue liquid loaded with multi-colored sprinkles.

—

Heath saw Mark flail as if the man had been burned. Cursing something unintelligible, he stumbled out the door to the tiered fountain in front of the shop and dunked his arms into the water to wash off the mess.

"You're not supposed to play in the fountain, mister," an obnoxious little girl with braids informed him, then huffed off with a disparaging smirk.

The vet sat at a table a few feet away from Mark and chuckled. "Looks like you had a collision with one of the crumb-snatchers."

Mark's response was an irritated look.

"I'm Heath Sinclair, Lucy Vega's veterinarian. I think we met up at the ranch a couple weeks ago. You were fixing the chicken coop, and your girlfriend—"

"Wife."

"Sorry, your wife, helps take care of Lucy's boy."

"Henry is Jaime's half-brother. We're watching him for the weekend while Lucy's in New York packing up."

"Nice of you. Our kids played together recently." Heath did a quick reconnaissance with a little wave to his daughter. Jaime caught his eye, too, and waved. Heath waved back.

"I'm Mark Wenter," the pastor said. "I'd shake your hand but..." When he shook his dripping, long-sleeve-covered arms, he seemed to realize that the vet probably got a good look at the rattlesnake tattoo slithering from beneath his cuff.

"Impressive ink," Heath said. "Northern Pacific rattler?"

Mark nodded, increasingly uncomfortable. He pulled down his sleeves and stuck his hands in his pockets. The wet white material was unfortunately translucent. "Lived up there for a while when I was a kid," he said. "They're beautiful creatures."

They are, for sure," Heath said. "Funny, we found one down in Lucy's barn a couple weeks ago. Bit her horse. Strange."

"Yeah, strange. Too bad about the horse." Mark's gaze left Heath and surveyed the crowd, obviously looking for Jaime, and to escape Sinclair's scrutiny

Gracie and Henry skipped out of the yogurt shop together, faces already smeared with chocolate. Jaime walked slowly behind them with two cups of the frozen treat.

"Doctor Sinclair, nice to see you."

"Hi Jamie, please call me Heath. Cool that you're taking Henry this weekend."

"Practicing for our own kids. I'm pregnant."

Mark flashed her an angry side eye.

Jaime frowned. "It's okay, Mark. Lucy knows, and the doc is a medical man." She handed her husband a cup.

"Wow, congratulations to you both. Very exciting. You doing okay, Jaime? Any morning sickness?"

She looked at Mark and then back at the vet. "No,

everything's great. Couldn't be better. No problems."

Mark nodded and gave a thumbs-up.

"Good to hear. Well, pleasure to see you all. Give a yell if you have any animal issues while Lucy's on the other coast."

"Yes, thanks. Your number is on the refrigerator," Jaime said.

As soon as they stepped away, Heath saw Jaime dump her yogurt in a trash can, bend over, and throw up. Walking toward the parking lot with Gracie, he wanted to text Lucy about the snake tattoos. But the last thing she probably needed right now was a far-out speculation that Mark was tied in with the snake attack somehow. Heath had nothing but unsubstantiated paranoia as a basis for concern. Maybe he shouldn't even mention it at all.

CHAPTER NINETEEN

Saturday before dawn, Lucy was still taping cardboard boxes together. There was much more than she'd remembered that she wanted to bring back to California. The company providing the moving pods had been alerted to the extra stuff, so all was fine.

Despite the heat, the windows to their vintage Brooklyn brownstone had been open all day yesterday to air out the place. With high ceilings and big rooms with hardwood floors, their digs here in this city were nice. Could she move back here? It would almost kill her, but she'd do it for their family.

This morning was already warm and humid in the borough, so she cranked up the air conditioning, poured herself a glass of iced tea and finally closed the windows. She was going to miss the bustle and diversity of the community they'd settled in. But definitely not enough to consider staying without Michael being here and working in the city.

Yesterday, she'd spent too much time mooning over every item she'd packed away—Henry's beloved monster truck, robots, magnetic blocks, an array of dinosaurs. Today, she was pretty much dumping drawers. Time was fleeting. Lucy was loading photography books into a carton when she got the call. Michael was on FaceTime.

Excitedly, she grabbed the phone and plunked down onto the couch. "Hey, darlin', I'm still in the city, packing up stuff to take to the ranch until you get back here."

"How was your flight?" His voice had a flatness to it. His hair was getting longer, and his eyes were bloodshot.

"Are you okay?" Lucy asked. Concern began to hum in her brain.

"We need to talk, Lucia."

His face looked strained. Her stomach tightened. "Okay, what's going on? Is your assignment going to be way longer than you thought? Or permanent? I can't say I wasn't expecting this."

He looked away for a moment. "This is hard to tell you." He chewed at his lip.

"So, rip off the bandage. I can deal with it," she said. "I'm sure we've survived worse."

He took a deep breath. Silence weighed long and heavy between them until he finally spoke. "I've been having an affair."

"What?" Lucy froze. Stars popped into her line of vision as if she'd been hit. "An affair? With who?"

He hesitated, tapping a pencil on the desktop. "With Lindsay."

It was a second sucker punch, this time to the gut. She gasped and clenched her stomach. It took her a moment to be able to speak.

"Lindsay." she repeated. Bea's former intern. Lucy's supposed friend who Michael took with him to Fallujah to give her a big break as an international correspondent. Lindsay— Rio's soon-to be ex-wife. Lucy wanted to scream and break things. "It's not casual. We're in love." Michael's voice was a cold whisper. "She's smart, driven, and so supportive of everything I want to do."

"And I wasn't?" Lucy moaned and heaved a roll of packing tape across the room. It crashed into an expensive ceramic sculpture of two lovers that Michael had purchased at a west side gallery. Teetering, it crashed to the floor. "I stuck with you and still loved you when your drinking was out of control, when you were on the network's trash heap of failed journalists." Angry tears blurred her vision. "And we worked together, too. We were an awesome team. Our documentary won a goddamn Emmy. And I moved to New York so we could be a family. You swore you wanted that, too."

Michael rubbed at his whiskery chin. "All of that's true."

Lucy groaned. "Unbelievable. How long has this been going on?" She wanted to force him into eye contact with her, but his face was hidden in the shadows of his dark office.

He paused, grimacing. "Maybe six months."

"Shit. We were still living in New York when it started? I thought we were happy." *How did I miss this? Is this my fault?* Lucy could feel herself start to slip into self-blame. But no, this was not her doing. She dug in her psychic heels and stopped the slide.

He said nothing.

"So, you took her with you to the other side of the world so you could, what? Test out the relationship without me in the way? I know you've been an incredible mentor to her. She has always put you on a pedestal. But I've seen deeper and forgiven you so many times. But not for this." Anger and resentment burned her insides. "It's over. Do whatever you want."

"I'm so very sorry, Lucy. I'm a total asshole. I should have leveled with you from the start."

"You're absolutely right. You're an asshole and a disgusting liar. But maybe that's what you want—lies, illusions. Someone who can see you in a shiny new, but phony, light."

Lucy looked at the half-filled box of their son's toys. "What are we going to tell our child?"

Michael rubbed at his eyes. "I dunno. He and I'll keep FaceTiming, as usual. You and me—we can talk later and figure it out. Who's taking care of our boy while you're in New York? Bea?"

"His sister, your daughter. Who is married to a minister and also pregnant, by the way.

Lucy wanted to laugh out loud at his shocked face.

"What the hell? Lucy, I told you—"

"You can stop telling me anything because you're not involved anymore. I have to go. Got even more things to pack knowing I'll never be back here again. I'll leave those nice black and white photos of our little family on the wall for you and Lindsay to enjoy." Actually, I'll take out the photos and leave sad, empty frames.

"Lucy, I'm sorry."

"No, you're not."

She disconnected from the call and resumed packing, hurling random items into the boxes like a woman possessed. She was taking her life back, all of it. That flicker hope about saving the relationship was finally an ash heap.

CHAPTER TWENTY

Bea arrived at Lucy's *Rancho de la Vega* early Saturday morning, wondering if Lucy and Michael had talked. Fingers crossed that he had manned up and shared what was going on. When they spoke, Bea made it crystal clear to him that he owed Lucy a second chance at a productive life, not one living in the illusion that they shared the same hopes and dreams. And more than that, he owed her honesty.

She left another message for her best friend, but no reply. She got out of the car and headed for the ranch house.

The dogs rushed to greet her. Henry was sitting on the front terrace with Omlette cuddled on his lap. The hen's golden head was tucked under the boy's chin as they lazed in the sun together. Bea was forever amazed at the range of emotion and sweetness in those birds.

"Morning, sweet pea." She kissed Henry on the forehead.

"Hi Bea-Bea. Mommy's still in New York. She's bringing my toys back."

"Yeah, she told me, very cool. I'm just picking up her photos. Gonna take them all to be framed."

"For the show?"

"You got it."

Jaime came to the door, her hair a frazzled mess like she'd just rolled out of bed. Likely she had.

"Hi Bea. I thought I heard somebody come up the drive. Forgot you were picking up the prints today." She didn't invite Bea in but stepped onto the terrace, the screen door snapping shut behind her.

Bea smiled. "Everything going okay this weekend?"

"All's cool."

"Sorry to drop by so early, but the framer called and wanted everything at his shop by 10:00. One of his staffers broke her arm so he'll be pushing to get this all done on time."

"Oh, okay. Mark's in Lucy's office working on his sermon right now. The prints, they're all in there. He hates to be disturbed. Let me go and check on him. I'll be right back."

The girl disappeared and Bea sat down next to Henry. She gave the yellow hen's downy wing a soft pat. "Does Mark work in your mommy's office a lot?"

"Yup, he likes to study. But Jaime plays with me."

Before the conversation could go further, Jaime returned to the door and held it open. "Come on inside. He's taking his laptop upstairs to work."

Bea followed Jaime through the foyer, across the living room and into the hallway.

"I told him I didn't think Lucy'd mind if he worked in here," Jaime said. "Was I wrong?"

"I think she'd be okay with it, except she told me she was trying to put the show catalogue together and had stuff everywhere."

"I'm sure he was careful not to disturb her things," Jaime said, a hint of defensiveness in her voice.

Bea immediately spotted the forty prints in two acid-free archival paper boxes on a sprawling work table. Mark had cleared out fast. She glanced around the room. It was pretty much how she had seen it last, except for a couple file cabinets ajar. As a long-time investigative reporter, she always looked for the little things. They could sometimes be clues to the big things.

Jaime followed Bea's gaze so Bea quickly shifted her attention out the window. "Beautiful view from here, isn't it?" she said.

"Yeah, this is a pretty blessed place. So peaceful." With sad eyes, the girl peered toward the pool and meadow.

"You look exhausted, Jaime. Are you doing too much, with the pregnancy and all? Early days can really take it out of you."

She sniffed back tears. "I'm fine, just a little overly emotional, which is typical, right? Hormones."

Mark appeared at the office door in his usual long-sleeved shirt and black jeans. He put his arm around Jaime. Her body language tightened, then loosened as she leaned into him. He pulled her closer.

"Hi there. Beatrice, right?" he said.

"You got it. Thank you and Jaime for taking care of my Godson this weekend. I had to go to a conference yesterday and couldn't get away. Have donor meetings this afternoon. Getting a new business started is tough. Keeping it going is even tougher. Probably the same with your camp."

Mark nodded and winked at Henry, who was still cuddling the chicken he'd carried into the office. "Our pleasure to take him," Mark said. "We love Henry. Sorry to be a pain with my sermon, but I really need to concentrate, and this office is perfect. God willing, I'll have one like it someday."

"Yeah, it's great." Bea picked up the two boxes. I'm sure Lucy would be happy to know you're enjoying it."

"You're in a hurry. Let me help you with those." Mark took the prints from her arms and trotted down the hall to the front door. The two women followed, with Henry holding Omlette just behind.

Bea frowned—Mark certainly didn't want to spend any more

time than necessary chatting. She wasn't even offered a cup of coffee. He'd been very helpful to Lucy, but he held Jaime a little too close for comfort. Something was off with the guy, but Bea had no idea what it was. She should like him, but she didn't.

Once out the door and onto the terrace, Bea gave Henry a hug goodbye, then crossed the yard and slid into the driver's seat of her BMW SUV. Mark had placed the boxes on the floor in the back seat. It felt like she was being hurried away from the ranch, but after all, she'd told them she had to be at the framer's in Santa Monica. They were just being conscientious and helpful. Right?

"Thanks, guys," Bea said. "And Jaime, call me if you want to discuss pregnancy stuff or anything else."

"Thanks, Bea," she said.

Mark pulled his wife close again. They waved goodbye together looking like some weird version of Grant Wood's classic painting, *American Gothic*. In Bea's vivid imagination, all Mark Wenter needed was the pitchfork.

CHAPTER TWENTY-ONE

Anticipating her joy at seeing Henry, Lucy's desolation eased at being discarded by the man she thought she was going to spend her life with; the one she'd foolishly imagined to be a lovingly present daddy to their son. But in a dark corner of her mind, she had known that would never happen. Your partner doesn't disappear to the far side of the world with barely a word unless something isn't right.

When Lucy picked Henry up at his Malibu pre-school, she checked in at the office. That done, she walked beneath a bougainvillea-draped arch past pots of sunflowers and tomato plants to where her son stood at an easel, painting marigolds.

"Henry!"

He looked up, dropped his paint brush and came running. "Mommy, you're back!" He dove into her arms.

Her son's paint-speckled face was the most beautiful flower in any garden. "Yes, baby, I'm back. I missed you so much." The briny Pacific breeze stirring up the children's playground smelled like heaven. Purple jacaranda petals danced in a tiny whirlwind.

"Did you bring my monster truck?" Henry asked, his face shining with anticipation.

"Yep, and two of the robots and your Bluey books. Everything else will come in a couple days. How was your time with Jaime and Mark?"

"Good. We saw Doc and Gracie at the yogurt store. She's on a soccer team. Jaime said she could come and play with me again."

"That sounds like fun. I'll set it up with Heath." Lucy helped Henry take his painting from the easel and ready it for a prime spot on the refrigerator.

Home at last. This time for good. The weekend away had felt like a month. Along with deep sadness and anger, she felt an unanticipated sense of relief. She was breathing more freely. It seemed like she had always been half holding her breath with Michael, and not realizing it. Lucy hummed along with an old Beachboys hit as she tooled down Pacific Coast Highway with her son. Focus on the goodness, the blessings, she admonished. There are so many.

When Lucy arrived at the ranch, Jaime's old Corolla was parked at the corral along with Heath Sinclair's veterinary truck.

"Uh-oh, what's going on?" Lucy said. She let Henry out of his car seat and they both jogged over to where Jaime and Heath stood together, looking her way. The dogs bounded at Lucy's ankles and Odin nickered.

"Hi guys. Everything okay?" Lucy asked, stroking her pup's silky heads. "Don't tell me there's been more vandalism."

Jaime wrung her hands. She was wan and appeared to have lost weight on her already slim frame. "I couldn't find Omlette. I saw feathers scattered over by the pool, like something had been eaten, so I called Doctor Sinclair. I didn't know what else to do."

"Is Ommy dead?" Henry's eyes were big and terrified.

"The chicken's fine." Heath patted the boy's shoulder. "Alive and healthy—followed your cat into the barn—they were holed up on a couple hay bales."

"The feathers were from, like a crow or something," Jaime said. "Black, not yellow like Omlette. I feel like such a fool. I'm so sorry Lucy, and Doctor Sinclair—Heath."

The yellow hen clucked from her usual place above the front door. Henry ran over to her. He reached into the can of tasty grubs by the window box and tempted the hen down into his lap.

"Thanks, for coming over, Heath," Lucy said. "Sorry for the false alarm but I told Jaime to call you with any animal issues."

"No problem."

"And Jaime, I thought you were heading back to camp with Mark this morning."

"I, uh, didn't want to go just yet. I don't want to see that awful midwife, May Lou. She follows me around because I'm the Chosen One."

"Chosen one?" Was this part of Mark's religious beliefs? "What does that mean?"

Jaime hesitated like she'd said too much. "Uh, you know, like Pastor Mark's special woman. He's a big deal in our church. So is being his wife. But would you mind if I stay with you for a few more days?"

"Sure, no problem, but are things okay between you two?"

"Oh, yes, we're doing great, but Mark is really busy with worship services and camp chores—I get a little restless and bored out there." She laughed and shifted from foot to foot. "And there's a whole host of people that look after the campers. I'm not needed."

Not sure she completely bought Jaime's explanation, Lucy welcomed her, nevertheless. "Yes, please do stay." The thought, however, of filling Jaime in on how her dad had fallen for another woman was overwhelming. But now, especially after the painful conversation with Michael, she had zero tolerance for dishonesty and the withholding of information. It was the root of so much pain and turmoil. Jaime was an adult, she needed to know what was going on in her family. And Lucy didn't have the mental energy to pretend that all was well.

The day was hot and breathless as Lucy walked toward the house. Stress and lack of sleep was closing in. Between the emotionally wrenching news of the relationship ending, non-stop packing, and flying with her borderline phobia about airplanes—it was too much. She suddenly felt faint. The barn began to spin, and she stumbled. The ground was coming fast.

CHAPTER TWENTY-TWO

H eath grabbed her arm and steadied her. "You okay, Lucy?"
"Just need to sit for a minute." She dropped onto the porch couch. Heath slid next to her, his arm around her shoulders. "A glass of water and something to eat would be good. I don't think I've had anything since yesterday. My blood sugar's probably about zero." She looked at Jaime, then at her son who was involved in a chat with the hen and the cat. They were both mini versions of their father. Lucy's heart filled with sadness.

Jaime turned to go inside and wrangle some food, but Lucy grabbed her hand and lowered her voice so Henry wouldn't hear. She couldn't hold it back. Not another second of duplicity. "Something's happened between your father and me," Lucy said. "You need to know."

"What's up? Is he coming back?" She chewed at her thumbnail.

Lucy took a deep breath. "We've separated. Permanently."

"Oh no." Jaime perched on the edge of the couch.

"He left me for another woman—a supposed friend who is

with him in Fallujah." Her throat tightened with repressed tears.

Jaime's hands clutched into angry fists. "That son-of-a bitch. I knew this was going to happen."

"I'm sorry to hear this, Lucy," Heath said.

"I'll get her some water and something to eat." Jaime stood and moved toward the front door, tapping Henry on the shoulder as she whizzed by. "Come help me make some lunch, Henry." They disappeared inside.

Lucy sat with Heath on the couch. She was relieved to have her son out of ear shot for a few moments. She was not ready to involve him in this mess. How could he begin to understand?

"Life's a brutal business," Heath said with knowing eyes.

"Bea's been telling me for a long time that he and I were never going to work," Lucy said. "I didn't want to hear it. I've been obsessed with creating this traditional, day-dreamy little family. After my mom and dad, my little brother, and my uncle, all passed, I think I went from survivor's guilt and an occasional death wish, to obsessively wanting Henry to have what I didn't—a storybook family, come hell or high water. I guess I just need to be grateful that Michael and my paths crossed long enough to create him. Maybe that's enough."

"Wise words."

Lucy shrugged. "I'm a long way from feeling those words in my bones. I've always been good at dealing with things in my head but not my heart. At this point, my supposedly *wise words* are all talk. Know what I mean?"

"I do." Heath's smile was wistful. "My wife left me and Grace for my cousin, a New York stockbroker with serious Broadway contacts. My ex is a theatrical set designer. Very good, very sophisticated and, I later learned, not a maternal bone in her body."

"I'm so sorry. And leaving her daughter? I can't imagine that."

"Yeah, well, we're much happier apart, so is Gracie. The

kid's thriving. Two years later, I can see that it was the best thing that could have happened for all of us."

Lucy nodded as Jaime and Henry came through the door carrying a tray of peanut butter and jelly sandwiches, a bag of tortilla chips and cans of sparkling lemon water. Heath pulled up the coffee table and the siblings laid down the lunch.

Heath popped the top on a can of soda water and handed it to Lucy. "Drink. You're probably dehydrated." He looked pensively across the yard. "I'm taking a few days off—going on a little vacation while the clinic is having some electrical work done in the surgery center. Tomorrow morning Gracie and I are heading up north to Mammoth. My family has an old hunting lodge my great grandparents built in 1908. Incredible spot. All updated about five years ago. There's a stream with a swimming hole surrounded by pine forests, incredible sunsets, and a stone fireplace you can practically stand in. Perfect for s'mores." He smiled at Henry.

"Sounds very special," Lucy said.

"Sounds incredible," Jaime echoed, her pale face animating.

"It's my version of your ranch. Do you and Henry, Jaime, too, do you want to come with us? Get out of Dodge, so to speak. We'd love the company." He turned to Lucy and whispered, "there'll be no old memories there."

"I dunno," Lucy said. "I just got back. I feel so exhausted."

Henry and Jaime's faces shone with excitement.

"I have a vet tech intern who'd probably be happy to keep an eye on the animals for a couple days. If you'd like, you can bring the dogs, too."

"Please, mommy," Henry begged.

Lucy looked over at Heath.

"Friends, totally friends," he said, reading her mind.

Why not? A new, neutral environment might be just what she needed to begin to kick start a new perspective on things.

"What do you think, kiddos? Anybody want to go to the mountains, the big mountains—the Sierra Nevada's for a couple days?" Lucy asked.

The verdict was hooting and claps.

"Okay. Looks like we're all in," Lucy said. From now on, she'd do whatever the hell she wanted. And she wanted the mountains, and the scent of pine, and maybe Heath Sinclair. On one hand it was all coming at her too fast, things were just over with Michael. But Bea was right, maybe they'd been over for a long time.

CHAPTER TWENTY-THREE

It was a five-hour straight shot up the highway into the eastern Sierra Nevada range. As a fresh breeze gusted lightly through the open sunroof, the morning sky was clear as the crystalline mountain lakes they were heading toward. Traffic was minimal. Heath merged the car onto Highway 14 toward Lancaster and then California 395.

"I haven't been up to Mammoth Lakes since I last skied. That was about, oh, fifteen years ago." Lucy shook her head. "Can't believe it's been so long."

"We'll have to remedy that next winter," Heath said. "Be good for Henry to get on the slopes as a kid, when they pick it up fast. Gracie's a good little boarder. Learned back East."

"I can shred powder," a little voice from behind piped in.

"Impressive, Grace." Lucy was distracted for a moment by Heath's handsome, proud papa face. Nothing sexier to her than a man being a good father. Then, her chest tightened with grief, but she refused to give in to it on this beautiful day. Focus on the present was required. "So, Heath, tell us more about where we're going."

"Okay, well, the Catriona and Cormag Sinclair Lodge is named after my great grandparents who built it. They wanted to provide a comfortable place to stay for hunters and fishermen. Now it's just a family retreat. Their much younger cousin, Sean Sinclair, was involved in obtaining the land—he was a lawyer, but they had a big falling out. Lost touch with him completely. "

"Families can be so complicated," Lucy said.

"That's for sure. Ye olde skeletons in the closet, eh? But anyhow, the place thrived and was designated a historic landmark a couple decades ago. It's about an hour from Mammoth Lakes in the Inyo National Forest. It's real wilderness, not like wilderness in L.A. County where you can go over a hill and fall into a TV production unit. We're talking seriously off any beaten path."

"What's it near?" Jaime asked from the back seat. Bugle was nestled asleep on her lap. Maddie and the Sinclair's pup, a sweet Scottish Terrier named Conn, were also along for the adventure. The two kids were watching the movie Frozen for the umpteenth time.

"We'll see Mount Whitney in the distance. It's at about 14,500 feet. We drive through the Mojave Desert, Owens Valley, and past Manzanar, the concentration camp where they held Japanese Americans."

Lucy nodded, recalling the tragic place and her connection to it. "I contributed to a photo essay about it for the *Times* years ago."

Jaime said, "We studied it in middle school. Is your lodge nearby?" She fiddled with her phone trying to get a signal with no luck.

"About a hundred miles northwest. We turn off 385 between Bishop and Lone Tree, then travel through ancient Bristlecone forests. The gnarled old trees are between three and four thousand years old. Mind boggling, huh? The history they have seen—wow."

"It's like another planet up there." Lucy said, remembering.

"That's why I love it." A wistful smile flickered across his face. "There's a transcendence about it. Puts things in perspective."

Lucy nodded. It was just what she needed. They drove without conversation for another half hour until Jaime said, "I could use a pit stop. Bathroom break?"

"Me, too," Henry called. "Me, three," said Gracie, laughing at her joke.

"Inyokern isn't far. Good bathrooms. Can everybody hold it for fifteen minutes?" Heath asked.

The back-seaters all voiced affirmative. Bugle whined.

"The dogs told me they can use a break, too," Jaime said.

At Inyokern, everybody took advantage of the restrooms at the Indian Wells Brewery. Heath let the kids buy a few snacks for the rest of the trip. Soon they'd be leaving the semi-arid desert behind and head up winding mountain roads into cool, lodgepole pine and juniper forests. Lucy oversaw the dogs going about their business and checked her watch. An hour and a half to go.

Jaime's face was pinched with worry as she joined Lucy.

"I'm bleeding." She chewed at her nails.

"Bleeding? Like a lot?" Was this a precursor to a miscarriage? A pang of worry pressed on Lucy. She was thinking worst-case scenario as she tended to do lately.

"No, just spotting, but heavy spotting."

"That's not unusual during early pregnancy. Any pain?"

"It always aches."

Lucy nodded. "Okay, love, keep me posted if it gets worse. We can go over to Mammoth Lakes and have you checked out."

"No need for that." Jaime anxiously pulled at a loose strand of hair. "Mark would be really angry. He's not into regular medicine. You know, we're more into God's will and all."

"It's your life, your body, not Mark's. And for some reason, *God's will* placed you with us this week. We're going to make sure you're okay."

She nodded and seemed relieved. "Alright, thank you. I'm sure I'll be fine. I'm just so nervous these days."

Lucy gave the girl a warm hug offering reassurance she didn't completely feel.

CHAPTER TWENTY-FOUR

Sinclair Lodge was stunning. Lucy swooned—no HGTV home show could have come up with a more beautiful setting. She couldn't wait to take photographs. The large two-story log edifice had a wide, screened-in porch replete with rocking chairs and vintage rattan sofas. Mason jars filled with wild iris and columbine sat on a long picnic table. Hot pink geranium-filled flower boxes flanked the massive front door.

From one of several nearby log cabins, an older woman in jeans and a red golf shirt ambled their way with a welcoming smile. Her white hair was tied into a braid and a chunky turquoise bracelet encircled her wrist. "Hey, darlings, so thrilled to see you," she called.

"Nana Ruthie!" Gracie yelled and ran to jump into the woman's arms, almost knocking her over.

"Gracie Rose, you are getting so big. My goodness! I've missed you so much. The lodge is all ready for you."

"We've missed you, Ruthie," Heath said, joining the hug. "Tons. Now that we're in California permanently, you'll be seeing way too much of us."

"Never, ever will that be true." She patted his cheek. "And who are these lovely people with you?"

Introductions were made. Long-time lodge caretaker Ruth O'Hara, and her husband Cal, a custom saddle maker who was in Mammoth Lakes with a client, gave Lucy, Jaime, and Henry a tour of the lodge. Heath unloaded food and supplies from the SUV while Gracie played with the dogs on the porch.

Inside, the lodge featured a two-story great room with a huge fireplace and panoramic windows overlooking the valley. Above, five bedrooms, each with recently updated *en suite* bathrooms, surrounded the main living area and looked down from a wraparound balcony. Native blankets hung over the railings. Landscape paintings of the area and photos of the early hunting lodgers and the Sinclair family lined the walls. Their Scottish family crest hung above the river stone hearth and half-log mantel.

"This place is amazing," Jaime whispered to Lucy.

Lucy was again grateful she'd agreed to let them all come. The day passed uneventfully as the children played in the swimming hole created by a small dam in the stream. The water was cold, but they didn't care; neither did the dogs. Dinner was spaghetti, salad, and s'mores roasted in the fireplace.

After dinner, Jaime complained that she didn't have cell reception, but Heath assured her he had a satellite phone if she needed to make a call. Jaime hiked up to a ridge to see if she could catch a signal.

So exhausted from the New York trip and the emotional stress of a relationship coming apart, Lucy barely remembered tucking Henry in. He and Grace shared a room with single brass beds. The sheets held the scent of pine boughs. Her boy smelled like fresh water from the clear creek burbling just beyond the house.

The fire in the hearth crackled. Lucy returned to the great room to thank Heath again for bringing them to the lodge and bid him good night. She climbed back up the stairs to the balcony and her bedroom, pausing for a moment to watch him as he sat reading. He looked up for a moment and smiled at her. He was disturbingly beautiful in the firelight.

After a glorious hot shower, Lucy burrowed under the down comforters and tried not to think of Michael in bed with Lindsay, or Heath in bed alone. She simply thanked God for another day and was out.

—

The next thing Lucy was aware of was that the sun was coming up and Jaime was moaning in the room next door.

Throwing off the blankets, she ran into the young woman's bedroom. Lucy gasped. Jaime lay in the midst of blood-soaked sheets.

"Lucy, help me," she begged.

"Oh my God." Lucy tried not to choke on fear. The scene was dire. She pressed

Jaime's hand. "I'll get Heath, he'll know what do."

She sprinted to Heath's room and burst through the door. "Jaime is hemorrhaging.

Blood is everywhere. Please come."

He grabbed the SAT phone on the bedside table. In cut-off sweatpants, he followed her into Jaime's room, then paused for a moment to take in the situation. He turned to Lucy. "Would you get my medical bag? It's downstairs by the back door."

She returned minutes later toting the leather case. He was on the phone with an emergency dispatcher. Grabbing his stethoscope, he assessed Jaime's vitals, reporting as he went.

She was crying and agitated. Lucy held the girl's hand and tried to calm her.

"Lucy, get towels from the hall closet," Heath directed.

His in-charge demeanor was comforting.

"And then run next door and tell Ruthie we need her to come over and watch the kids right away. I have to stay on the line with the paramedics."

His attention went back to the phone conversation with the dispatcher. "MedEvac is an hour out? Shit." He moved from the bedside and paced, then stopped. "Okay, here's what we're going to do. We'll leave here and meet the ambo at the Columbine Meadows scenic turnout. It's a half hour in opposite directions for both of us. Here's the medical situation..."

Lucy stopped listening, whispered encouragement in Jaime's ear, then followed Heath's requests, grateful that Henry and Grace were not awake to witness this horror.

Fifteen minutes later, Nana Ruthie was gathering up the bloody sheets. The children were still sleeping. Heath and Lucy loaded Jaime into the SUV. Gravel flew as he gunned the engine and rocketed onto the narrow county road.

CHAPTER TWENTY-FIVE

L ucy was in the back seat with Jaime's head on her lap, trying to stabilize them both as they jostled slide-to-side on the winding mountain road. She pressed towels between Jaime's legs and on her lower abdomen. The pale blue terrycloth was staining red, and the metallic smell of blood filled the car. Lucy gulped to stem a pang of nausea.

In ten minutes, Jaime had soaked four bath towels and began to lose consciousness. The girl's skin was cold and clammy, her breathing labored. She was no longer responsive to Lucy's attempts to keep her awake and talking. "Heath, we're through all the towels and she's fading."

He removed his gray fleece hoodie and tossed it back to Lucy. "Use this. And there are some old clothes and a maybe blanket behind your seat. Do the best you can."

Lucy pieced together what she could find then squeezed in to kneel on the floor behind the driver's seat, putting her whole weight on Jaime's abdomen. Were they going to lose her? She tried not to go there but this was bad.

Heath had the phone on speaker with the emergency

medical folks. His voice was steely, in full professional mode. "She's bleeding out. We're going to need a transfusion STAT. What've you got?"

"Two units of O-neg," a female paramedic said. She'd introduced herself as Lauren.

"Universal donor. Great," Heath said. "Hook it up and have it ready to go. My ETA's ten minutes."

"Roger that," Lauren said. "We're pulling into the turnout now. Are you a doc? You seem to know what you're doing."

"I'm a veterinarian."

"A vet?" She sounded disappointed.

"Who spent three years as an Army Special Ops Medical Sargent in the field during the Afghan war. I've seen a lot. A whole fucking lot."

"Whoa," the paramedic said. "That's like the Delta Force of military trauma personnel."

Lucy was surprised to hear this. Now, his cool, disciplined demeanor made sense. "Did you treat many women?" she asked.

Heath nodded and took a long breath. "Along with military, we treated civilians from surrounding villages—men, women, kids, animals. You name it, we dealt with it the best we could." He pressed his eyes as if trying to dim the vision. Then, laser focusing again on Jaime's crisis, he said, "Lauren, we're going to have to tie off the bleeder or she's not gonna make it."

"Yes, sir. How do you want to proceed?"

"I've done this a couple times before. Can you get the general surgeon from the medical center to Zoom in and oversee?"

"I think so, maybe," Lauren said. "Hartman may not be working this morning."

"Find her. Now. And be ready to go. My guess is it's a ruptured ectopic pregnancy."

"Oh, shit," Lauren said. "On it."

"You have an ultra-sound onboard?

"Brand new. Just got it."

"Okay, and call MedEvac to meet us."

"Done," she said.

Lucy felt warm liquid wicking through her T-shirt. She'd scrounged up a camp blanket that smelled of dog from the back seat. It was doing a pretty good job of absorbing the blood. With all her weight on Jaime, the gush seemed to be slowing just a bit. Or was it was just backing up into the woman's abdominal cavity?

"How much longer?" Lucy asked, beginning to lose feeling in her arms from pressing so hard. Out the window, the landscape blurred by.

"There they are, just ahead."

Lucy stayed glued to Jaime as Heath's SUV barreled across the parking lot.

"Hang in there, Jaime, we're pulling up to the ambulance. You'll be okay," she whispered, desperate to believe it.

The paramedics were at the car door in seconds with a gurney. They loaded the young woman onboard and rushed her into the ambulance. Heath jumped in behind them.

Lucy, drenched in blood, lunged out of the back seat. She felt a short-lived sense of relief that the medical people now could work on stemming the hemorrhage. She watched as Lauren, slim with short hair beginning to gray, gave Jaime Oxygen, hooked her up to the IV, hung a bag of blood, and then brought up her vitals. Even a layperson could see the numbers didn't look good. Lucy took a deep breath to try and calm herself. Jaime couldn't die.

Lauren's assistant, a young male EMT, held a laptop. His name plate said Raul Bautista. "We've got Christa Hartman coming on any second," he said. "She's head of surgery at Mammoth Lakes Med. A really good doc."

Heath, palpitating Jaime's abdomen, nodded as Lauren prepped what Lucy figured was anesthesia.

Soon the surgeon's face filled the screen. Blond-haired, in

her late forties, she'd seen the vitals and immediately began to talk with Heath about the impending operation. Lauren worked on providing a sonogram.

Lucy glanced at her watch. It was 7:30 a.m. "How can I help?' she asked Raul. He was positioning the camera on the laptop, so Hartman had full view of the surgical target.

"Keep anyone from driving into the lot here so the chopper doesn't have to waste time finding a spot to put down," he said. "And pray."

Lucy nodded and stepped away. The ambo door closed, and she prayed.

Traffic was light. Only a few tourists attempted to drive into the scenic overlook during the half-hour wait for the MedEvac chopper. One driver was outraged because he and his wife had driven all the way from Utah. They demanded to pull in.

Lucy finally stuck her bloody hand through the car window, grabbed the man's shirt and hissed, "Is looking at a meadow you can see just as well a few hundred yards down the highway, worth the death of a young pregnant woman who can't get into a rescue chopper because you're in the goddamn way?"

He drove off fast, almost catching Lucy's arm in the window as it rolled up.

Then she heard, it—the *whomp, whomp* of helicopter blades coming from the North. First an insect-like blot in the blue sky, it was soon positioning to land on its skids in the parking lot. The atmospheric pressure seemed to drop, and dust boiled in the air.

Lucy glanced at the ambulance; the back doors were still closed. First out of the helicopter were two men pushing a gurney. A dark-haired woman was in the pilot's seat.

To avoid the downwash, the medics ducked and moved out of blade range fast. They met Lucy by the ambo.

An older man with weather-worn skin said, "The dispatcher filled us in. They're almost done with the surgery. Got the bleeder tied off but she's critical."

Lucy nodded. "I'm going with the patient to the hospital." Given her flight phobia, the ride was her idea of hell on earth, but she had to do it for Jaime.

"You family?" the weathered man asked.

"Step-mother."

The other paramedic, short and young, nodded.

Lucy wasn't really a step-mother, but who cared. It got her in. Jaime was going to need caring support to survive this.

The door to the ambulance opened. Heath and Raul brought out unconscious Jaime on the blood-soaked gurney. Lauren was on the laptop with Doctor Hartman. The men made the transfer onto the MedEvac cot with its clean light blue sheets. The younger tech grabbed the half empty bag of blood and carried it alongside, attached the patient.

Lucy ran to Heath. "I'm going with her."

"Okay, good. She'll need all the moral support she can get."

"Is she going to be alright?" Lucy asked.

His eyes held a wary, haunted look. "It's a crapshoot. Surgery went well but she's lost so much blood. She has a fighting chance. I'd put my money on her making it. But the pregnancy is over."

Lucy nodded, worry and grief souring her stomach. "Okay, I'm outta here."

"We'll talk later this afternoon," Heath said. "God speed."

She hugged him then went to the SUV to grab her day pack. The vehicle looked like a major crime scene.

Lucy sprinted to the chopper as the engines revved and the spinning blades began to whine. In minutes they were racing east toward Mammoth Lakes Med with Heath and the ambo receding in the distance. She held Jaime's cold hand in hers and went back to praying.

CHAPTER TWENTY-SIX

Jaime's eyes fluttered just as the chopper touched down with a big bump at the Medical Center. She had regained consciousness and was trying to speak.

Lucy pulled off her headphones and leaned in close.

"Am I dying?" she asked. Her eyes were slits trying to open to little avail. The chopper noise was too loud for conversation.

"You'll be fine," Lucy mouthed, pressing the girl's hand in both of hers. Jaime turned to her side and vomited into a bag the tech held at the ready.

"Anesthesia will do that to you," Raul shouted.

The pulsing blades began to slow. In moments, the two medics had the young woman out of the chopper, rushing her toward the ER entrance with Lucy at their side. The double doors wheezed open.

Inside the facility, the staff was ready for the incoming patient. Jaime was whisked into an exam room, transferred to a bed, and hooked up to another IV, wires, oxygen, and electrodes. Soon Dr. Hartman entered the room with a coterie of nurses and technicians. After she and Lucy shook hands,

Hartman gloved up in blue nitrile.

Lucy reminded the doctor that Jaime was a recovering addict and shouldn't be prescribed opioids. Then, she stood back against the white tile wall, out of the way, as the staff went to work.

"Lucy," Jaime called, her voice plaintive.

"Right here, honey. The doctors need room to do their job but I'm not going anywhere, not leaving you."

Two hours later, Jaime had been checked into a regular hospital room where Lucy sat quietly at her bedside. The patient monitor droned with a reassuringly consistent beep. The sounds of talking and the wheeling of carts in the hallway was occasionally joined by laughter from a TV game show playing several rooms down.

Since Jaime was awake but groggy, Lucy explained to her what had happened in the simplest way possible. Tears of loss oozed down Jaime's cheeks when it was confirmed that she'd lost the baby. Lucy knew that a failed pregnancy, even though not unusual in the larger scheme of life, was a personal blow from which one never quite recovered.

"Call Mark, please, right away." Jaime's voice was a weak whisper.

"Yes, of course. The signal is spotty in this part of the hospital, sweetheart, but I'll get him as soon as I possibly can." She brushed the tangled hair from the exhausted girl's eyes as she fell asleep. Lucy didn't have a chance to mention that she was also going to contact Jaime's father as well. He and her mother needed to know what was going on with their daughter.

In the meantime, Lucy left a message for Heath on his SAT phone that the patient had stabilized, still in serious condition but out of the trauma unit.

Dr. Hartman checked in again with just a single nurse this time. Hartman was a tall, fit woman who could star in a Scandinavian Noir mystery series. Great bone structure, no make-up, the kind of natural beauty that Hollywood found difficult not to plump, fill and sculpt into a boringly perfect stereotype that lost all unique appeal.

Hartman studied Jaime's chart, then looked at Lucy with a tired smile. "Doctor Sinclair did a fabulous job," she said. "Barring anything unforeseen, your girl here should recover fine. Still has one lovely and functional fallopian tube so decent chance she can get pregnant again when she's ready."

"That's great to know," Lucy said, relieved to finally get the definitive word on Jaime's condition. "Thank you for the amazing care from you and your team."

"Was pretty crazy there for a while." Hartman smiled again. "I think we'll keep her another day or two for observation. Recovery is around six weeks—no lifting, light activity, and lots of rest. The first few weeks she'll be very sore. And the emotional fallout from this experience is not going to be easy. She's going to need a lot of patience and support."

"Yes, for sure," Lucy said, personally recalling the trauma of a pregnancy gone wrong.

Hartman glanced at her smart watch. "This afternoon, the nurse will be back to go over everything with both of you."

"Thank you so much," Lucy said. The adrenalin rush of the last hours was ebbing, she was feeling both relieved at the prognosis and totally spent.

"And tell Sinclair, if he ever wants to go back and get his medical degree, the human one," the doctor chuckled, "we'd hire him in our trauma unit in a hot second."

Lucy nodded. "I'll pass on your compliments, but my guess is he's had enough trauma in the military to last a couple lifetimes."

The nurse, an older woman with short curly hair said, "I have something for you, Miss Vega." She handed over a pile of light gray scrubs. Lucy looked a bit mystified.

The nurse patted Lucy's arm. "We got you fresh clothes, socks, shoe covers, a warm flannel blanket and a biohazard bag." She topped it off with a kit that looked to contain toiletries. "Feel free to use the staff locker room down the hall. Take a shower, get on those fresh clothes and stow all that bloody stuff of yours in the bag."

"You are so thoughtful. Thank you." Lucy was suddenly aware that she was covered in dried blood. Her hair was matted with it. She reeked of it. "A shower sounds like heaven."

"Come on then," the nurse said. "Jaime will be sleeping for a while. I'll take you to the locker room, then you can grab a late breakfast in the cafeteria."

"Has a beautiful view of the mountains, good cell reception, and excellent blueberry pancakes," Hartman said.

"Fabulous." Along with wanting a shower, Lucy was starved. She'd clean up, grab coffee and pancakes, then make the tough phone calls.

CHAPTER TWENTY-SEVEN

Mark put down the phone, face grim. A vision out of the 1950s, May Lou, in her usual simple house dress and apron, stood near him in the kitchen, drying dishes.

"Jaime lost the baby," he said. "Up in Mammoth. I should never have let her go, but I figured it would be a chance for her to get closer to Lucy Vega and the kid."

"Was that Vega on the phone just now?" the woman asked.

"Yep. Jaime's in the hospital, still asleep. Lost a ton of blood. Probably would have died here."

May Lou's mouth puckered into a lemon-eater grimace. "We can't have that. Without the girl, we got no access to the ranch. Guess it was good luck that she was with that bunch for a few days. Must have been God's will. Wants you to have the success you've always dreamed of and get that property. But the miscarriage—you got plenty other children. Most of them in the camp's your progeny. And anyhow, maybe she'll get with child again soon."

Mark nodded.

"So, stop lookin' so glum, boy. Have you gone over to the

laundry and welcomed that Miss Tanya Lee Riggs, the gal cousin Clement sent up from Tennessee last week? I put her to work washin' an foldin' sheets and towels. Nobody stays here without a job. Colossians 3:23 says, *Whatever you do, work at it with all your heart, as working for the Lord, not for a human master.*"

Mark acknowledged the scripture quotation with a slight bow of the head. "But about Clement's girl, I haven't seen her. Got a lot on my mind." Mark listlessly finished the last of a pile of bacon and buttered grits.

May Lou took off her glasses and cleaned the lenses with her drying cloth. "I told you a week ago to git over there, introduce you'self like a gentleman. Clement sends lots of money every year to help keep this place goin'. We take care when he asks for a favor."

"Yeah, okay, I'll go now, need a distraction." He stood, tucked in his shirt, pulled down the sleeves and moved to the kitchen door. "Why'd he send her up here?"

May Lou picked up his plate and shrugged. "Ain't the first woman he's sent needin' our shelter. Like the others, she's in some kind of trouble with the law."

"Like what?"

"Dunno. That's for you to find out. I run the business of this here community and you take care of the other stuff. That's the way it's been since we sent your parents to God. Now, off with you. Make sure she feels welcome and comfortable. Clem needs to know we're treating her right. Remember Romans 13, *Share with the Lord's people who are in need. Practice hospitality.*"

"Yes, ma'am. I will practice hospitality." Mark shook his dark wavy hair like a wet dog and headed to the laundry building wondering what this woman on the run would have to offer his ministry.

—

The converted double wide trailer sloshed and hummed with

the sounds of washers and dryers. All the windows and the screen door were open as Mark crossed the playing field to reach the other side of the compound. A soccer ball rolled his way, and he kicked it back to a pint-sized player. Mark smiled. The kid had his athleticism and lush, brown hair.

"Miss Tanya Lee Riggs," he called as he opened the screen door and stepped into the trailer. With the appliances belching humidity, the big room felt like Tennessee in the summer.

Behind the long folding table stood a woman about Jaime's age. Her light brown skin was shiny with sweat and her brown hair was up in a curly ponytail. "Miss Tanya Lee?" he asked.

"Why, yessir, Pastor Wenter. At last, a chance to meet you." She continued to fold white towels.

At first glance, she was attractive but not beautiful. Until she smiled. And then it was hard to pretend not to notice her lovely face and basketball-sized bosoms. His loins stirred.

"So sorry I haven't been around to greet you personally, ma'am. It's been a busy week. I trust May Lou has seen to your comfort?"

"Yes, indeed. Your cousin Clement was happy to hear I'd arrived safely. Although, he described this place as being practically in Hollywood, where he was hoping I might eventually find a career."

"We have plans to move in closer, develop those theatrical relationships, but for now, I hope you can find some respite from your troubles with the law in these parched hills."

Braless, she pulled at the straining buttons on her thin white blouse. "Clement said you'd want to know the details of what happened. That man always hangs around the club looking to save the sinners. But most sinners ain't interested in followin' The Word. Gotta give him credit for trying though. He always protected me—you can imagine how handsy a bunch of horny, red neck drunks can get."

"Must be awful."

"Uh-huh. And two weeks ago, it went too far. I shot Foster

Eagerton between the eyes. Bang, bang. It was self-defense. He'd raped me when I was fourteen and I was not about to let the asshole do it again. Happened at the Honeysuckle Inn outside of Klapperville where I work weekends."

"Honeysuckle Inn, the strip club? I heard of it." Mark knew it well and could envision her on that pole. Cousin Clement took him there the first time on the boy's thirteenth birthday.

"I was the only act keepin' that place afloat," Tanya Lee said. "Don't know what the owner's gonna do now I'm gone. People come from miles around, pay good money to see me dance and see the girls unbound." She pushed aside the pile of newly folded towels and walked around the table. Leaning against it, she arched her back striking a pose that Mark guessed she'd done a whole bunch of times.

He sucked in his breath. The girl was wearing Daisy Dukes. She might be just a little too fleshy for the cut-off jeans, but a man couldn't look away. "Again, ma'am, I'm so sorry about what you gone through. We'll treat you well here, I promise."

She smiled her brilliant smile. Her teeth were perfect. Her pink tongue flicked like those of his beloved rattlers.

"Is there anything more you need here during your stay that we can provide?" he asked.

Her caramel-colored eyes narrowed. "Well, Pastor, I seen you in church last week, shakin' and a preachin'. I say to myself, Oh Lord, I gotta get me summa his religion. I've seen your other cousin, Jethro Smiley, do the snake handling at the Snell Corners Revival Church, but it ain't nothing like what you do. Oh, Lordy. You know how to put on a show, like me."

"Thank you, ma'am. I try to engage my parishioners."

She arched her back again and stretched. Mark broke into a cold sweat as the buttons on her blouse looked ready to pop. He was ready to pop.

"It's nice and calm out here in the desert," she said, "but I's used to a little more activity. None of the boys here look too lively, but you look really fine, Pastor Wenter. I could use a little poke once in a while, you know, to steady my nerves."

"A poke?" He knew exactly what she meant.

Tanya Lee nodded and sucked on her finger.

"I guess I could manage that, for your nerves," he said.

"What about that tall pretty blond I see you hang 'round with? I hear she's the Chosen One."

"Yes, she is, for now. She can help move our ministry closer to L.A., to the film and TV studios. To your career. "

Tanya beamed at the thought and edged in closer to Mark. "Then you must take good care of her."

"Yes, for sure." He could feel his snake tattoos beginning to crawl. "But she's not like you." He touched her cheek. "She could never pull a trigger."

Tanja Lee grinned, made a shooting motion with her hand then stepped away to lock the trailer door, then leaned back against it. "Just one more thing," she said.

"Yes, what is it?"

"I'm not really the laundry type." She moved close to him and undid every one of her buttons except for one. The dam holding back the anticipated flood of magnificent tits was about ready to burst.

"We all honor the Lord with jobs here at the camp," Mark said, his voice husky. "Something you'd rather do than laundry?"

"Uh huh. I used to bake part-time at the Klapperville Bakery making donuts and sweet pastries a man could really wrap his lips around. I want to work in the kitchen, be in the bakery." She pressed her body against him.

He moaned. "I think we could manage that, Miss Tanja Lee. Yes, indeed we could."

She undid the final button.

CHAPTER TWENTY-EIGHT

Lucy remained at Jaime's bedside until just before midnight, text messaged Heath that all was copasetic, then crashed for the night at a modest hotel across the street from the Medical Center.

The next morning, she called just to hear his comforting voice and get the latest on the children.

"How're the kid's doing?" Lucy missed both of them.

"They're busy making get well cards for Jaime," Heath said. "And this morning they put away enough waffles to feed an infantry platoon."

Lucy smiled and felt a flood of relief knowing they'd been mostly shielded from the trauma. "Sounds good. Maybe I can FaceTime with them later." She paused. "And how are you?" She drew in a quick breath remembering Heath's beautiful, half naked body as he dashed along the balcony to Jaime's room the previous morning. She chastised herself—how could she think about such a thing given the awful circumstances?

"I'm okay," he said. "The whole situation was kinda—what do you call it—was triggering. But I'm fine. Dealt with most of that crap a long time ago. Could've used a better sleep, though. There was a wolf howling up on the ridge around midnight and both the kids were scared—ended up in my bed and wouldn't leave."

Lucy laughed, "Nothing like a four-year-old's foot in your face to help you relax."

"Yeah, and your kid has sharp heels. Grace, on the other hand, tosses and turns like a banshee. And has three stuffies she has to have with her. Then the dog joined us. I finally left them all in my room and slept in one of the twins."

Lucy laughed again. "Hate to say it, but I envy you. I'm on my way back to the hospital. Jaime was sleeping peacefully when I left last night. If all goes as expected, she's due to be discharged tomorrow, mid-morning."

"Okay," Heath said. "I cleaned up the truck as best I could. Gonna need some major detailing inside at some point. Might even be considered totaled."

Lucy knew he'd be forever haunted by the bloody interior. Maybe a new truck was in the cards.

"I'll have the munchkins packed up, we'll grab you and Jaime around noon and head to L.A.," he said. "She can lay across the back seat. I've got sleeping bags and pillows."

"Sounds good. I'll have more information after I see Doctor Hartman again. By the way, the doctor wants to offer you a job."

He chuckled. "Thanks, but no way in hell would I want to do that kind of work every day. You hanging in there?"

"Yep, just counting my blessings. One of which was some fresh scrubs from a nurse yesterday, so I'm good for now. My shoes are still so bloody you could throw them on a plate with a baked potato and they'd be mistaken for a sirloin."

Heath groaned. "That's a pretty disgusting image, Miss Vega."

"Sorry, gallows humor. I soaked the shoes in the sink all night and then tried to dry them with a hair dryer. Made things worse."

"I think you might have to ditch those kicks before we arrive."

"Will do."

Anxious to see Jaime, Lucy ended the call. She checked her watch—it was almost eight. She grabbed coffee and a slightly stale muffin at the hotel breakfast bar, then headed across the street to Mammoth Lakes Med. The sky was cloudless and at almost eight thousand feet above sea level, the air held a faint nip of coolness.

Beelining through the main entry, Lucy signed the visitor's log and took the elevator up to Jaime's floor. Attendants were delivering meal trays and doctors were making their rounds. When she walked into Jaime's room, Lucy's heart almost seized up. The room was empty, the bed was freshly made and the equipment stashed away.

No, of course she didn't die in the night. Jaime must have been moved to another area. Lucy rushed to the nurse's station. The woman who had given her the scrubs greeted her with a smile.

"Morning Lucy, you look upset."

"Jaime Burleson, is she okay? She's gone. Where has she been moved?"

"She was discharged into her husband's care an hour ago," the nurse said.

"What?" Tension ratcheted in Lucy's chest.

"She said you knew."

"No, I didn't know anything about her leaving early. My God, she practically died yesterday."

The nurse nodded and scrolled down her patient discharge screen. "Mark Wenter—that the husband?"

"Yes, that's him."

"I told Mister Wenter we highly recommended she stay one more night, but he was adamant that a local midwife could provide all the care Jaime needed."

Lucy wasn't at all sure that was true. Between Jaime taking

off with Mark and the bad hotel muffin, she felt sick to her stomach. "Well, you can't keep her here if she refuses to stay."

"Very true. We wish her a good recovery," the nurse said.

"Deep gratitude to you and your team for your help and kindness." Lucy smiled, trying to mask her distress at Jaime's disappearance. She turned away and tried to call the girl but received no reply. She left a text message asking Jaime to get in touch.

With nothing more she could do, Lucy headed to the hospital gift shop where she bought a pine green Mammoth Mountain sweatshirt, a pair of black sweatpants, and two stuffed wooly mammoths for the kids. The only footwear available were rubber shower slippers which she snapped up. Changing into her newly purchased clothing in a restroom, she dropped her shoes in the trash and the scrubs into a laundry cart that sat outside the restroom door.

Returning to the hotel, Lucy called Heath to tell him about the latest turn of events.

"Oh, shit, seriously? They left? That was a major piece of surgery. Plus, a transfusion. She should have stayed," he said, clearly unhappy.

"Yeah, and Jaime isn't responding to my texts."

"Such a bad decision on their part." Heath let out a growl of frustration, then abruptly changed the subject. "So, life goes on. They made their choice. I'm in the middle of helping Cal, Ruthie's husband, replace rotting boards on the fishing dock. Too much for him to do himself, although he doesn't agree with me. When we're done, I'll pack us all up and we'll meet you at the hotel. We can have an early dinner and head for L.A. Decent plan?" Heath asked.

"Sounds perfect," Lucy replied. "Feels like I've been gone for days, and it's only been about twenty-four hours."

Heath chuckled. "Some days are minutes and some are damn eons."

CHAPTER TWENTY-NINE

This last week had brought Lucy a major move from NYC, the dissolution of what she thought was a life-long relationship, and the near death of Michael's daughter. She was distressed that Jaime still hadn't contacted her. Lucy was, however, more than relieved to finally be home. Not only did the ranch always offer her a sense of solace and security, but there were still plenty of details regarding the upcoming photo show still hanging unattended.

After much planning and preparation, the exhibition was finally happening the following weekend. She'd just been on the phone with the caterer to finalize the menu and then checked in with the gallery to confirm the number of café tables they had on hand. Then, a text popped up from Bea. She was on her way to the ranch—the photo framing had been completed early. Bea had to be in Calabasas soon for an interview, so she was dropping the work off at the ranch on her way.

Lucy had barely spoken to her friend since the surreal Zoom breakup with Michael. It was an hour and a half before Lucy was scheduled to pick Henry up at pre-school. Her old-fashioned tea pot had just begun to whistle when Bea called through the door.

"Hey, girl, I've got four boxes—can only lug one at a time. You want them in the office?"

"Please," Lucy called back. "Be right there." She turned off the burner, met Bea in the living room, and followed her into the office. "On the table is good."

Bea deposited her frames then turned to her friend. "How are you doing, my sister?"

"Day at a time." Lucy rubbed her neck.

Bea smiled a sad smile. "After all you've just been through, I'm surprised you're still functioning. Good for you."

Lucy paused for an instant, then tearfully threw herself into Bea's strong arms. "Life just totally sucks sometimes."

"Understatement of the century. We should have it tattooed on our foreheads." Bea led Lucy to a loveseat across from the work table. "Crying your eyes out is good. Also staying productive, like you're doing now with the show. And remember the ancient adage, *this, too, shall pass.*"

Lucy nodded, pulled a tissue from her pocket and blew her nose. "I love you, Bea."

"Love you, too, Lucia. But baby, I'm glad Burleson and those doomed hopes for the fantasy family are in the rear view. Maybe you'll see more clearly what's right in front of you. And it's never going to look like the Brady Bunch."

Lucy laughed and blew her nose again. "Oh, bearer of hard truths, you're at it again."

"And you've done the same for me so many times." She hugged Lucy close and kissed her wet cheek.

Bea's phone sounded and she took a look at the text. She held up a finger to pause their conversation. "Pete just got a call—possible homicide up the road at Leo Carrillo Beach Campground. He's going to stop by here for a sec to hand off some tickets for his daughter's volleyball tournament."

"Sounds nice, the tickets part, anyway." Lucy stood. "Enough tears. Let's go grab the rest of the boxes. Thanks for your love and support, my friend."

They each brought in one more box, then Lucy went back out to grab the last carton from Bea's trunk. As she was about to lift the box, Pete's beat up Crown Vic, the unmarked car he'd been driving forever, turned off Kanan Road and accelerated up the drive. Smiling, she paused and waited for him.

"Hey, my lovely." He slammed the car door behind him and jogged toward Lucy, petting the dogs as he approached. "Lemme give you a hand with that."

"Thanks, Pete." Lucy was happy to let the burden go. "Can't believe the opening is a week from Friday. Never thought I'd actually get around to doing it."

"Yeah, well, with Miss Beatrice on your ass for a decade, it was bound to happen. I'm even kinda getting to like that soup photo of us. Thanks for sending it to me."

"I hope you hung it in the bedroom," Lucy said with a smirk.

He smiled and followed her across the Spanish-Mediterranean style living room and down the hall to the office.

"Hey, Lover," he called to Bea, setting the box down next to a new print of Jaime and Mark standing with Henry. Lucy had taken it just before leaving for New York the previous week.

"Hey, handsome," Bea said. She gave him a smooch. He smooched back.

It looked to Lucy like their on-again/off-again, was seriously on again.

"These are for the tournament finals." He passed Bea the tickets she'd been waiting for. "We'll be coming from the valley, so we'll meet you at the field house. Okey dokey?"

"Thank you, hon." Bea pocketed the tickets. "Can't wait."

"My baby girl Gianna's team is in the regional volleyball championships," Pete said to Lucy with a proud swell of his chest.

"That's fabulous," she said. "If I didn't have a lecture at the gallery, I'd be lobbying for me and Henry to come along with you guys."

"Cool. I'll keep you posted for next time." Pete turned back to the photo on the table, which seemed to be pulling him in. He tapped his fingers on the image. "That's Burleson's kid, Jaime, right?"

"Yeah, that's her," Lucy said. "And her new husband. He's a youth pastor at a private Bible camp somewhere in the Simi Hills."

"Uh huh." Pete narrowed his eyes and moved his fingers to the young man's face.

Lucy edged up next to him. Bea peeked over his shoulder.

"I'm pretty sure I've seen this dude before," he said.

"Really? Like where?" Lucy asked.

"I dunno. Can you email me a copy of this? Your resolution would be better than a pic from my phone."

"Send it to me, too," Bea said. "We have a new research assistant from USC's Journalism program who's amazing."

"Yeah, sure," Lucy said. "I'll send it to both of you today." A little shiver of cold tightened Lucy's chest. "You think he might be a criminal or something?"

Bea shrugged. "You know I've had a sketchy feeling about the kid from the beginning. Nothing solid. Maybe he's the next coming of Yaweh, for all I know."

Pete held up his hands. "I don't have anything specific either. Might run him through facial recognition though."

Lucy felt anxiety start to rattle her already anxious cage. "He's been very kind to me."

"Chill, my raven-haired beauty. Just doing my due diligence for a hot friend." He winked at Lucy. She frowned, knowing both Bea and Pete had excellent track records when following suspicious hunches.

Pete kissed Bea adios and headed to the office doorway. "Okay, ladies, gotta bounce. We got something nasty in the Leo Carrillo campground and I need to beat the coroner to the scene."

"I gotta run, too," Bea said. "Interview with the new

congressional rep over in Calabasas. Ran as a green candidate, then it turns out he's a major stockholder in a very naughty pesticide company."

Lucy shook her head. "Go get 'em Bea." She took a quick peek at a text coming in. "Uh-oh, the show programs were sent to the wrong gallery. Always something. Will be so relieved when the opening is over."

She scrolled through her messages once again. Lucy still hadn't heard from Jaime and was becoming increasingly concerned. She tried to push the Jaime situation to the back of her mind. Mark was a good guy who loved his new wife. They lived at a religious camp with people who cared about her welfare. All was well. The young woman would be fine. Right?

CHAPTER THIRTY

Eden's Gate Camp Community

In the cottage's screened-in porch, Jaime sat on a rocking chair, a pillow clutched to her abdomen. A bible and a glass of orange juice rested on a stand next to her. She felt like screaming and knocking everything to the floor but she knew May Lou and Mark would be upset. They were trying to be kind. Why was she unappreciative? What was wrong with her? She needed to pray more.

Joylessly, she gazed at the pool where Isabella, the woman who had once approached her with a warning, helped conduct swim lessons for a half-dozen toddlers. Jaime moaned. Would she ever have a child of her own? Sinking in depression, salty tears burned her swollen eyelids. Who knew that losing a microscopic clutch of cells could be this traumatic? The hormones, her changing body—Jaime needed to talk to someone who might understand. She wanted to talk with Lucy, but May Lou wouldn't give her phone back, so Isabella was the next best option. She'd somehow felt a connection to the woman.

Gently pressing her wound, Jaime rose from the chair and headed outside to the swimming pool. The kids were scrambling from the water toward a new resident, a young woman carrying a tray of snacks for the little swimmers. May Lou had said the woman's name was Tanya Lee. Jaime had noticed that Mark paid her a bit too much attention. She feared that if she didn't get healthy soon, he would find a more willing recipient of his holy adoration. Maybe she would no longer be the sublime Chosen One. The thought terrified her. Mark was the first man in her life who truly made her feel valued. She couldn't lose that.

Slowly, she walked across the grass toward the pool deck and the picnic tables just beyond. She called out as she approached. "Hi there, Isabella."

The woman looked up. Jaime gave her a wave. Isabella recognized her and turned away. Jaime walked faster in her direction.

"Isabella, please, just a few minutes." Tears welled in Jaime's eyes again—she'd rarely felt so isolated and alone. Old fantasies about the warm oblivion of past heroin dreams stirred, but she refused to fall back into its thrall. That chapter was done. She had worked too hard to beat the Sirens that lured addicts to their demise. From the terrible loss of the fetus and almost of her own life, Jaime knew she wanted to live.

She reached an imploring hand toward Isabella. "Could we talk? Just a little? I lost a pregnancy, I'm so depressed. Mark is clueless, and May Lou, she scares me. She's like a ghoul in a housedress."

Isabella snickered, paused, and turned around. "Don't let anybody hear you say that. But so true."

Jaime felt an unexpected surge of joy and relief. At last, someone who could acknowledge her reality.

"I had three miscarriages before my son," the woman said.

"Oh, I'm so sorry. That's awful." She was not the only one

here who grieved.

"Was worth the wait, though." Isabella's hand lightly grazed her belly.

"Is one of these kids yours?" Jaime asked.

Isabella pointed to a handsome dark-haired child around Grace's age."

"He's beautiful."

Isabella nodded. "He's my life."

"I wonder why May Lou never had children," Jaime said.

"She considers Mark her own." Isabella frowned. "Just make sure you never get between them because you will lose."

"What do you mean?"

In the distance, Jaime spotted Mark coming down the hill from the dining hall. Isabella saw him at the same time.

"We can't talk, Jaime. Don't come to me again."

"I don't understand."

"Understand this, I don't want any trouble, and if you try to hang around me, bad stuff will happen." She glanced at her son. "Now please, leave." Isabella scowled, walked away and slid onto a picnic bench among the children.

Jaime shivered as Mark approached.

"You okay out here by yourself?" he asked. "Anyone bothering you?"

"Of course, I'm okay. I'm not totally incapacitated." Jaime bristled in frustration. "And if you're referring to Isabella as someone bothering me, she's the only person who has ever been kind enough just to say 'hello' and acknowledge my existence. I feel like a prisoner here sometimes, Mark. At least when I take care of Henry, I'm in the world and doing something helpful."

She spun around and hurried toward their cottage. Mark ran to catch up. He grabbed her arm.

She winced. "Mark, you're hurting me."

"Come now, sweetheart, you're way over-reacting." He loosened his grip. "You're not a prisoner, but being the Chosen One among others is a heavy burden. I prayed to the Lord you would be one who could flourish with this honor, who would be at my side as we go forth to promote my ministry. Was I wrong?" Mark snuck a side-eye at Tanya bending over to clear the picnic table.

Not missing the glance, Jaime straightened and wiped her eyes. "No, you're right. I should be stronger. I'm sorry, Mark."

"I love you so much, darling, I'd never hurt you in any way, or make you feel unappreciated. I want to be supportive."

Jaime sighed. "I know you do. And you are."

He took her into his arms and held her close. She snuggled into his warm shoulder.

"I'm so sorry, Mark. Forgive me. I will do better. Your ministry is more important than anything."

"Good girl." He kissed her forehead. "Now go back to the cottage. May Lou made a nice lunch and then you'll rest. It's important to recover your strength. We have much to do."

—

As soon as Jaime left him, Mark turned, scanning for Isabella. She was collecting the swim toys and stowing them in the pool shed. When she saw him coming, she shut the door and began to walk away.

"Isabella, we need to talk," he called. "Now."

She froze, her hands clasped together.

"Let's walk up to the music building," he said.

"I was just being a decent human being," she blurted, following him across the lawn and up a low rise. "*Blessed is one who is kind to the needy.*"

"She's not needy."

"But the girl is in pain. She doesn't have anybody to talk to who has been through what she has."

"She has May Lou and me to talk to. That's enough."

He opened the door to the music building, another double wide trailer like the laundry, but this one was filled with instruments, amps, sour-smelling choir robes, and rumpled sheet music. Isabella seemed to shrink as she stepped into the room.

Once inside, Mark stopped short and turned to her, his expression ominous. "If I see you speaking with the Chosen One again, you will go away, and the child will stay. Do you understand me?"

Isabella paled, her hand went to her throat. "No, please. I'll never talk to her again, ever. Don't take my, our, son. I beg you. I've been such a good mother, you know that. And I've been clean for years."

"A good mother can lose any hope of child custody if she's found over-dosed, with fresh tracks on her arms, in the Greyhound bus station bathroom."

"Please, Mark, I will never cause any problem again. I will renew my commitment to the ministry in every way." Her mouth quivered.

Mark took Isabell's face in his hands, pulling her close so she could feel his breath. She grimaced as he ran his thumb over her generous lower lip. "I always loved that lip. It's your best feature. I haven't experienced its pleasure for way too long."

She shuddered. "No, Mark, please. I'm no longer chosen. You have others to, uh, enjoy."

"But I want you." He smiled, catlike, batting at his prey and enjoying her humiliation. He stripped off his shirt. The tattoos undulated across the muscles of his chest.

The door to the music building opened. Mark spun to face the intruder.

Tanya Lee stepped in, shutting the door behind her. She pulled her sundress over her head, revealing her outrageous endowment. "Mind if I join y'all?" Tanya Lee asked.

Isabella recoiled as if she'd been struck and edged away.

Mark smiled. "Behold, a woman who knows how to service the Lord. Come and worship, my dear. The snakes are roiling." He flipped the switch on a small sound system and pulsing gospel music banged away.

Isabella attempted to flee. Mark grabbed her by the hair, grinned, and locked the door.

CHAPTER THIRTY-ONE

Lucy's phone pinged. She checked her caller ID. It was Jaime. Finally.

Unwilling to hide her frustration and hurt, Lucy started talking before even saying hello. "Jaime, why haven't you called me? I've been so worried. You disappeared against the orders of the trauma team. I'm really upset with you."

"I'm so sorry, Lucy," she said, voice contrite.

"You never even bothered to let us know you were okay. You almost died in my arms, and then, nothing."

Jaime didn't respond right away. Lucy could hear her sniffling.

"I feel terrible about not calling," Jaime finally said. "But Mark and May Lou, they took my phone. They thought it would be better if I totally relaxed without it. They were just trying to protect me."

"Protect you? From what? From the concern of the people who saved your life?" Lucy huffed. "If you couldn't talk, then Mark should have called."

"Don't be too hard on him, he's been so sweet, trying to help me recover. He can be a little controlling but it's for my own good."

Lucy didn't feel comfortable with that response at all. Sounded like Jaime was being gaslit by her oh-so-caring husband. A long silence hung uncomfortably between them. Lucy could hear Jaime crying again. Maybe she'd been too hard on the girl. Jaime was obviously still in a very vulnerable state.

Lucy looked out across the meadow and tried to calm herself. "I'm relieved to finally hear from you. Thank God you're on the mend. I'll let Heath know."

"Lucy, I can't begin to tell you how grateful I am to you and Heath." Her voice was shaky. "I owe you both my life and I should have insisted Mark give my phone back. You needed to know I was okay. I was weak. Again."

"Stop beating yourself up, Jaime. You're not weak. You're just recovering from a major trauma. And before that, you battled addiction but you're clean now. That's kick ass stuff." Lucy took a deep breath and tried to let her aggravation go. "Hey, I get it if you can't get to the ranch to see us anytime soon, but maybe we can come visit at the camp. The kids made get well cards and are anxious to see you."

Jaime hesitated again but the crying seemed to have stopped. "So sweet, but we don't have visitors very often, or ever. I'm ready to start back to work at the ranch, though."

"Isn't it too soon?"

"No, I'm good. I just have to take it easy. I thought maybe you'd need somebody to stay with Henry when your show opens on Friday night. I can go see it another time. It's at the gallery all month, right?"

"It is." Lucy knew her son would be bored to death at the opening even though there was a children's area sponsored by an arts organization she supported. She also had a sense that being at the ranch and doing something helpful would raise Jaime's spirit. "You really think you're well enough?"

"I am. It would do me good. I feel like a prisoner here half the time."

Lucy heard Jaime draw in a quick breath. "I'm just kidding," she said. "This place, these people, are wonderful. They're the reason I've been able to recover so fast."

"Okay, well, it would be really nice to have you here. Henry would be thrilled."

"That would be amazing. It'll be my first time out since the ectopic. When do you want me?"

"I'll text you the details," Lucy said.

"Great, thanks. I miss you guys."

"We miss you, too. I'm so glad we could finally connect. See you Friday."

Lucy hoped Jaime wasn't stepping into action too early. And was she being paranoid to think that the girl's conversation was being monitored?

—

At the kitchen table in the cottage where they sat, Mark took Jaime's phone. She hesitated to relinquish it, but understood her husband was only looking out for her, trying to keep her safe and stress-free so she could regain her health.

"Good work, sweetheart," Mark said, lightly kissing her forehead as he stuffed her phone into his pocket. "You're back in the fold now with Lucy. That's great."

May Lou appeared less than enthusiastic. "Now take your vitamins, dear." She stood, laid a bony hand on Jaime's shoulder, and offered up the pills on a China plate. Jaime winced but swallowed them with a chaser of water. The vitamins tasted bad and made her gag. She forced a smile and nodded at the midwife but couldn't suppress a pang of regret at having to lie to Lucy. Mark and the ministry, however, were everything. Weren't they? She squeezed his hand.. "Your vision is my vision. And you are His shining instrument, my handsome husband."

"You're beginning to truly understand the righteousness of

our mission here on Earth, my Chosen One," Mark said. "That brings me great joy."

"But I still feel bad about Lucy," Jaime admitted out loud this time. Or had she just thought it? Beginning to feel a little woozy, she needed rest.

May Lou looked heavenward in a gesture of supplication. "Of course, you feel some regret, my dear, but the Lord smiles on your effort to gain custody of the child and claim this ranch in the name of Eden's Gate Community. It is all for the glorification of Him and obedience to His will."

The midwife sounded all certainty as Jaime's thoughts began to blur.

"The ranch is in your family," the woman continued. "It's practically yours already. And the boy is your brother." She puckered her lips and then recited, "As Proverbs says, **Honor the Lord with your wealth, with the first fruits of all your crops; then your barns will be filled to overflowing, and your vats will brim over with new wine. It is God's Will that we build wealth. And you lost a child, you are meant to have your brother, just as I had mine.**" She smiled at Mark.

"Yes, of course," Jaime agreed, not at all sure what May Lou was talking about. She yawned. "I feel a little dizzy."

"You're exhausted. You must rest, my love." Mark stood and helped Jaime up from a kitchen chair. He guided her through the living room and into their bedroom where her thoughts quickly dissolved to blackness.

CHAPTER THIRTY-TWO

The Sigrid Bergmann Studio Gallery in Calabasas was a Mediterranean style collection of three high-ceilinged exhibit spaces containing Lucy's work, and an art classroom, all in an exclusive outdoor shopping mall. The galleries opened onto a flagstone patio surrounded by metal garden arches dripping with fiery bougainvillea and fragrant jasmine. A five-tiered fountain splashed in the center of the patio where cocktail tables were set up next to a bar. Black-attired servers passed out hors d'oeuvres and poured wine as a string quartet played light classical fare.

"The show is fantastic," Bea said. "Everything is perfect. I'm always stunned by what an incredible eye you have, particularly for observing relationships." She stood next to Lucy, both were dressed for the artsy event—Bea in a silver sheath and Lucy in skinny black pants, short red boots, and an over-sized gauzy white shirt. Silver earrings dangled from her ears and a stack of bracelets jingled on her wrist.

"Thank you, my friend. None of this would have happened without your kick in the derriere."

"Glad my Manolos could provide the impetus," Bea said. "But what else is going on? You look beyond excited."

Lucy bounced on her toes. "I just heard from the Curator of Contemporary Photography at the Getty."

"Whoa." Bea pressed her hand to her heart. "And?"

"And they want the entire collection! It's so insane! I can't believe it!"

Bea screeched with joy and wrapped her friend in a hug. "I'm not surprised at all! Congratu-frickin-lations, sweet pea!"

"What's all this noise?" Pete nabbed a couple jumbo shrimp from a passing tray as he joined the two women.

"The Getty's acquiring Lucy's whole portfolio!"

Pete grinned. "Even the sexy soup?"

"Even the sexy soup. That's what probably sold it," Lucy said, laughing. "I think you'll be the first LA County Sherriff homicide detective in the J. Paul Getty Museum collection!"

"Holy shit," he said. "Better not let my people know that or I'll never live it down. Only other public place that ever posted my mug is the dart board at the Hog Town Hippie Grill."

"That greasy biker joint near Palmdale?" Bea asked, wrinkling her nose."

"That's the one, baby cakes." Pete winked at Lucy. "Friends in low places, as they say."

Before the conversation could go further, an event photographer stopped to snap candids of Lucy and her friends, then several guests were at her side with questions and to chat.

An hour in, Bea and Pete left to pick up his son for the weekend. The gallery was still hopping half an hour before closing time. That's when Heath Sinclair walked in.

Lucy intuitively felt him check her out as he slowly approached, taking in the images on the walls as he ambled her way with a glass of dark red wine in hand. He was freshly scrubbed, hair still damp, and wearing a retro Bob Seger T-shirt, black blazer, tight jeans and cowboy boots. He looked ready to line dance or maybe hop on a bronco and ride. She flushed and grabbed a glass of Chardonnay from a passing server, took a gulp, then caught her breath for a second before turning to greet him with a smile. "Doctor Sinclair, so happy to see you."

He reached for her, pushed a stray strand of curly dark hair from her face, then embraced her in a hug. Her electrons hummed.

"Amazing show," he said, releasing her. "I heard you were talented, but this is really impressive, Lucy. So cool."

"Thank you," she said. "It's been a successful evening. I have some awesome stuff to tell you. I'm so glad you could make it."

"Wouldn't have missed this. Had to get Gracie squared away with mom and dad for the night or I would have been here sooner. Who's with Henry? I almost called you to bring him over."

"Jaime finally contacted me. I texted you."

"Sorry, dropped my personal phone in a horse trough out at one of the ranches. Just got it replaced at the phone store on the way over."

"Oh no. Well, I let Jaime know we were both really upset about her leaving the hospital early and then ghosting us. Turns out Mark took her phone to try and keep her relaxed and focused on recovery."

Heath frowned. "There's something I meant to mention to you about that husband of hers, from when you were in New York."

"What's that?" Lucy asked, but patrons interrupted to bid her goodbye and offer compliments on the show. Lucy whispered to Heath, "Can you stay for a bit after we close? We can go for a stroll, talk."

"I've got the whole night free," he said, smiling.

Friends gathered around Lucy pulling her into the crowd. She was whisked away, fantasizing about spending a night with the hot vet.

THE SNAKE HANDLER'S WIFE | 139

CHAPTER THIRTY-THREE

Mark sat at Lucy's desk organizing his papers.

"Henry's asleep," Jaime said as she entered the study. "He's such a sweet boy. Sorry you missed seeing him."

Mark glanced up at her with a perfunctory smile. "Glad he likes you. Will make everything much easier. And it's best Lucy doesn't know I was here."

Jaime sat down across from the desk, resting her bare feet on the coffee table. "So, my love. What exactly is the plan to get this property? You seem to be pretty vague when I ask you about it."

"Sometimes, the less you know, the better," he said with a wink. "Isn't that what they say on all the cop shows?"

She shrugged. "Nobody's going to get hurt, right?"

Mark's eyes narrowed. "Grow up, Jaime, of course somebody's going to get hurt. Christ died on the cross, he got hurt for us, right? No different than what we're doing." His jaw clenched and unclenched. "It's called sacrifice for the eternal life of our followers." He sighed, clearly aggravated by her constant need for reassurance. "With the help of my dear parent's long-time lawyer, I have all the paperwork completed to transfer the ranch to Henry and give you custody and power of attorney over his affairs. Once the property transfer is complete, you'll immediately hand over authority and ownership to Eden's Gate Camp Community."

"Okay, but Bea is his godmother. She's going to fight for Henry." She rubbed her eyes. "She's not going to want me in charge."

Mark's smile was sly. "I went through all of Lucy's paper files and hacked into her PC. There's nothing that gives Bea any legal right to the boy. Plus, he's going to want to be with you, his sister. Your father, the big shot international correspondent who's finally free, won't want custody. He has a new life and a new woman. But I have a plan if he does go after the kid."

Jaime chewed at her fingernails then stopped herself. "No way will Lucy abandon Henry and travel to Iraq after my dad, if that's what you have in mind."

"She may not, but someone will. And the local gendarmes will look to your father as the culprit when she disappears. You don't need to know any more, my love. You will only worry your pretty head, and I want to shelter you from any unnecessary strain."

Jaime squirmed in her seat. What the hell had she gotten into? Making Lucy disappear and framing her father for murder. WTF? She couldn't stand him, but he wasn't a killer. She felt Mark scrutinize her carefully, like he could read her innermost thoughts and didn't like what he was seeing. She had to put the brakes on any bubbling up of doubt.

"If you can't do this," he said, "I need to know now. The future of our entire movement depends on you being strong and committed."

Abject fear of losing this man tightened in Jaime's chest.

"And that sometimes means doing things that aren't comfortable, my sweet. I know you're really emotional right now, and that you may not fully understand what we are trying to do here for the good of His disciples."

Jaime struggled to let her resistance fade. *Let go and let God,* as they said in her AA meetings. She reminded herself that Mark was the best thing that ever happened to her. "Okay, I understand, I do, sweetheart. Many lives will be enriched at this place, lots of people will be saved through the sacrifice of a few."

He sat on the arm of the chair, his fingers stroking her throat. "Like I saved you."

"Yes, like that." Her eyes shut and she breathed in the scent of his power. "I can do it. I *will* do it," she declared with conviction. "You don't have to ask me about this again. I'm committing, here and now."

Mark nodded, his smile angelic. "I adore you, Jaime. And God adores you even more."

They made love in Lucy's bed.

—

The opening night of the photography show finally came to an end. As the caterers loaded the last of their equipment into a van, Sigrid, the gallery owner, a handsome German woman in her sixties, bid Lucy and Heath goodnight.

The movie theater next door had just let out and the palm-lined sidewalk filled with chatting audience members heading for bars, restaurants, or their cars. The night was soft and perfect as Lucy and Heath passed a popular eatery's outdoor terrace. Light jazz played and the sound of silverware clinking felt homey and comfortable. Heath reached for her as they walked.

"Okay if I hold your hand?" he asked.

Lucy had a flash of guilt and anxiety, that she extinguished as fast as it came. She was a single woman, free and unattached. "That would be nice," she said.

Heath interlaced his fingers with hers. "I've been wanting to do this for a while." He smiled down at her. "Just didn't want to be too forward."

"A little forward is just fine. In fact, let me be a little forward, too." She let go of his hand and slipped her arm around his trim waist. He put his arm around her shoulders and gave her a gentle hug. They leaned into each other like lovers as they strolled. Lucy couldn't remember the last time she'd felt both so peaceful and so aroused at the same time. Heath Sinclair was gorgeous, smart, kind—he was someone she wanted more of. Maybe it was just the rebounding desires of a broken heart, but she didn't care if it was.

Lucy checked her watch, disappointed. "Sorry to say, I've got to get back to the ranch so Jaime can go home."

Heath nodded. They turned down one of the dimly lit pathways to the parking lot where hibiscus flowers glowed fairy-gown white in the evening shadows. Lucy turned and looked up at Heath. He took her face in his hands and kissed her. Tentatively at first, until she responded making clear she wanted to be kissed, thoroughly, passionately kissed.

Lucy caught her breath and grinned. "What a night. A terrific show opening, the Getty acquisition, great press, and kissed by the multi-talented Doctor Heath Sinclair."

He laughed and held her close as they walked to her car. Then he stopped, the warm animation in his face fading. 'There's something I've been meaning to tell you."

CHAPTER-THIRTY-FOUR

Lucy tensed. Of course, everything good in her life usually came with nasty caveats. "What's wrong?" she asked, shrinking away from him.

"I've been wanting to tell you what I saw when Gracie and I ran into Henry, Jaime, and Mark at Malibu Yogurt when you were in New York."

"Okay, go ahead." She leaned back against the car door.

"Two kids running with smoothies collided with Mark. Covered him with blue gunk. He had to rinse his arms off in that fountain in front of the place. He was wearing a white long-sleeved shirt, all buttoned up. Seems to be his usual look."

"Okay, what happened? Did Henry fall in or something?"

"No, Mark had tattoos. He tried to hide them, but his sleeves were pushed up." Heath released her hand and began to gesture. "The tats wound around his arms, probably his whole upper body. I could see them through his wet shirt."

"I don't understand. Lots of people have tattoos."

He shook his head. "Not of rattlers the same unusual species as we found in Odin's stall."

"Whoa, bizarre." Lucy tried to tamp down prickles of apprehension.

"It could be nothing, Lucy. But it could possibly be something very, very bad."

He took her hand again, but the magic had been replaced with worry.

—

Tanya Lee gazed at Mark. Naked except for his tattooed flesh, he lay splayed across the couch in the music trailer. He was a beautiful man. His brown eyes sparkled with serpentine glints of yellow, and his mouth—A-listers would pay dearly for fillers and never achieve that beautiful kisser. Even his feet were perfect.

Tanya Lee smiled, pulled on her shorts and T-shirt, then re-tied her ponytail. The music trailer hook-ups with the insatiable snake man over the last few days, had become increasingly frequent and imaginative. And whiny Isabella, evidently uninspired by threesome sex, had finally been allowed to run off to her cottage. Good riddance.

 Rising from the couch, Tanya began to pick up scattered sheet music and organize it into a pile. "You know," she said, "we could make a lot of money together in the adult film business. We could do a weekly show about having sex in risky, forbidden places."

Mark chuckled. "You are certainly an entrepreneurial thinker, aren't you? And ambitious. I like that. And I like you. If I didn't need Jaime to get possession of our new venue, I'd replace her with you as the Chosen One."

Tanya Lee finished stacking the papers and turned to him, frowning. "I don't need to have you choose me. I make my own choices. I learned that a long time ago."

Mark sat up straighter, looking acutely aware that she wasn't his usual drug addicted, broken bird, desperate to be saved that he was used to. "I meant no disrespect. Just the opposite. But no pornies, I'm a pastor."

Tanya Lee laughed wickedly and slid onto the couch close to him. Stroking his body, she said, "That would make it even more exciting. You'd pull in a whole new group of sinners to save."

She knew Mark was ready to have her again, but she stood and crossed the room to the fallen choir robe rack. She pulled it up from the floor where they'd kicked it over and returned the disheveled golden robes to their hangers.

Mark glanced at the wall clock and slowly began getting dressed. "Jaime will be back soon."

"What ever happened to your parents?" Tanya Lee asked, not responding to the news of Jaime. "Some say they died of COVID. Others say they were killed in a car accident."

"It's complicated." Mark said. "They had COVID, but they died in a car crash. My father had poor nighttime vision. They hit a rockslide on the road."

"So, a collision."

"Yep. Trying to avoid it, they bashed through the safety barrier along the arroyo just west of here. Dropped down about a hundred feet into the gorge. The car turned over, gas tank was ripped open and caught fire." He paused and watched her work.

Tanya Lee nodded, completed her clean-up task, then watched him finish dressing. Buttoning the top button of his shirt, he always looked a little bit strangled to her.

"When the bodies were discovered," Mark continued, "the cops got involved. Found some paint from my SUV on their back bumper. They thought I'd might have run my folks off the road, but it was never proven."

"Never proven, but did you do it?"

Mark opened the music room door, and they stepped outside. The night was dark, and the sky was splashed with stars, sharp as broken glass. They walked down the rise together.

"So did you?" she persisted.

Mark stretched and looked out across the playing field and pool. The cabins were lit from inside like lanterns. The two continued walking.

"They controlled everything, treated me like a slave, abused me in every way," he said. "I had big dreams they were obsessed with crushing. I'd just turned eighteen and they were about to cast me out, that's what we do with the boys. But my congregation was growing, even bigger than theirs. Then God spoke to me. Guided my actions. May Lou came to my side and encouraged me. I'm sure you could never understand."

Tanya stopped where the path turned off to the cabins. She looked up at Mark, his face slashed with shadowy dark planes. "So, you did do it. I can understand more than you know."

"I doubt it."

"The murder I'm on the run from? Cause I shot a man dead, right between the eyes?"

"Yeah."

"He was my pappy."

CHAPTER THIRTY-FIVE

Just returned from dropping Henry off at a friend's house, Lucy tossed a striped Navajo-patterned blanket over Odin's back. He pranced and snorted. With the nod of approval from the veterinarian, Lucy and Odin were both ready to test the leg. Would they be able to hit the trail together like old times?

Lucy secured and mounted the hand-tooled Western saddle her uncle had brought north from his childhood home in Guadalajara. She looked toward the ocean, savoring the warm sunshine and the scent of horse and leather as she steadied her nerves. The snakebite had done a nasty number on Odin. Would he limp? Shy? Have a hard time with the weight of a rider? It was time to find out. She climbed aboard.

"Let's go, big boy." Pressing her heels to his side, Lucy clucked to urge the horse forward. He didn't hesitate. They walked around the corral several times then ambled out the gate, across the yard, and up a gentle rise to the trail. Lucy's body loosened and swayed in tandem with Odin's familiar rolling gait. She closed her eyes, completely in the moment as they moved comfortably together along their usual path that wound its way from the chaparral into a cool glen along the creek. She gave Odin's neck a loving pat. He swished his tail with pleasure. He was fine. Lucy felt a lost piece of her soul falling back into place.

It was an easy several mile round trip, perfect for their first outing. Black scars from the fire almost five years ago marked the bases of the mountain oaks but their foliage was now gray-green and healthy. Acorns crunched underfoot and the generous clumps of mistletoe hanging from high branches sparked Lucy's warm recollection of her recent kiss with Heath.

Tugging the reins, Lucy and Odin turned back toward home. As they did, she caught a glimpse of a long-haired man dressed in black, hustling from behind a clump of century plants. He glanced their way, then disappeared into the dimness of the trees along the creek. With the area being just off Mulholland Highway, a popular biker route, it was not unusual for riders, both of the motorized and pedaled varieties, to find their way to the lush riparian grove shrouding this part of her property. She shrugged off the momentary disruption and focused again on the

trail ride. It ended way too soon but was a total success in terms of marking Odin's return to health. That was everything.

As they approached the barn, despite her efforts, Lucy's peaceful mindset dissipated. She began thinking about Jaime and Mark and the tattoos Heath had seen on Mark's arms. She would ask Jaime about them when she came to the ranch the next day. But what motivation could Mark Wenter possibly have to drop a snake in a stall to hurt her horse? It made no sense.

She guided Odin back into the corral and dismounted just as the parent who'd hosted Henry to play, drove up to return him back home. After a quick chat and promises of another playdate soon, the friends drove off and Henry was at his mom's side helping groom Odin with a curry brush.

When they finished with the horse's beautification and

snack, Henry asked, "Can I go swing, mom?"

"Of course. I'll call you when lunch is ready. Won't be long."

His head bobbed as he ran past the corral to the swing that hung from the big olive tree.

Five minutes later, Henry walked into the kitchen with a gun.

—

Lucy, on the phone with Pete, tried hard not to sound hysterical. She closed her eyes and took deep breaths while panic gnawed her innards.

"My four-year-old child came into the kitchen with a fucking revolver." She paused and breathed deeply again. "I'm sorry. Stopped using the f-bomb when Henry was born, but Pete, he had this deadly thing in his little hand and was staring down the barrel. I ordered him not to move, terrified he'd try to run away with it, as little kids can do. Or, my God, he could have pulled the trigger. He must have seen the horror in my eyes because he let me take it away from him without complaining. He knew it wasn't a toy. I stashed it in a cupboard where Henry can't reach it. It's still there, I didn't touch it again. Didn't want to compromise the evidence."

"Whoa, scary shit," Pete said.

"Terrifying."

"What kind of gun is it?"

"It's a revolver, a Kimber, and it's frickin' loaded!"

"Fuck."

"Yeah." Lucy tried not to hyperventilate while imagining Henry, bloody and dying, on the kitchen floor, or by the swing, from a self-inflicted wound. Irritation and fear about the previous vandalism on the ranch flared, burning hot in her belly. The harassment had stepped up. Somebody messed with her kid. She would find out who, and they would pay.

"Did you check your security cameras?" Pete's voice held a matter-of-fact calm that Lucy needed.

"The camera doesn't quite cover that area." She muttered, "I have nothing. I need more cameras."

"There a serial number on the gun?"

"Scratched off."

"Shit...stolen. Notice anybody wonky around the area?"

"Down the trail this morning I saw a guy near where the creek goes under Mulholland. But that's not unusual—people stop there. You know the spot."

"Yeah, okay. Should be checked out. I'm up at Leo Carrillo campground finishing up with the crime scene. I'll be at your place in around an hour."

"Thank you, Pete." Lucy ended the call. With shaking hands, she picked up the lunch tray and walked out to the porch where Henry was assembling magnetic blocks in the shape of a gun.

—

Bea and Pete showed up together in separate cars. Bea hopped out and ran to embrace Lucy. "Girl, you okay?"

"Not really, but I've talked myself down. Pete's very calm, that helps."

"You think whoever left the gun is the same asshole who messed with you earlier?" Bea asked.

Lucy shrugged. "Yeah, probably. But it's getting worse—first they try to kill my horse, then all my animals are let out and put at risk, and now this. Henry could have been killed. Or he could have shot me. Can you imagine what that would do to a child?" Lucy trembled and Bea pulled her close.

"The gun still in the kitchen?" Pete asked, joining the women at the front door.

"Yes," Lucy said. "In the cupboard next to the sink." She and Bea followed him inside, trailed by Maddie and Bugle. Henry met them at the refrigerator. Lucy's heart sank. She didn't want her son to hear any of this.

"Are you here to see the gun?" he asked Pete. "Hi Aunt Bea-Bea."

"Hey, sweet pea." She gave him a kiss on the head.

"I'm gonna take a good look at it," Pete said to Henry, "and bring it to the police station."

"Guns are not for children," Bea said to the boy, voice stern. "Ever. Detective Pete will find out who it belongs to. They're in big trouble for putting it where a kid could get it."

Henry nodded. "I just made a gun out of my magnetic blocks. Wanna see?" he asked Bea.

"Sure, my little man." She sent a look of concern Lucy's way, then took the child's hand. They disappeared onto the screened porch.

Pete examined the revolver, rotated the cylinder and ejected the chambered rounds, one at a time. He secured them and the firearm in evidence bags. "Do you know exactly where he found it?"

"I'll show you." They left the house and walked over to the swing.

"Henry said it was resting right here in the crotch of that first branch. Low enough on the trunk so a kid could see it right away."

Pete nodded and looked around. "Notice anything else?"

"Nothing. No footprints other than the kids' scuffing the dirt. The ground's hard here. I've been meaning to buy some of those rubber playground mats. But I guess we all survived without them." She sighed. "I took pictures with my phone and texted them to you. Not much."

He pulled out his cell and nodded. "Received. Thanks. Okay, I'm gonna call for uniforms to check out that area of your property just off Mulholland and the creek. I'm wondering if this gun could be tied to the Leo Carrillo shooting. Same caliber."

"Oh my God," Lucy gasped. "The guy on the trail might be a murderer?"

"Dunno, Luce. But we'll find out," Pete said. He immediately radioed for assistance.

CHAPTER THIRTY-SIX

Lucy and Pete were walking back to the house when Heath Sinclair's truck pulled into the barnyard.

She groaned. "Oh no, I totally forgot. How could I screw up like this?"

"What did you forget, Lucerino?" Pete asked.

"My vet and his daughter are here to swim and have supper tonight. I thought it was Wednesday, not Tuesday." Lucy ran her hands through her wild hair. "This gun thing has totally blown what bit of brain function I have left." She picked up her pace. "Let me introduce you, real fast. I told you how he saved Odin."

"Okay, but make it quick, I've got to get over to where you saw this trespasser. I'll hike in from here. The other units will hit it from Mulholland."

Lucy did the introductions. Bea called Grace inside, giving Lucy a chance to provide Heath a summary of what was going on without frightening the kiddos.

"Maybe you and Henry should stay with us for a few days until this gets sorted," Heath said.

Pete nodded. "Great idea. I like you already, Doc."

"Maybe we'll do that," Lucy said, turning to Pete, "but first, I'll go down the trail with you, point out where I saw the guy."

Bea joined the group before Pete could respond. "Young'uns are eating fruit salad on the porch and watching *Dino Dana*," she said. "I'll go with y'all," she said, "'cause I'm covering the Leo Carrillo story for my news source. In case there's a tie-in with the gun like you suggested, lover, I'll be all over it." She winked at the detective.

Pete grumbled and scrubbed at his whiskery chin. "Let me warn you, Heath." The detective regarded the vet with a beleaguered expression. "These two women here are the stubbornest chicks in LA. Also, the smartest. And the hottest. So, what's a man to do?"

The vet looked at Lucy with a concerned half-smile.

"I don't wanna be responsible for you civilians tracking this guy," Pete said, deadly serious. "And how many times have I told you both not to get involved, and you completely ignored me? How many times have you two Annie Oakley's put yourselves at risk on my watch?"

"We'll stay out of your way and do whatever you tell us," Bea promised with a modest bow of acquiescence. "I know that Lucy and I have caused you heartburn in the past, supposedly interfering with your investigations—"

"Supposedly?"

"Okay, interfering, but I don't want us to split up over this again, Pete. My sheets would weep. But also, your bouillabaisse is better than mine."

"Yes! You finally admit it. Maybe times are changing after all. And we can't have weeping sheets."

Bea smirked.

"We'll respect your authority, I swear," Lucy said, crossing her heart.

Pete rolled his eyes. "Okay, let me get with my people and plan the approach. We have to pull the logistics together fast."

He eyed Bea and Lucy again. "As soon as Lucy IDs the spot where she saw the guy, you ladies return to the house. I don't want anyone getting hit with a stray bullet if things go sideways."

The two stood together, heads nodding reassurance.

"I can take the kids to my folk's place right now and get back here to help however you need me," Heath said to the detective.

"Great idea, doc. Get the kids outta harm's way. When you return, you can keep an eye on the ranch house and barns while we're on the trail."

Everyone spun toward the screen door as it slammed shut, sounding like a gunshot. The kids emerged from the house, smiling like cats who'd just eaten the family canary.

"We heard what you said about the bad man," Henry announced.

The children giggled.

"Oh, Lord." Lucy's nerves were jumping like grasshoppers when she'd walk through the meadow.

"If you don't catch him, he could come here and try to steal a car to get away," Gracie said.

"But he won't take my toys, will he?" Henry asked, very concerned.

"He won't take your toys or our cars," Lucy said. "He won't come to our house at all. Detective Anthony will catch him so don't worry."

Pete nodded. "Your mom's right."

"You two go get in my truck," Heath said to the munchkins. "Right now." They raced toward the truck, laughing. The dogs bounded at their side.

Lucy was horrified at the thought of the children being privy to a possible crime. And worse than the cars, the thought of a horse being snatched away by some fool trying to use one of them to mount an escape, had her pressing her temples, hard.

"Can never hide anything from kids," Pete said. He glanced at Lucy then turned to Heath. "Okay, doc, I'll leave a radio for you on the kitchen table for when you get back here. Lock yourself in. Call me immediately if you see anything and don't engage in any way. You being at the ranch house will free up a uniform to be in the field where we need them."

"Roger that, Detective," Heath said. "Got your six."

"Now that's the kind of response I like to hear," Pete said, glaring at the two women.

CHAPTER THIRTY-SEVEN

Several hours had passed and the long summer day was slowly dying. Misty ocean gloom was beginning to shroud the landscape as Pete, Bea, and Lucy headed down the trail. The trees and shrubs lining the creek leaned in together like dark-robed Druids gathered in ancient oak groves.

"ETA fifteen minutes," a voice crackled through Pete's radio.

"Roger that," Pete said. "On my way along the back trail."

"I see it on the SAT image," the voice reported.

"Okay, good. When you get there, pull into the turnout where the creek goes under Mulholland and wait to hear from me."

"Ten-four, Sarge."

Lucy began to talk as soon as Pete signed off from his comms. "I'm sure this gun-in-the-tree thing has nothing to do with Mark Wenter, but…"

Pete looked at her and frowned. "You know better than to ever assume anything."

"Duly noted," she said. "Anyhow, have either of you had time to research the guy yet?"

"As soon as we make some headway on the campground shooting, Wenter's next on my priority list," Bea said.

"Actually, I got a text message from the crime lab on the facial rec," Pete added, scanning the meadow and the track ahead. He did a little hop-skip, narrowly missing a fresh pile of coyote scat. "Haven't had a minute to read it."

"Can you take quick look? Please?" Lucy asked.

"Yeah, okay." He pulled out his cell phone, studied it, then let out a soft whistle. "Shit. Mark Wenter's in the system but was never convicted. Was a long time ago."

"What was he accused of?" Lucy asked, concern mounting.

"Murdering his parents."

She stopped short and gasped. A montage of her own dead family raced through her brain. "He said they died of COVID."

"Nope, was a car wreck. A rockslide out in the Simi Hills. Suspicious paint scrapes and dents on the kid's car."

Pete continued. "The parents ran kind of a fringe Christian cult-like community out there. Snake-handlers."

"Snake handlers?" Lucy felt red flags snapping like whips.

"Mark Wenter, and an older cousin named May Lou Wentworth, they weren't completely sure about the relationship, anyhow, the two inherited the whole operation," the detective said.

Lucy gulped, her mouth dry. "The snake tattoos that he hides...and lying about his parents' death. And I think May Lou is the supposed midwife who ignored Jaime's symptoms."

"All sounding increasingly wonky. And Corinthians forbids tattoos amongst the faithful." Bea plucked at a stray strand of her curly hair. "How old is Mark?" she asked.

Pete glanced at his phone again, then out ahead. "He's thirty-one. The woman is late fifties. Both from Tennessee originally." He stuffed the phone back into the pocket of his cargo pants.

"I thought he was closer to Jaime's age," Bea said. "May be more experienced than he looks. And this May Lou's old enough to be his mother."

"That's true," Lucy said, thoughts beginning to spin like shaky plates on a stick.

"These cultish family groups have been known to be pretty incestuous," Bea said.

Pete interrupted. "Okay, people, focus. We'll talk about Wenter and Wentworth, and all the Went derivatives, later. Are we near where you spotted the dude, Luce?" Pete clutched and unclutched his fingers like he was getting ready for action.

"Yeah, just ahead." Lucy pointed. "See that clump of century plants, maybe ten of them? Agaves are beautiful but they can really slice you up. That's where he was."

Pete stopped. "Okay, ladies, I got it. Thank you for your help. Time for you to head back to the ranch." His radio came to life.

"We're in place," the voice said.

Pete replied, "you descend along the creek bed and head west and meet you coming up from the trail."

"Copy that, Sarge," the voice said.

Lucy and Bea stood by, listening. Pete turned to them, face grim.

"Go straight back to the ranch," he commanded. "Now." His voice left no room for negotiation. "And keep your lovely heads up. *Capiche, bellas?*"

As promised, Lucy and Bea, however reluctantly, headed back down the trail.

CHAPTER THIRTY-EIGHT

Heath Sinclair parked behind the barn. He took a moment to scan the area, his hand on the holstered revolver hooked onto his belt. Then, heeding the detective's request, with the key Lucy'd given him, he entered the ranch house and secured the door behind him.

He'd been in her home before but never walked through it as an unaccompanied observer. It felt uncomfortably intimate, but he needed to be the detective's eyes and ears around the house and out-buildings.

He took a route through Lucy's living room, a comfortable, traditional Spanish-style space warmed with fine art, Oriental carpets, leather furniture and a stone fireplace his grandparents would have approved of. Also on the main floor was the kitchen, Lucy's office/studio, the porch, and a bedroom where Elsa lived, the elderly woman who had helped raise Lucy. Heath made the rounds, keeping watch out the big windows, trying not to become distracted by the myriad little details that spoke of the Lucia Vega he was getting to know.

The radio crackled to life. "Doc?" It was Pete.

"Roger, Heath here."

"Lucy and Bea should with you soon. I sent them back about twenty minutes ago."

"Ten-four, Detective. Eyes out for them."

"Let me know when they show up."

"Will do." Heath signed off from the communication.

Relaxing into his task by the fourth time he walked the route—which he did every ten minutes—Heath heard a horse whinny from near the barn. He stilled, listening. Madison whined at his side. Bugle raised his head from his dog bed.

The horse whinnied again, more stridently. Heath went to the kitchen window. Across the yard, a long-haired teenage male had the paddock gate open and unsuccessfully was trying to mount Odin. The saddle was seriously listing.

Pulling out the radio, Heath shouted, "Pete, a guy's trying to take Odin. Gonna stop him. I'm carrying."

Heath took one last look out the window and saw Lucy rocket across the yard. He dashed through the house to the front door and ripped it open.

"Get away from him," Lucy screamed. Bea sprinted behind her.

Odin snorted and danced away from the would-be thief. The young man, maybe eighteen, with dark, dirty clothing, spun around, bug-eyed and ready to bolt.

Heath dashed toward the paddock, gun drawn. "Put your hands up," he bellowed, "or I'll shoot."

The kid's eyes popped even wider. "Please, don't shoot me!" he wailed.

"Back away from the horse," Heath ordered.

"I wasn't gonna hurt him. Just a borrow." He dropped the reins and raised his hands.

"Looks like horse theft to me," Bea shouted. "Three years in prison and a big fat fine."

Lucy hurried to Odin, grabbed his halter and did a cursory check. She looked over at Heath and nodded. The horse was unharmed.

The young man seemed to wilt. Slowly, his hands went skyward. Bea disappeared into the barn and came out moments later with a fistful of plastic zip ties.

"Don't move." Heath approached the perpetrator. "Are you armed?"

"No, no, I swear," the kid whined.

"Keep your hands up, legs wide. I'm going to frisk you." Heath went through the pat-down procedure he'd become familiar with in the military. "He's clean."

"Turn around," Bea instructed. "Move your hands to your head.

The kid complied. After she cuffed him with the zip-ties, Heath lowered his gun and slipped it back into his belt holster.

Seconds later, in a LA County Sherriff cruiser, Pete arrived on scene with a uniformed officer. In the rear sat two males about the same age as the captive with the same hungry, disheveled look.

"I'm sorry, Pete. But I couldn't let him take Odin, I had to get involved," Lucy said as he walked up to the young thief. The officer stayed by the car.

Pete said nothing to Lucy but nodded, then turned toward the perpetrator. "What's your name?"

The young man toed the dirt, looking desperate and miserable.

"Name?"

He didn't speak, just kept licking his dry, chapped lips. It wasn't clear if he was being uncooperative or was just so scared he couldn't get words out.

Pete did another search of the detainee, came up empty for weapons or drugs, then pulled a wallet from the kid's back pocket. He went through it.

"Fifty-three dollars. Name's Wentworth, age eighteen, address Simi Valley."

Lucy's eyes narrowed. Wentworth? Same name as May Lou.

And a Simi address? Same area as Mark's supposed camp. What did this mean?

"Why did you leave a loaded gun in a children's play area, Elijah?" Pete's voice was low and threatening. The detective circled the guy like a wolf narrowing in on its dinner.

No response.

"Where were you the night of July 11th?"

Nothing.

Pete crossed his arms on his chest, raised his chin and looked down on Elijah. "I think you were at the Leo Carrillo Beach campground. And I think you killed a man and his son who were camping there to get this fifty-three-fucking dollars."

CHAPTER THIRTY-NINE

The young man gasped, quaking. "No, no. I, we..." he looked toward his cronies huddled in the back of the cop car for some kind of support. They were even younger than him. "We were near the campground, sleeping rough, stealing food, but none of us killed anybody. I swear to God."

"Then you better tell me what the hell happened and how you got the gun you planted, or you and your buddies will be going to prison for a long time. They might get juvie, if they're lucky." Pete nodded at the cowering detainees. "But you, you're of age and will do hard time. Ain't gonna be no Malibu Conservation Camp, I'll promise you that." Pete folded his arms across his chest and planted his feet.

The young man looked about to faint. "Okay, okay. Some older guy, never seen him before, had the gun. Gave it to me. Said he wanted it put somewhere the lady who lived here would find it. Gave us each fifty bucks and a shitty bicycle." He wiped sweat from his forehead. "We were starving and sick of walking everywhere." Tears welled in his eyes, and he blinked them away.

"We're gonna take you to the station and show you some pictures. You think you could ID this man?"

Elijah hesitated then nodded affirmatively.

"Where do you live in Simi?" Pete continued.

"Nowhere, now. Homeless. We all grew up in kind of a commune. The boys, when we turn sixteen, seventeen or so, we're thrown out, on our own. There's a head pastor and he doesn't want any competition, if you know what I mean." He raised his eyebrows suggestively.

Lucy moved close to Heath. "Every new piece of information seems to somehow bring in the Simi camp," she whispered.

He nodded and gave her shoulders a quick hug.

After an intimidating pause, Pete said, "Don't lie to me or it will go badly for all of you. Did Mark Wenter give you the gun and ask you to plant it?"

The boy's eyes went wide. "No, no, not Pastor Wenter."

Pete glanced at Lucy and Bea. The connection with Mark Wenter had been made—they knew him. The women were both twitchy, trying hard not to interfere to ask their own questions.

"So, you lived at Pastor Wenter's camp?" Pete continued.

"Yeah, Eden's Gate. Our whole lives. But it was time for us to be men in our own right, so we had to follow the scriptures and leave." Elijah pushed his hands so deep into his pockets it looked like they'd pop out the ankles.

"They just dump you on the street?" Pete asked.

"We each got a hundred dollars, seemed like a lot at the time. We'd never handled money." He chewed at his lip. "We were left at the Camarillo Wal-Mart, in the parking lot. Or we could've chosen to take a bus ticket to some small-ass town in Tennessee." His shoulders sagged. "Should've taken the bus."

"There a lot of guns at the camp?" Bea asked. "They teach you how to shoot?"

Elijah paled. "I don't know anything about no guns at the camp."

A second cruiser crossed the bridge and pulled up next to

Pete's. He nodded as the officers got out.

"We're taking you to the Malibu-Lost Hills Sheriff station where you'll be booked and we'll talk some more," Pete said to Elijah. "We'll get you some grub, too."

The kid nodded, resignedly.

Pete instructed the latest uniforms on the scene. They secured Elijah in the back seat then both cruisers pulled away with the three young men.

"You have enough to get a search warrant for the camp?" Lucy asked Pete.

"Naw, we got nothing. Not yet anyway. But this kid didn't do the murder," he said.

Lucy frowned. "Seems like just a hungry teenager who doesn't have any idea what he stepped into."

"Too bad they just abandon the boys," Heath said.

"Yeah, people suck," Pete said. "Anyhow, thanks for the help, Doc. Glad Lucy here is hanging with you."

"Glad to do it—hang with her and help the County Sheriffs."

Pete continued. "And ladies, it's the least interfering you've ever been, so thank you for your restraint."

"You're not mad at me for going after the guy trying to steal my horse?" Lucy asked.

"I'm sure as hell not happy about it, but I understand why you did it. I expect cooperation, not that you're suddenly going to change who you are." He smiled and gave Lucy a gentle punch to the shoulder.

"Thanks, Pete." She hugged him.

"Yeah, and only a tad of uninvited questioning." He side-eyed Bea. "And one attempt to run down a perp," he looked at Lucy. "Not bad for an evening with you two." He laughed. "I gotta boogie, get those kids some drive-through and then see what I can squeeze out of them. Find out more about who handed off the gun. And yes, my lovelies, I'll keep you posted."

—

Lucy packed a small duffle containing clothes and basic toiletries for the night. She was looking forward to being held in Heath's strong, warm arms. Whatever was in the cards for their relationship, tonight she was ready to take a leap of faith.

She pulled her car up the driveway to his modest ranch house, painted bright white with green flower boxes overflowing with vining red geraniums. The place was well-kept and inviting.

As Lucy climbed out of her Jeep, the porch lights came on. She passed Heath's truck and a silver sedan with a car rental decal on the bumper. Friends visiting? Climbing the steps to the front door, she pressed the bell. Conn began to bark. Maddie and Bugle were still in her back seat, whining to be let loose. Hearing Henry and Gracie laughing from inside, Lucy couldn't wait to turn off the nightmare of a loaded gun in innocent hands and just enjoy the evening with Heath and the kids. Was it barbeque she smelled wafting from the back yard? Suddenly she was starved.

Footsteps. The door swung open. A beautiful ginger-haired woman, likely in her late thirties, greeted Lucy with an assessing smile. Lucy almost fell off the top step in surprise.

"Hi, you must be Henry's mother," the woman said. "Come in. He's such a cute kiddo."

"Yes, thank you, I'm Lucy. And you are?"

Gracie came tearing into the foyer. "Hi Lucy. My mom just came from New York to surprise us. Isn't it great?"

CHAPTER FORTY

The pill sat on a plate in front of Jaime with a glass of water. "I don't want any more of these." She frowned at May Lou who sat across the chipped yellow linoleum-topped table, sipping tea. "They make me dizzy and give me weird dreams."

The woman put down her cup and scowled at Jaime as if she were dealing with a naughty child. Enunciating each word slowly she said, "They are important vitamins and supplements for healing, my dear. Magnesium and melatonin—those ingredients guarantee you a good sleep."

Jaime pushed the remnants of meatloaf and potatoes around her plate with a fork, fantasizing about stabbing the woman with the gravy-covered tines.

May Lou continued her lecture. "It's important to get extra rest after what you have been through. You're doing very well under my directions. Let's keep it up."

"Your directions, ha." Jaime huffed, disgusted. "Your directions almost killed me. You said the pains were just part of a normal pregnancy."

"Even a physician could have made that misdiagnosis,

dear." The woman's eyes narrowed. "We do our best."

"Ever since I lost the baby, you and Mark are treating me like I don't exist. You're so totally consumed with getting the Vega ranch, but you don't tell me anything. I'm sick of not being included. I'm not just a means to an end that you can manipulate." Jaime stood and walked away from the table, shocked that she had somehow managed to confront the nasty bitch. Could she have done it if Mark were here staring at her? Probably not, but he wasn't.

"I'm going to bed." She stood and pushed in her chair.

"Okay, dear, sweet dreams." May Lou's lips disappeared into a thin, tight slash.

"By the way, where is my beloved husband tonight?" Jaime asked.

"Music practice, dear. He's auditioning a new soloist. As the book of Psalms says, *Sing to the Lord a new song, for he has done marvelous things.*" She picked up the leftovers and took them to the sink.

Jaime walked away and got ready for bed. It had been several weeks since the surgery and her husband had barely laid a hand on her. Something wasn't right. She crawled beneath the cool sheets and turned off the bedside lamp. But sleep didn't come. Her mind kept racing. She'd promised Mark that she was all in, completely committed to his ministry, but that resolve was slipping. Again. What was wrong with her that she couldn't stay faithful and stalwart?

An hour later, Jaime crept out of bed and into her bathrobe. Mark still wasn't home. She was going over to the music building. Maybe soulful melodies were what she needed to help settle down.

Barefoot, she padded quietly out the porch door. Lights were on in several of the cottages, but most were dark. Pole lights illuminated the open playing field and the swimming pool. The music building sat dark and still. Her husband was obviously not rehearsing or trying out a soloist, it was too late in the evening for that. Maybe he'd fallen asleep inside or was in the chapel practicing his sermon.

Jaime proceeded toward the music building, feeling like a restless spirit, a ghost in her filmy white nightgown and robe. Mark insisted on virginal white nightclothes for her. As she passed the double-wide music trailer on her way to the chapel where a light still shown, she heard a moan. Was someone hurt? The sound grew louder. She rushed to the window and peered inside. Through the slats of the dusty, bent mini blinds, in the weak ambient light of the silent sound system console, was her husband. His snakes were violently thrusting between the legs of the big-busted new resident, Tanya Lee Riggs.

Jaime gasped in shock and revulsion. She turned, staggering, back toward their cottage. She had nowhere else to go.

—

A short time later, Mark sat on the side of their bed in the darkness. "Sweetheart, you are way over-reacting," he said.

Jaime had wrapped herself in the sheets and turned away, refusing to look at him. Between sobs she cried, "I see you having sex with another woman and you say I'm over-reacting? You must be kidding."

He moved a little closer. "You are the one I love, darling, but I have needs that I don't want to burden you with until you have recovered."

"I have needs, too. Like to be respected by a faithful husband. I'm sure May Lou has a Bible verse or two about that."

"Listen sweetheart, you're very fragile now, very emotional. It's not like it seems. It's not the catastrophe you're creating here." He put his hand on her hip.

She pushed it away. "Don't touch me. Never touch me again. I want a divorce."

"Jaime, my love, you are wounding me to the core."

She heard a note of fear in his words and smiled. "Good,

then you know what it feels like."

"Darling, everything I do, I do for you and our ministry. My meaningless fling with that woman was to protect you. I'm not having an affair with her, it was nothing."

"You screw someone who is not your wife, it's called an affair."

"I didn't mean to hurt you."

"You betrayed me."

"You're making this way more than it is—don't do that to me, to us. I can't live without you, beautiful Jaime," His voice softened. "I will never go near her again."

His fingers grazed Jaime's shoulder and rested there. She gritted her teeth but allowed it, ashamed and disgusted with herself for giving in.

"I beg you to forgive me." he said. "As God forgives us all."

"If I hear another out-of-context Bible verse, I'm going to scream," she hissed.

Silence lingered between them until Jaime's sobs slowly began to subside into soft hiccups.

Mark spoke first. "I've done so much for you, my love. Took you from the street and recognized the shining miracle that you are, taught you His word, provided you an opportunity to contribute to something meaningful."

Spent from all the weeping, her voice was husky. "And I'm grateful, never doubt that." Was this pain and confusion what real love felt like? She made a deep swallow. "I will try to forgive you."

Soon she was in his arms, but the taste of the other woman remained on his lips.

CHAPTER FORTY-ONE

In a marked LACSD cruiser, Pete drove down a rutted, gravel road to Eden's Gate Community Camp. On the surface the place ahead looked like any other summer camp—modest cabins, kids in a pool, sports fields, and arts and crafts under a sprawling oak tree.

He pulled to a stop at a guard shack staffed by a bald, skinny octogenarian male. Pete lowered the window.

The fellow stepped from the shack and leaned over to peer into the driver's side.

"Can I help you?" the man asked, adjusting his eye glasses. His breath was sour.

"Hello, sir. Detective Peter Anthony, LA County Sheriff." Even though his cruiser was testimony to his legitimacy, he flashed his badge for the old man. "Here for Pastor Mark Wenter."

"Do you have an appointment, officer?" The guard checked a note pad.

Pete was getting antsy. After hours with the *lost boys* the previous night and their stories significantly changing in the wee hours, his patience was thin. "No appointment, but I need to meet with him."

"Well, he's very busy today."

The detective frowned and leaned out the car window. "I need to see him. Now. Or this camp's gonna be crawling with police. Understood, sir?"

"Oh, goodness gracious. We don't want that." The guard adjusted his glasses again, his eyes huge rheumy saucers through the lenses. "We're running a law-abiding, God-fearing organization here. May I tell Pastor Wenter what this is about?"

"A murder."

The old man blanched. "Let me call and find out if the Pastor is available."

"You do that."

He retreated into the shack. Through the window Pete could see him on a walkie-talkie.

A few minutes later, the guard returned. "Go on down to the chapel, he's inside preparing for worship. Just follow this road to the left."

"Appreciate your cooperation," Pete said, trying to rein in the irritation he was feeling. He still had the shithead pastor to contend with.

"Have a blessed day, officer." The old man waved arthritic fingers.

"Yeah, you, too," Pete replied, eyeing a 360-security cam high on the light pole next to the shack. There were likely many more.

—

High on a hillside above the camp, Lucy and Bea sat on the hood of Lucy's Jeep. They watched Pete's entry into the camp with binoculars.

"He's in." Bea released the field glasses and let them hang around her neck. "I'm feeling just a teeny tiny bit bad about this little foray of ours after we promised we wouldn't interfere with my honey's operations."

Lucy shrugged. "Well, we could call it a day and go home."

They both laughed.

"He can't get a search warrant so the cops can't check out any part of the property. If we get caught nosing around, we're just a couple of lost hikers," Lucy said. "I think we've had luck with that ploy before. And I wore my Santa Monica Hiking Club T-shirt for a purpose." She patted the logo on the front of her khaki-colored top.

"I mean, we can't just sit around and do nothing, right?" Bea said. "Not our style, for sure." She smiled and took another quick look through the glasses. "Sometimes Pete needs our help even when he doesn't know it."

"We're incorrigible," Lucy said.

"Let's roll, girlfriend, it's getting hot." Bea slid off the hood of the car and adjusted her ballcap. "So, what did Jaime have to say when you asked her about the snakes and what this group believed in? I mean the name alone, Eden's Gate, conjures visions of Eve offering the apple to Adam. He takes the fateful bite."

"Sounds like Snow White and the Seven Dwarfs with the poisoned apple," Lucy said, following Bea across a rocky flat. "I guess most fairytales are based on ancient history and legend."

Bea smiled. "Yes, indeed. But in Eden, when Adam gets in trouble with the Big Guy for eating the apple, Adam blames Eve. *'Oh Lord, she made me do it.'* Soundtrack of every abusive relationship, right?"

"Remind me, what happened to the snake?" Lucy asked.

"He lost his legs, had to slither along the ground and be a dust eater for eternity."

"I'm so glad your dad was a Baptist minister," Lucy said, smiling. "So randomly interesting sometimes."

Bea laughed. "Couldn't start Sunday dinner until we kids had all recited a Bible verse and discussed the context. Daddy was big on context."

"That's pretty cool, actually," Lucy said. "So, about Jaime, she told me Eden's Gate is just a conservative Christian community. What makes them unique is that they continue the tradition of snake handling during services. She was told it started back in rural Tennessee in the early 1900s. Mark's family is from there, probably long-time snake people."

"God's commandment to take up poisonous serpents is in Mark 16, somewhere," Bea said. She took off her hat for a moment and wiped her forehead. "Had to look that one up. Supposedly, true believers won't be harmed. How did Jaime react when you asked if one of Mark's snakes could have found their way into your barn?"

"Totally freaked out. Got teary and started pacing. I know she's still dealing with the lost pregnancy, and will be for a long time to come, but it seems like something else is going on."

"You planning to continue letting her take care of Henry?" Bea asked.

Lucy sighed. "Frankly, I don't know what I'm going to do on the Jaime and Henry front. The two clearly love each other. They're bonded for life, brother and sister—I have to honor that. But I don't want Mark Wenter around, that I know for sure."

CHAPTER FORTY-TWO

"On the satellite image Pete showed us, you could see remnants of a barn and corral just over this hill." Lucy looked up the low, gravel-strewn rise. She pointed to a faint, narrow, animal trail. "Let's follow that." They grabbed their water bottles, took a drink, and started up the dusty hillside.

"So, regarding the hot and highly desirable Heath Sinclair, I'm sorry to hear about last night with his ex-wife and all," Bea said.

Carefully, they walked a wide berth around a stand of prickly pear cacti.

"Yeah, thanks for letting me and Henry crash at your place. There was no way I could stay there with her. I sure as hell didn't want to get in the middle of anything domestic. Who knows, maybe they'll reconcile."

Bea laughed. "Reconcile? Hard to believe with the way he looks at you, sweet pea. Has he called this morning?"

"Yeah, but I'm not ready to talk. Haven't even listened to his voice mail. I mean, I had no right to expect anything, but I did. My bad. I'll touch base with him later."

"Be sure to do that, and soon." Bea gave Lucy a stern look before she stopped to grab her binoculars and scan the area again. "So far, no action out this way at all. Nice."

"I think I mentioned Heath told me his dad knew about a religious community here in the hills way back when," Lucy said as they continued their hike. "Old Doc thinks he visited several times in the eighties when they had horses."

"Interesting. Maybe there's more to learn from Old Doc."

Lucy nodded. "We need to talk with him."

The day was already a scorcher. Lucy could feel the heat through the soles of her hiking boots. Twenty minutes later they'd crested the rise. Below was a dilapidated barn and corral.

Lucy wiped sweat from her face with her sleeve. "Looks ancient but it's not falling over."

"Yet." Bea followed Lucy down through sagebrush and across a low sandstone spine bordering a ravine. All along the corral, the fencing was rotted and broken. A rusted metal gate entangled with barbed wire lay toppled in the dirt. A tiny lizard skittered into the shadow of a cholla cactus.

Bea took another long drink of water. "Let's peek in the barn and then get the heck out of here. Place is creepy."

Lucy turned toward the building, then stopped. "Look, Bea, fresh motor bike tracks."

"These hills are full of dirt bikers," Bea said, unimpressed.

They approached the barn. From the whoosing of the gusty chaparral wind, the grating sound of a motor revved. Lucy froze.

The barndoor burst open, almost ripping off its rusted hinges.

"Hey, what the..." Lucy shouted. She and Bea stumbled into each other as a man came hurtling from the dark interior riding a motorcycle.

Silver helmet pulled low, he hunched down and accelerated, side-swiping Lucy and knocking her over.

Bea fumbled for her phone and managed a shaky video as the rider disappeared over the hill in a cloud of dust.

"You okay, Luce?" Bea helped her friend struggle up, shaken, from the rocky ground.

Coughing, Lucy grimaced and brushed herself off." I'm fine." She examined the long tear in her leggings. "Just a little road rash. The asshole."

"You sure you're okay?" Bea asked, eyes following the biker's route.

"Yeah. Let's go inside. See what he was up to." Lucy limped toward the open door.

"Wait a minute," Bea said, unzipping her fanny pack. She pulled out her Glock 19.

"I didn't know you were carrying," Lucy said, concerned.

Bea whispered, "Hell, I'm not going anywhere in the realm of these possible murderers without it." She clutched the gun with both hands and headed stealthily into the building, with Lucy at her heels.

Bright slices of sunlight, dust motes dancing in their stripes, shined between the old boards. The long-abandoned barn still held the scent of decomposed manure and rotting hay.

The two women inched their way through the building with Bea and her Glock in the lead. They discovered four horse stalls on each side of a center breezeway with an empty tack room and what might have once been an office at the front. Several moldering hay bales remained at the edge of the loft. The wooden rungs from a ladder lay shattered on the ground.

"We're clear." Bea slid her gun into the waistband of her shorts.

"I smell something. Like burning wax." Lucy sniffed the air.

"Maybe engine oil?" Bea said, eyes scanning the ground.

As they turned to leave, Lucy pushed open the office door more fully. Bea, gun redrawn, stepped inside first with Lucy close behind.

Lucy's throat tightened at what she saw. A single bed was jammed against the wall behind the door, topped with a rat-gnawed mattress streaked with what appeared to be dried blood. A chain with a metal neck collar was bolted to the wall.

A cold, dank gust suddenly filled the room, as if the space itself was drawing an evil breath.

"Lord have mercy," Bea said, backing away. "Really bad juju in here. Awful things happened."

Then they saw it. On the floor at the foot of the bed, a candle had recently guttered out amid a ritualistic array of amulets—feathers, rocks, and a rodent skull surrounding a recently killed rattlesnake. It had a nail hammered through its head.

Goose bumps rose on Lucy's skin. Immediately, she began to snap photos and took a short video with her phone. Her attention kept returning to the frightening, blood-marked mattress. "I think I'm going to take a sample of the fabric," she said. "Who knows, by the time Pete can get a crime scene crew up here, all this could disappear."

"Good idea." Cautiously, Bea leaned over to inspect the dead rattler. "Heath should be able to tell if this guy is the same variety as the one that bit Odin."

"Nail through the rattler—nicely symbolic." Lucy pulled a Swiss Army knife from her fanny pack and pried open the scissor tool. That's when a loud, percussive bang hit the front of the barn.

She gasped, almost cutting herself. Was the motorcycle asshole back? The front door to the barn had wrenched open and was banging in the wind against the building. The Santa Anas were picking up, making the already hot temperature rise. The barn creaked and groaned like a person in pain.

"Get that sample fast, Luce." Bea crept from the office while Lucy snipped out a four-inch square of bloody mattress cover, wrapped it in a tissue, then rushed outside after her friend.

"Those devil winds are gonna blow this place down," Bea said. "Let's get out of here. Not in the mood for a confrontation if the motorcycle dude decides to come back and play *Road Warrior*."

They found the faint trail where they'd come in and hustled up the hillside. Sand and grit blasted their skin as the desert dragon roared in.

CHAPTER FORTY-THREE

The camp's place of worship was an unattractive rectangular building built of dusty, once white-washed cement bricks. Over the door, a peeling sign proclaimed *Eden's Gate Community Tabernacle*. Homicide Detective Peter Anthony entered.

Inside, the place smelled of gym locker room, cleaning products, and wilted flowers. Several dozen rows of folding chairs were set up along a center strip of aging purplish carpet. Religious paintings on black velvet hung on the windowless side walls, reminding Pete of portraits he'd once seen of Elvis. A low riser in front held an electric keyboard, a guitar, and a drum kit, all dominated by a rustic cross, inscribed with a quotation about serpents. "They will pick up serpents with their hands; and if they drink the deadly poison, it will not hurt them. Mark 16:18."

Broad shouldered Pastor Mark Wenter stood at the pulpit studying an open Bible. In his buttoned-up white shirt and dark trousers, he looked like what Bea would probably call *a hot Amish dude*. For an instant, Pete thought of her and Lucy and tried not to wonder what they were up to this morning. With those two, it was usually better not to know.

"Detective Anthony, welcome to Eden's Gate. What an unexpected surprise." Mark smiled. "The whole camp will be wondering what brought the L.A. County Sheriffs to our humble community." Mark placed a silver bookmark between pages in the Bible, then closed it. Pressed a hand on the cover as if drawing strength.

"We picked up three of your community members last night on the Vega ranch property," Pete said, all business. "Elijah Wentworth, Jared Wentworth, and Hosea Wenter. Evidently, at least one is a relative."

"A very distant cousin," Mark Wenter said. His tongue flitted from between his lips.

"Elijah planted a loaded gun next to the children's swing by the corral. You know the area. In fact, you did some repair work for Lucy Vega up there."

"Yes, I know the ranch. A loaded gun? How horrible." Mark shook his head. "But I'm sorry, it has been months since those three severed their affiliation with Eden's Gate to spread the Word and seek meaning for themselves as young men in the outside world. It's been our policy since the beginning of the community in the late sixties to initiate men into adulthood at around sixteen."

"Teenaged boys are still total idiots," Pete said.

Mark shrugged.

Pete continued. "Anyhow, they've been living in a stolen tent near the Leo Carrillo State Beach campground for a good three weeks. They said a fourth guy, Cain Hensley, bought the gun in a Camarillo alley and used it to murder two campers to get their money and supplies. They don't know why Hensley wanted the gun planted at the ranch. The kids, and I call them kids because the oldest is only eighteen, were literally starving. They say you gave them each enough cash for dinner at Micky D's and dropped them off at a Wal-Mart parking lot. Child Protective Services might call that fuckin' child abuse."

Wenter gripped the edges of the pulpit so tightly his knuckles turned white. His voice raised an octave. "They're lying. We cared for those boys. Gave them plenty."

Pete stepped closer. "Those kids were set up to fail."

Wenter puffed his chest and tried to hold his ground but finally stepped backwards. "They failed because they made bad choices, Sargent." The pastor took a breath and lowered his voice to a calm drone. "Along with the Bible and teachings on how to live a righteous life, they learned job skills here—property maintenance, food service, landscaping. In this post-COVID world, businesses are begging for those skills. Whatever trouble those former community members found themselves in, it may be unfortunate, but they're responsible."

"It doesn't change the fact that your former congregants, or whatever you call them, are out causing havoc."

Wenter fidgeted, then looked heavenward for a moment. "Hensley was a bad seed from the beginning. Came to us from a broken, meth-addicted home in rural Tennessee at age thirteen. We did our best."

Pete stood quietly, arms folded on his chest and eyes roving the chapel, for just long enough to make the pastor begin to twitch.

"Do the women all stay here?" Pete asked. "Or are they aged out, too?"

Remaining behind the pulpit like a shield, Wenter opened and closed the Good Book multiple times, then slammed it shut. "Most of the women and their children have been rescued from abusive situations, drug addiction, prostitution. They mostly stay with us, caring for their children and running the camp. We do the Lord's work here, detective, we raise people up."

"Good to know it's working so well." Pete took a last look around. Mark Wenter was convincing, in an oily salesman sort of way. Pete could see how he could gain the trust of desperate people. "Thank you for your time, Pastor Wenter. If you hear from Hensley, call me right away. The other three will be in custody for a while." He handed Mark a business card. The man was probably more comfortable taking one of his snakes.

Pete turned to leave, then stopped and spun back around. He pointed to the image of the serpent on the cross behind the pastor. "How do you think a rattler got into Lucy Vega's horse stall?"

Blanching, Wenter said. "I have no idea. And if you're looking at me as the perpetrator, you are sorely mistaken. My serpents are used only to worship the Lord."

In his most ominous voice, Pete said, "I want you to stay away from the Vega ranch. Do you understand?"

Wenter froze, then said, "I've done nothing but help Lucy and her son. My wife is a relative, the boy's sister. Technically, that makes me his brother-in-law." His smile was sly.

Pete crossed the floor, stepped onto the dais and leaned in, close to Wenter's smug face. He took a fistful of the pastors' freshly ironed shirt. "I don't care who the fuck you think you are to that kid—stay away from the Vega ranch. "Do. You. Understand?"

Scowling, Wenter finally nodded, but said nothing.

The detective released him, patted the shirt back into shape, then walked down the center aisle and out of the church.

Returning to his cruiser, Pete slid in and started up the air conditioning. Had to be twenty degrees hotter out in these hills than nearer the city. Checking his messages, he spotted a text from Lucy with an attachment from her and Bea. He grimaced, then played the video, and immediately texted them back. "Might give us enough for a search warrant. Meet me at Lost Hills Station in an hour. I'll sched CSI to check out that barn ASAP."

CHAPTER FORTY-FOUR

Mark stormed through the screen door, letting it slam hard, then strode into the kitchen where May Lou worked on the accounting books.

She looked up and frowned. Her reading glasses slid to the end of her narrow nose. "What happened? I heard a detective wanted to talk with you. What was that about?"

He scrubbed at his dark hair. "Looks like Cain Hensley shot and killed two people over at the Leo Carrillo campground. Cops are looking to me..."

"Mercy!" May Lou interrupted, almost falling out of her chair. "They think *you* did it?"

"No, no, just wanted some background information."

She removed her glasses and nervously fingered the lenses. "I told you we needed a more permanent solution for that boy. The epistle of John says, *Do not be like Cain, who belonged to the evil one...*"

Mark nodded and began to pace back and forth in front of the kitchen stove. "The damn detective suspects I planted the rattlesnake in Lucy's barn."

"What?" May Lou's eyes widened.

"They're getting too close." He rubbed his tattooed arms.

She shut the books and pushed them away. "We need to act. Now." May Lou poured another splash of the recipe into her tea. Grabbed a mug from the counter and did the same for Mark.

"Yes, it's all coming too fast. We can't lose this opportunity. Gotta move our plans forward. You book the plane reservations, and I'll go get Tanya Lee. Time to make the arrangements." Mark locked his hands around his mug like he wanted to strangle it.

"Her passports should be done by Friday," May Lou said.

"Then we engage with Vega on Monday." He wiped perspiration from his forehead. "We'll fly Tanya out that night. The hour is nigh." He gulped down the contents of his mug in a single long swallow.

"For everything there is a season..." she began.

"Enough, May Lou. Enough," Mark growled.

"As you wish, my dearest one." Despite the hot day and a lack of air conditioning, May Lou turned up the fire under the teapot.

Mark nodded. "Jaime will be working at the ranch Mondays and she's there today. It's Thursday? I'll fill her in with as few details as I can. In the meantime, we need to get Tanya Lee up to speed."

"You think the girl can pull this off? She's a wild card," May Lou said, preparing another cup of Earl Gray and adding a splash from a bottle labeled *Tennessee Torchlight*.

"She has to," Mark said, backing toward the door. "She's smart, ambitious as hell. She'll make it happen. Everything depends on it, including her plans for a career in film. That's enough to keep her focused." He hustled from the cottage.

—

Lucy leaned on the kitchen island watching Henry and Jaime interact. They were frosting cupcakes and laughing at each other's attempts at decoration. Sprinkles were everywhere. It pained Lucy to let Jaime go, but given the young woman's relationship with Mark, she didn't trust her. Yet, she and Henry were siblings, and the relationship had to be preserved. Lucy sighed, still not sure how to approach the situation. But she wanted to address it before Jaime left for the day.

Lucy's phone buzzed. She glanced at the caller ID. It was Sigrid Bergmann from the gallery. "Hey, Sigrid," Lucy said. "How are you?"

There was a way too-long moment of silence. Lucy's stomach tightened.

"Sigrid? All good on the gallery front?" she asked.

"Lucy, sorry, I'm in shock. I just came in, you know we open late on Thursdays—at one o'clock. Somebody broke in last night. Trashed everything. Glass shattered, photos slashed."

"What?" Lucy almost dropped her phone, reeling at the news. "Oh no, no. Unbelievable."

"The police just arrived. They want to talk with you. Can you come down? Like now?"

"Yes, hold on for a second." She turned to Jaime. "Can you stay with Henry for another couple hours?" So much for letting Jaime go today.

"Yes, sure, what's going on?"

"A problem at the gallery."

"What kind of problem?" Henry asked.

Lucy's mind scrambled for a plausible line that wouldn't further upset her child. "Oh, uh, a couple of the photos fell off the wall and got broken. We have to re-hang them," she said. "No biggie. Be back soon." She fought tears of fear and anger welling in her eyes.

"Sigrid, I'm leaving now. See you in a half hour."

Lucy grabbed her purse, kissed her son and hurried toward her car, heart palpitating. The vandalism, the gun, the Eden's Gate lost boys, and now the Gallery. Did the MIA Eden's Gate castoff, Cain Hensley, do this? What did he have against her or the ranch? Lucy was beyond confused as she left a distressed message for Pete and Bea.

CHAPTER FORTY-FIVE

"I poured my heart and soul into this collection." Lucy choked back tears.

It looked like a bomb had gone off inside the once beautiful gallery. Sigrid greeted Lucy with a hug and then went to huddle with a black-suited insurance adjustor that Lucy thought looked like an undertaker. She almost felt like she was ready for the slab herself. So much work, all in shambles.

Bea picked her way through glass shards sparkling like crushed ice on the gallery floor. "The show wasn't just trashed, it was savaged."

Pete's eyes scanned the wreckage. "This is personal. If this is Cain Hensley's work, what the hell does he have against you?"

"I have no clue," Lucy said, trying to wrap her brain around a motivation. "But maybe it's not against me, maybe it's against Wenter. Hensley could be taking it out on me because the pastor's wife is working at the ranch and Mark has helped us out, too. That's the only connection I could possibly have to this guy. Could be Cain hates Mark Wenter because he and his friends were dumped on the street. So, whatever Wenter might be attached to, Hensley wants to destroy it."

Bea bent over and picked up the ripped photo of her and Pete from the floor. She ran her thumb over the black and white image of her lover's torn face. "I don't think that's it, or not completely. Why would he go after Mark for a policy that's been in place since the elder Wenter's time?" She carefully placed the ruined photo on the counter. "Feels more personal. Could it be that he and Mark had some kind of a romantic triangle going on, and Hensley lost?"

"That seems like a stretch," Lucy said, shaking her head.

"No, listen to me, Luce. A competitive sexual dynamic is common in cults led by males, and Eden's Gate sure sounds cultish. Jonestown, the Moonies, NXIVM, the leaders all used sex to manipulate and control—was a total power trip. I covered the Children of Heaven's Ridge trial in San Diego about ten years ago," Bea said. "This thing smacks of the same patterns."

Pete nodded. "Could be you got something there, babe. A young fool in love, disrespected and beat out by a more powerful rival like the cult leader. That could drive somebody to do crazy shit."

"Okay, you could be right. Were you able to get a search warrant for the camp?" Lucy asked Pete. "I'll bet it was Hensley who ran me down at the barn. And any news on the blood sample?"

Pete glanced at the mutilated photo of he and Bea. "Just heard. The warrant is a go. Good for the barn area only, not the camp."

"It's a start," Lucy said.

"Definitely. But the sample you sliced out of that mattress cover? It isn't human, it's rabbit blood." Pete looked over at a crime scene analyst who'd been motioning to him. Excuse me, ladies." He stepped away to join his colleague.

Lucy felt a bit of relief. "So, a ritual sacrifice of some kind and not a torture murder scene?"

"Maybe, but Pete said he wants the whole mattress

analyzed," Bea said. "A small square of material doesn't tell the whole story. I mean that neck shackle...somebody was held in there and very bad things happened."

Lucy shuddered.

Moments later, the detective rejoined the two women. "Some good news—they found blood on a couple pieces of broken glass. We'll see if it's Hensley's." He turned to Lucy, eyes intense. "You still staying with Doc for now?"

Lucy shook her head. "No, his wife's in town. Ex-wife. I, uh, want to stay away from any, you know, domestic issues. I've got a good security system at the ranch."

Pete frowned. "Not good enough to have grabbed a picture of the asshole planting the gun. I don't like you being out there alone."

"I'll readjust the camera coverage." Lucy knew Pete wanted her away from the ranch. Bea had offered her a guest room in Santa Monica for however long was needed, but Lucy would not be pushed out of her home. She'd walked away from the ranch once to be in New York with Michael, but she wasn't doing it again.

"By the way, girlfriend, have you called Heath back yet? Bea cast a side-eye, guessing the answer.

"No, but I will." Lucy didn't want to hear about him reconciling with his wife.

Bea's hands went to her hips, chin up.

Lucy winced. She knew the look.

"What is this?" Bea asked. "High school? Woman up and call him."

"Yeah, yeah. I'll do it." She turned to Pete who was being beckoned by the crime scene folks yet again. "Is it okay if I leave now?"

"Yeah, you can take off. Watch your back, baby cakes. Hear me, *Lucia mia*?" he asked.

Lucy hugged everybody goodbye and returned to the parking lot with ugly visions of the trashed photography show stuck in her brain like one of the glass shards.

Even though she'd managed to park in the shade of a tree, the hot leather of the driver's seat burned her legs as she slid in. Opening the windows, Lucy cranked up the air and closed her eyes, welcoming the coolness.

She texted Jaime that she was on her way home. A thumbs-up icon appeared seconds later.

Then, she called Heath.

CHAPTER FORTY-SIX

In the empty dining hall, Tanya Lee Riggs examined her two U.S. passports, both featuring her picture. One was marked as belonging to Lucia Ingrid Vega and was photoshopped to look a little more like Lucy who she'd be impersonating. The second was issued to Terrie Lynn Wente of Los Angeles.

"I don't look too bad," she said to Mark. "Would be nice to have more of a full-body shot."

"Face-only for passports," he said, studying his laptop.

"I've never been on an airplane let alone to an airport." Tanya shuffled the two booklets like playing cards. "This is crazy, it's like a spy movie." She grinned. "So cool."

"May Lou and I have carefully thought through everything, but you have to play your part to the max. Your role is critical."

"I'll be awesome." Tanya regularly fantasized about winning an AVA, the Adult Video News award someday. Or maybe an Emmy or an Oscar.

"Okay, so you have to start watching the YouTube videos I sent you," Mark said. "Familiarize yourself with LAX and the security and boarding processes. Check out the general info about airplane travel and the stuff about Muslim culture. All very important. I'll print out your tickets. You'll have a burner phone which is un-trackable."

"Does it have a camera? I have to document my trip."

"One thing you do NOT want to do is document this trip. Calls and text only."

"You must be kidding."

"No, Tanya. You're a ghost. No record of anything."

She felt her eyes narrow, and her heels begin to dig in. This trip was sounding less fun by the minute. And Mark was becoming irritatingly bossy.

He continued. "And you won't be checking any luggage, you'll have just a rolling carry-on, a fanny pack which will stay attached to you at all times, and whatever small purse you want to bring. All valuables stay in the fanny pack including passports, the phone, and money." Mark held the pack up for her to see. "It never leaves your person. Understood?"

"Yeah, okay. It's not too cute, though. I would have liked an animal print."

Mark groaned. "It's black, it's supposed to be totally innocuous, inconspicuous. We draw zero attention, never want to be a target of interest to anybody. That's how we're going to pull this off and how you're going to stay safe. Do you understand how important this is, Tanya Lee?"

"Yeah, of course." She let out an exaggerated sigh and jotted something into a notebook.

"Glad you're writing all this down," Mark said.

"I'm not taking notes; I'll remember everything. I'm creating my screenplay for the first of the *Pastor and the Deaconess Do the Deadly Sins* adult film series. She pushed the pages toward Mark. "Read it."

Visibly frustrated, he examined the pages, gritting his teeth.

"Pornies are not known for brilliant scripts, but I think this one is totally lit," she said, smiling with pride.

Mark banged the table with his hand. "Tanya, you

absolutely must focus on our long-term goals. Forget the script for now. If you mess this trip up, you can kiss your film career goodbye. And it won't be pretty or sexy, I guarantee you."

"Okay, okay. I'm sorry." She frowned and grabbed the notebook from Mark, shoving it into her backpack. "Chill, Pastor Mark. I've been listening, I'm a great multitasker. You drop me off as Lucy Vega, on Thursday afternoon at the LAX International Terminal. The plane leaves at 3:30 p.m. for New York. On arrival there I go to the Quatar Airlines gate to board my flight to Baghdad where fake Lucy disappears. See, I was listening."

She pulled a tube of pink gloss from her pocket and slathered her puckered mouth, then took a drink of water. Her greasy lip print remained on the glass. "For the trip home, I become Terrie Lynn Wente. I kind of like that, could be my stage name." She glanced at Mark then wiggled her shoulders seductively, reminding the pastor of what he was going to miss while she was gone.

"Okay, good summary." Mark appeared a bit reassured. "Over these next couple days, review your itinerary carefully."

"Will do." She smiled. "Now, what about the money?"

"You'll have two hundred U.S. in cash and a similar amount in Dinar for miscellaneous use—meals, or maybe a small souvenir. You'll have three prepaid, untraceable Visa cash cards of $500 each, in case you get in a jam."

"Like the flight is delayed and I need a hotel room or whatever, right?"

"Exactly. I expect to have two of the cards back and major change left on the third one. You'll basically never leave the airports so expenses should be low. Spending a lot of money is not an option. Understand?"

She nodded. "I'm getting excited, planning what I'm going to wear. I love the idea of being a world traveler, so sophisticated."

"May Lou will have your clothing ready."

"Oh, no. A little daisy-patterned housedress and slip-on sneakers?" She laughed.

Mark found no humor in the situation. "You're dressing as a conservative Muslim woman; dark clothes—an abaya and a hijab"

"A what?"

"Like a headscarf to cover your hair and a loose-fitting robe-type thing."

"Loose fitting?" Tanya leaned across the table toward Mark, a cougar ready to tear off flesh. "No way. I laid out my hot pink leggings, high heeled boots, they're silver, got them on that online luxury goods discount site. Cousin Clement sent me some money. I also found a black Prada halter top and a leather bomber jacket. It's actually plastic but you could never tell. It looks like one Rihanna wore."

"Rihanna?" Mark's face went red. If steam could explode from human ears, it would've erupted out of his.

"You clearly do not understand the meaning of the words unobtrusive and *innocuous*?" he rasped. "You bring zero attention to yourself and remain bland, innocent, and low-profile."

"None of the things that I am." She puckered her lips, this time into a pout.

"Tanya Lee, you are not going to a strip club in Klapperville or to an awards show in Hollywood. You are sneaking, unseen, in and out of a Muslim country where people can be put to death for viewing pornography."

She swallowed hard, frowning. "Really? To death?"

He nodded. "Really. This is serious shit. Now go back to your cabin and study the websites I sent you. I'll quiz you in the morning. It's critical that you understand you're entering a very different culture, and you must play by their rules. May Lou will be over with your clothing shortly. Are we on the same page?"

She grimaced.

"I know how hard it is going to be to *keep that light of yours under a bushel,* as Matthew 5:14-16 tells us," he said. "But when we finally own the ranch, the first thing I will do is build you a movie sound studio."

Tanya's frown turned into a tentative smile. "And you'll be the Pastor to my Deaconess?"

"You pull off this trip and I'll read your screenplays and be the Pastor to your Deaconess forever."

CHAPTER FORTY-SEVEN

Lucy climbed into her car and made the phone call before pulling out of the Calabasas Shopping Center parking lot. When Heath didn't pick up, she felt a mix of relief and disappointment. She left a voice mail. "Sorry I haven't called back. I truly appreciated your offer to put Henry and me up for a few nights, but I didn't want to interfere with your time with Grace and your wife. We're fine at the ranch. Not going to let some creep intimidate me out of my own home. Anyhow, call when you can."

She hesitated to say more but he deserved to know that he mattered to her. Why was it so difficult to tell him? Avoidance of rejection? For sure. Fear of another failure and loss? Hell, yes. All those things kept her paralyzed. Lucy knew in her gut that she had to take the leap, at least a little one, or risk losing something that was good and hopeful.

"I miss you." It was a short, innocuous comment but terrifying to make. There was a fragile heart beating in those three words.

Forcing aside her anxious thoughts, Lucy cranked up the air

conditioning and pulled her vehicle around a gaggle of cruisers and the crime scene van in front of the gallery. Choosing to take the less traveled Agoura Road home rather than the busy freeway, the light was losing its daytime intensity, tinting the rocky landscape through the Santa Monica Mountains soft and golden. As she turned onto Kanan Road toward the ocean, her phone pinged. She glanced at the caller ID—it was Heath. She felt a school girl fluttering in her chest as she answered.

"Hey, Doctor Sinclair, sorry again I took so long to get back with you."

"It's Doctor Sinclair now, is it, Ms. Vega?"

"Sorry, Heath, I'm feeling a little awkward. I had no idea your wife would answer the door the other night."

"Ex-wife. And neither did I. She arrived fifteen minutes before you did, immediately acting like she owned the place. That's her *modus operandi*. Anyhow, she's gone. Has a swanky apartment downtown. She's doing the art direction for a play at the Mark Taper Forum. She'll be in town for a month."

"Gracie must be thrilled."

"She is, and it breaks my heart. There'll be a whirlwind of activity, lots of expensive presents, then mama will disappear again until the next random drop-in. A month? Six? More? Shit." He sighed. "Anyhow, Grace is with her for the next couple days. I know nothing beyond that."

"I'm so sorry, Heath. Sounds like both our children have an unreliable parent to deal with. We do our best to compensate, right?" Lucy slowed down as a truck carrying alfalfa bales pulled out from an equestrian center in Triunfo Canyon. "Care to join me and drown our sorrows together? It's taco night at *Rancho de la Vega*."

"I'd love to."

"I'll be there in fifteen," Lucy said. "I'll send Jaime home, Henry and I will feed the critters, then start on dinner."

"See you soon," Heath said. "And I'll take margarita duty."

"*Perfecto, nos vemos luego, señor.*" She lost connection

through the first of three tunnels through the mountains. No matter, she'd be with Heath soon.

Despite the horrible day, Lucy's dark mood began to dissipate. But she needed to talk with Jaime, let her go, or something. She groaned out loud, refusing to douse the warm spell conjured by the anticipation of seeing Heath. She'd deal with Jaime soon, but not tonight. This evening was going to be *especial*.

Back at the ranch, Lucy decided to put her car in the garage for once and not risk tampering or whatever the next act of intimidation might be. The trashed gallery was more of a psychological blow than she cared to admit.

When she came into the kitchen, Jaime and Henry were frosting another couple batches of sugar cookies in red, white, and blueberry. Jaime was doing the frosting; Henry was licking the spoon and scraper. How they loved to bake together. Lucy'd have to find a few less sugar-intensive recipes for them to tackle.

"Hi, Lucy. Can't believe it's nearly the Fourth of July." Jaime sounded in good spirits despite Lucy's tardiness.

"Yeah, and speaking of time flying, I'm really sorry about getting back so late. Everything took much longer than I expected."

"No prob." Jaime finished the last cookie and put down the knife. "So, what happened with the gallery? Vandalism, right? I never got to see the show."

Lucy sighed and hung her purse on the back of a bar stool. Ran her finger along the rim of the frosting bowl and took a quick taste.

"Very good." She turned to Henry, "Hey, sweetie pie, would you mind going into my office and grabbing one of those show programs off my desk? I want to give it to Jaime."

"Yup, but don't eat all the sprinkles."

"Pinky swear. I won't touch them." Lucy hooked fingers with her son. He slid off the stool and scampered away.

When Henry was out of earshot, Lucy turned to Jaime. "The

show was totally trashed, broken frames and glass, the photos slashed. It was scary. It was like whoever did this—hated me. I mean big time anger, rage. I don't have a clue as to who that could be. Is there anyone at your camp that might resent you or Mark? Maybe it was Cain Hensley, and he came after me because you both help here at the ranch." She rubbed her stiffening neck. "I'm grasping at straws."

Jaime tugged at a long strand of her straight blonde hair. "I mean, some people always resent the leaders. They don't realize how hard it is. They just complain about the privileges. For instance, I'm the only person working outside the community."

"I didn't know that," Lucy said, sensing how hard it would be on Jaime when she lost her childcare job with Henry and was relegated solely back to camp life. Of course, she could still visit her brother when Lucy was around to oversee. It was heartbreaking not to be able to trust a family member whom Lucy had begun to really care about.

"Everybody else has jobs on site," Jaime continued. Childcare, gardening, maintenance, security, cooking, worship programming—there's so much that needs doing. We hadn't expected that you would be kind enough to let me help here." She gazed warmly at Henry as he came back into the kitchen holding a slightly frosting-smeared show program.

"Thanks, Henry. And Lucy." Jaime took the booklet and as she smiled at them both, she was unable to hide a tremble to her lips. "So, I'm late for our evening supper, gotta run." Grabbing her backpack from a hook next to the kitchen door, she headed out fast, not stopping for her usual quick peck on her little brother's cheek.

CHAPTER FORTY-EIGHT

Returning to the kitchen island, Lucy finished cleaning up the cookie project and laid out the taco ingredients. Henry lingered by the door.

"My sister is sad," he said, face worried.

"Sad? Why do you think so?" Lucy shut the refrigerator. He rarely called Jaime, *my sister*.

"She cried."

Lucy turned all her attention to her son. "How come she cried?"

"She said it's about being married—things kids can't understand."

Lucy nodded and hugged her son. "It's tough being a grown-up sometimes." Sounded like all was not well in Eden with Jaime and Mark. She wondered what was going on between them.

There was a knock at the door.

"We can talk more later, honey, but Heath is joining us for taco night." Lucy checked her phone's security camera. It was, indeed, the man. "Would you let him in?"

"Oh, yea!" His concerned little brow unfurrowed and he bolted off to welcome their guest.

When they entered the kitchen, her son was happily up on Heath's shoulders, sticky hands skimming the ceiling. "Where's Gracie?" the child asked.

"Grace is spending the night with her mother in downtown L.A." He dropped the bag of Margarita fixings onto the counter while still hanging onto Henry. "Her mom lives in New York, like you and your parents did. She works there, doesn't see us too much."

Henry rested his chin on Heath's head, gripping the man in a strangle hold around the neck. "Like my dad. He works far away. Sometimes I don't remember what he looks like."

Lucy swallowed hard. She took a deep breath to quell the stab of pain. Her first instinct was to defend Michael, but she let it go. There was no defense. The man had made his choices.

Heath put Henry on a stool in front of the bowl of shredded cheese. "Start loading up those tortillas, big guy." The doc reached across the counter and pressed Lucy's hand, his mouth was tight and his face pale.

"Are you okay?" she asked.

"I'm fine. We'll talk later. Let's enjoy dinner." His enthusiasm felt forced.

Lucy tried not to overthink or second-guess his mood. She reached for the tequila and took a swig out of the bottle before handing it over to him to mix the drinks. He grimaced and took a hefty swig as well.

The tacos, assembled by all, were delicious and the Margaritas tasted like summer nights in Southern California—bittersweet, salty, and sensual. After dinner, they saddled up two of the horses, including Odin, and went for a trail ride as the sun disappeared beneath the dusky lavender horizon. Henry rode behind the saddle horn tucked in front of his mom.

Cottonwood trees near the stream were dropping their multitude of seeds. Gossamer white, cotton candy parachutes, they danced on the breeze.

"They're really pretty," Henry said, raising his hands to catch one.

"California springtime snow," Heath said, smiling. His eyes were sad.

The soft poignant sounds of night creatures replaced the sharper tone of daytime fauna. Small bats flitted after mosquitoes and coyotes howled in the distance. A calm filled Lucy's heart. It was the blessing of the freedom to feel completely herself in this place that she adored. She would not lose it to anybody.

Later sitting on the porch, when the horses were back in their stalls and Henry tucked in and sleeping, the doc checked his watch.

Did he want to rush away? "Heath, you're somewhere else tonight. What's going on?" Lucy chewed at her lip then asked, "Are you thinking, like, maybe we shouldn't be spending time together? Maybe moving too fast?"

He shook his head then looked out toward the stand of eucalyptus trees on the edge of the field. Lucy could smell a tinge of their fragrant oil spice the breeze. It was indeed a perfect summer night—but she guessed a storm was brewing.

Rather than relax next to her on the couch, Heath crossed the porch and sat at the table, watching her with pained eyes. Lucy's heart constricted. Was he calling it quits already? She had been a fool to let herself fall like this. But fallen she had, and hard.

Then he said, "I'm crazy about you, Lucy. I hope you know that."

She gulped. Crazy about her but not enough to stay.

He rubbed his hands through his hair and moaned. "But papers came to the practice just before I left for your place tonight."

"What kind of papers?"

"My ex-wife is filing for custody of Grace."

Lucy gasped. "Oh my God, Heath. No." She rushed over and kneeled next to him, hugging him close. "You're a wonderful dad. She's an absentee mother."

He stroked her hair. "It doesn't matter. Even if the court splits custody fifty-fifty, that means Grace is in New York for six months of the year. I can't be away from her that long, I can't just be a visitor. I don't know how I'll manage my job and everything, but good chance I'll be gone from here, Lucy. I know that's not either of us want."

Lucy gulped. "We'll figure it out. New York is not Afghanistan. Let's wait until we see how the case goes. Bea knows a great lawyer that helped her keep custody of Dexter when her pro baller ex-husband tried to take him away. Sounds like a similar situation." She stroked his cheek. "I'll support whatever comes with you and your daughter anyway I can, Heath. I hope you know that."

"Thank you, Lucy." He kissed her deeply.

She tasted, fear, gratitude, and passion. "Do you want to stay tonight?" she asked.

Are you sure you want me to?" His handsome face was cast in shadows. "I have no idea where the hell my life is going."

Lucy touched his beautiful face.

He pulled her close and kissed her again, long and slow.

CHAPTER FORTY-NINE

The next day, outside the Eden's Gate chapel, Detective Pete Anthony handed the warrant to Mark Wenter. After a quick look at the document, the pastor crumpled it up like a used tissue and dropped to the ground.

Pete scowled.

The big ugly bodyguard at the pastor's side planted his feet and crossed his arms over his beefy chest.

"Okay, Detective," Mark said, "I will honor the warrant."

"Damn straight you will, or I'll arrest your ass right now." Pete's irritation grated in his voice.

"No need for that." Mark opened his arms like he was bestowing a blessing. "But Cooter Biggs, our Chief of Security here…"

Pete noted a self-satisfied smile flicker on Mr. Security's wormy lips.

"…he'll take you and your investigators out to the barn. The road's hard to navigate, has been washed out and blown over in a lot of places. And of course he'll oversee your search."

Pete cocked his head as if studying an insect and deciding

whether to step on it or release it into the brush. "Sorry pastor, I oversee the search, and your guard dog stays outside the warranted area." If Wenter wanted a pissing contest, Pete was only too happy to give him one.

Wenter's face flushed, but then his demeanor relaxed, conjuring the compliant victim role like a skilled thespian. He turned to his man. "Okay, Cooter, take the folks out to the old place. Call me if you need anything. Always happy to cooperate with law enforcement." He forced a smile and retreated to the chapel.

Pete watched him go inside. What the hell was that dickwad up to?

Cooter jogged over to the camp truck. Pete motioned for the CSI to follow, then returned to his cruiser. They trailed Cooter a few hundred yards along the main gravel road then turned off onto a barely visible trail into the dusty hills.

—

Lucy pulled her Jeep onto the same flat area where she and Bea had parked before.

"I thought it would be good," Lucy said, "for the two of us to hike in along the same route we took last time and meet Pete and his people at the barn. He's good with it. We can see if anything has changed along the path—additional tire prints, blood splatter, dropped detritus, whatever."

They both climbed out of the car.

Bea grabbed her water bottle and stuck it into her day pack. Her phone sounded and she took a look. "A text from Pete. They just left the camp."

Lucy nodded and slathered on sunscreen. She had her Mexican mother's dark wavy hair and fiery temperament, but her Norwegian father's blue eyes and pale, sunburn-prone skin. She tossed the lotion to Bea. They finished their prep for the hike, locked the car, and headed up the hill into the chaparral.

"So, sweet pea," Bea said a few minutes in, "I put your

boyfriend in touch with my lawyer, Siobhan Massey, this morning."

"Thank you so, so much. Heath's completely freaked out. The whole thing is terrifying."

"No kidding. Remember when my first husband tried to take custody of Dexter? But if anyone can hammer out a strong settlement, it's Massey. She can also really calm her clients down. The first time I went into her office I was a basket case. She even managed to settle my world class anxiety." Bea patted Lucy's arm. "But honey bun, you haven't offered a thing about your night with the sad Doc Hotness—healer of rattlesnake bites, savior of hemorrhaging women, and goat distemper eradicator—to highlight just a few of his prodigious skills. Beyond custody and family drama, was there amazement to be found in his arms? Spill, girl. I can't wait another sec."

Lucy laughed. "His ex-wife has Grace for a few days," Lucy grumbled. "So, I invited him over for taco night with Henry and me. They were delicious. I used tortilla crusted tilapia—"

Bea groaned and stopped in her tracks, turning to her friend. "You really think I give a damn about tilapia? The question is—was *he* delicious? Lucia, did you sleep with him? Finally?"

"No, no sleep." Lucy went dreamy and almost stumbled into a cactus.

"Why are you doing this to me?" Bea grumbled and continued to hike, still scanning for bike tracks. "I want details. Dee-tails. Now!"

Lucy felt her body heat spike and it had nothing to do with the high temps promising to cook the day. "Okay, okay. It was, he is, amazing. I've never felt like this before, Bea. I mean I loved Michael, but nothing was every easy. It was always a struggle, and I always felt like Henry and I were losing."

"What you and Michael wanted in life never matched up," Bea said. "But you kept trying to make it fit for way too long."

"I see that now. And at some level I knew it wasn't going to work."

"I feel that way about Rio, too," Bea said. "I'll love him forever, but I always had a sense, down deep in my soul, that something was off. Pete, well, he's rough around the edges as you say, but he's the most authentic and good man I've ever met. What you see is what you get. It goes both ways, and I adore him for that. That and his outrageous ass. But back to you and Heath, on a scale of one-to-ten? Ten being top-O-the-sheets? Or kitchen table, or whatever, wherever."

Lucy chuckled, smiling. "Let's just say if I died tomorrow, I'd know we'd blown the top off the ever-lovin' Richter scale."

Bea laughed out loud and stopped to high-five her friend. "I am so thrilled for both of you. Now we need to help him get the custody shit worked out." Then something caught her eye, immediately shifting her focus. "What the hell?"

The two women bent over fresh tire prints.

"A motorcycle again," Bea said. "A small dirt bike. Looks familiar."

Lucy snapped several shots of the indentations in the loose sand. "Good bet Cain has been back to the barn." She texted the images to Pete. "Let's get moving."

Lucy and Bea were the first to arrive. Off to the east, they spotted the camp truck, Pete's cruiser, and the crime scene van, stirring up dust as they approached the fallen corral fencing.

"Let's just take a peek." Bea pulled her Glock from the day pack and tucked it into her jeans pocket.

"We should wait for Pete," Lucy said. "I mean, we're pretty sure by the new tracks that the man's been back here."

"We'll be careful. Dude's probably long gone. C'mon." Bea moved quickly through the barn's central drive bay, past old tack and feed rooms, to the office.

Lucy hurried to keep up. The office door was wide open as they had left it. Stepping inside, it smelled of fuel and fertilizer. She wrinkled her nose.

Bea stopped short. "Holy Moses," she gasped.

Lucy looked over her friend's shoulder. WTF? Next to the bloody bed was a row of 10-gallon gasoline containers, all wired together and attached to an LED timer, live and counting down. 15-14-13...

"Bomb!" Bea screamed. "Run!"

Lucy turned and sprinted for all she was worth. Pete was approaching from the corral. "A bomb, get back!" Lucy shrieked.

The CSIs froze as they were about to climb out of the van.

"Where's Bea?' Pete shouted.

Lucy stopped and whirled around. Bea wasn't behind her. "Oh, shit!" Before Lucy could dash back in, her friend limped out of the barn. Lucy darted forward; arms outstretched.

And then it blew.

CHAPTER FIFTY

The force of the blast sent Lucy flying backwards into Pete. She felt the breath sucked out of her lungs as the barn exploded into a burning nightmare. Like a horde of devil fireflies, orange shrapnel, made of bone-dry barnwood, rained down on Bea's prone body.

Lucy and Pete stumbled toward Bea, grabbed her arms and dragged her away from the maelstrom. Lucy could smell Bea's hair burning and beat down the cinders with her bare hands.

The flaming building groaned as if it was human. The roof began to sag. In minutes, it collapsed upon itself. A raging inferno swirling with dense, gray smoke made the bright morning darken and stink of hell and death. Embers swirled in the air with the ability to travel miles and conflagrate distant, unsuspecting places.

"Simi Fire Department's on its way," one of the crime scene investigators shouted. She dashed up to Pete. "I'm a Medic. Let's get this woman to our rig."

Pete picked up Bea and carried her to the CSI van while Lucy watched the last of the standing barn walls surrender to the fiendish blaze.

Outside the crime scene rig, Lucy was almost paralyzed in the thrall of the inferno as heat scorched her skin. Her eyes stung and she began to cough as smoke shifted in their direction. If Cain was responsible for this disaster, they had to find him before he caused something else horrific to happen.

It felt like an eternity before sirens sounded, coming in fast. She came aware of Pete's voice nearby, "Come on, Luce, get in the van. We gotta get away from this smoke."

Lucy crawled into the CSI vehicle and wedged herself next to the barely conscious Bea and the medic who was administering oxygen. As the fire trucks rolled in, Lucy placed a gentle hand on Bea's arm and prayed her dearest friend would survive.

—

Mark nodded and checked his phone—it was just past four in the morning the day after the fire. Despite the lingering stench of the unfortunate event, the air, blowing away from the barn, felt cool and invigorating. As Mark and Cooter bumped across the chaparral in the camp truck, the pastor was charged up for the unpleasant but necessary task.

"Cain will still be asleep, never was an early riser." Mark gazed out across the coffin-dark landscape. In the distance, the town of Simi Valley was a dull glimmer. "I should have known he'd find his way to the old bomb shelter. He's on the run and feels safe there, which is to our advantage."

"He defied you a shitload of times and went against the sacred tenets of our community," Cooter said. "We gonna plant him out here permanently, right?"

"Actually, I have other plans in that regard."

"Like what?"

"Just wake him up, make sure he's subdued. I'll instruct you from there."

"I don't like not knowing the details." The big man began to drum his fingers on the steering wheel. "Don't know why you're so sure he's in the shelter. Shit, the place hasn't been touched in decades."

"Not true." Mark rubbed his arms, a sly smile on his face. "It's where I breed my serpents."

"Sheee-it," Cooter said. "So that's where the fuckers come from? Glad I never tried to go inside. Now I'm starting to see your plan."

"You're not as thick as you look, Coot." Mark said, chuckling.

The big man tried to manage a smile, but it was unconvincing.

"The only way Hensley knew about the bomb shelter was because I took him there once—thought he might be a good snake-handling preacher someday, my assistant, someone I could mentor. He's not bad looking, likes dangerous stuff, knows the Bible. But he fell in love with Isabella."

"Nuts for brains," Cooter said.

"Indeed, so I had to immediately put an end to that," Mark said. "Took her as my own, made him watch until he understood. Never forgave me."

"Fool. He should'a known better than to cross the pastor." Cooter turned on a religious country music station, the volume low.

As they passed the still-smoldering barn, the acrid smell roiled in through the open truck windows. Cooter coughed. "Lucky I wasn't killed in that explosion." He glanced at the dashboard clock. "Damn Hensley, what an asswipe. But too fuckin' bad the rest of 'em didn't blow up with the barn."

Mark looked over at the bald lug. The man's wide face was tinted with a green cast by the light of the console. "Your language is getting coarse these days, Coot."

"Oh yeah, sorry, pastor."

"And Hensley didn't plant the explosives, I did."

Cooter gritted his teeth and frowned. "Shit, pastor. I had no idea. You coulda fuckin—I mean freakin' killed me."

"But here you are, safe and sound." Mark put on his headlamp and adjusted it, ready for the dark foray. "The bomb was just a warning. I hope they got the message."

"How much further up here is it?" Cooter asked, voice tense.

"Like I said, been a while since I was anywhere near the place."

"Maybe a half mile. Easy to miss. Dirt-covered concrete entry surrounded by lots of boulders and cactus—it's almost invisible. I must confess, my parents did a good job with the construction. And it's where we'll dump the Vega woman real soon."

Cooter nodded and slowed to move around a gaping sinkhole.

The eastern horizon had begun to brighten. Driving carefully on the almost invisible path, the two hummed along with a familiar hymn. Then, Mark said, "Stop here. We'll walk the rest of the way. Can't hear much of anything from inside the shelter, but don't want to chance rousing him. This'll be a stealth op, Cooter, like when you were in the Marines—fast, furious, and final." The security man's glum face began to cheer up.

When they got out of the truck, Mark said, "Let's take a moment to pray." They bowed their heads, hands on each other's shoulders.

After their prayer for success in delivering the nonbeliever to the bowels of Hades, the men hiked toward a dark thatch of brush amid a pile of shadowy gray boulders. It looked like a hundred other similar scenes in the parched hills, but Mark long sensed this spot was different—somehow an instrument of His holy plan. They climbed through the rocks.

Cooter's flashlight picked up faint cycle tracks. They led to the small hatch that was the front entry to the cast cement structure. "You're right. He's here."

Mark nodded and turned off his headlamp, homing in on a bit of entry damage as they approached in the darkness. He fingered a rusty hasp. "Cain broke the lock."

"No seal from the inside? We can get in?" Cooter wiped his hands on his jeans.

"Rotted away a long time ago." Mark pushed the hatch open. Its moan was faint. "You ready?"

From a sheath strapped to his thigh, Cooter drew out his USMC Ka-Bar military combat knife. Dead gray, it wouldn't pick up a shine from any light source. "Ready, pastor."

Mark had a small handgun stuck in the waistband of his black trousers. He'd never had to use it; other means had been sufficient in the past. He expected tonight's outcome would prove no different, but he was always prepared for a change of plans.

CHAPTER FIFTY-ONE

M ark and Cooter ducked through the hatch, stepping into a high-ceilinged concrete vestibule. Hensley's motorcycle leaned against a wall. The temperature inside the structure dropped significantly. A weak yellow glow with wattage similar to a bedroom nightlight, cast a muted path on the shiny cement floor. The air smelled musty with age. There was also a faint scent of tomato soup. Mark felt vindicated as to any doubt he might have had. Cain was here.

Cooter, knife in hand, followed Mark down a narrow hallway, their backs against the cold wall. Electrical wiring ran overhead. As they moved along, the shelter opened into a large chamber. The sound of a generator droned, obscuring any inadvertent noise as they crept into the room.

On the far side, bunkbeds were lined up like in a camp dormitory or a military barracks. In a bottom bunk nearest the kitchen area, Cain Hensley slept in a dirty orange sleeping bag, probably snatched from his victims at Leo Carrillo. Mark gave Cooter the thumbs-up and the big man, who moved as stealthily as a spider, edged toward Cain.

Mark left the room and eased open a nearby metal door leading to what once housed the bomb shelter's water well. He lit a kerosine camping lantern that sat on the floor, then pulled aside the heavy, round metal top sealing the well.

Momentarily, he heard what he always listened for—the soft rattles of his creatures—like a comforting whisper in his ear. His blood pressure lowered, and he felt a sense of calm, like God's hand atop his head in blessing. This was all part of His greater design; Mark was His humble tool.

Then, he heard Hensley scream.

A moment later, Cooter dragged the infidel into the well room. In a ripped T-shirt and baggy underwear, Cain struggled hard, kicking and thrashing. Blood ran down his face where the knife had sliced his cheek. Cooter, twice his size, maneuvered the victim to the edge of the snake pit and pressed him forward for a full view of the contents in the pale light.

"One of my pretties just bore about twenty little ones to serve in His name," Mark said. "Did you know rattlesnakes give live birth?"

Cain gasped. "You're fucking insane." Spittle flew.

Mark laughed. "There are fifty-two mommas and daddies down there, rattling their tails, ready to discharge their venom to protect the snakelets. Did you know there's a den in Northern Colorado with almost two thousand rattle snakes living together. They're very social creatures and are good parents. When it rains, they coil into a bowl shape to catch rainwater to drink. So lovely."

Struggling again with Cooter, Cain roared, "Who the fuck cares about your moronic snakes?"

Mark's gaze contorted for an instant, then his focus moved from the dark pit to Cain's terrified and enraged face. "So, Cain," his voice was now calm and impassive, "I understand that you wanted Isabella, and you think her child, Asher, is yours. But even if the youngster has a bit of your DNA, the boy is mine, his mother is mine. They are *all* mine. End of story, end of your story. A shame you never understood that."

Cain tried again to break away from Cooter to no avail. The big man pressed his knife to the kid's throat. Red oozed. Cain gagged as he spoke. "You dipshit, your greed will devour you. It's a shame *you* never understood *that*."

"But I do." Mark shrugged, looking bored with the whole situation. "Regarding the *de la Vega* ranch, I will have it. And soon. I brought the snake to the horse and did a bit of vandalism. No, let's not call it vandalism, I'd rather call it *aggressive* evangelism. It was all to help the Vega woman begin to depend on me and my chosen one. But the gun you planted, the gallery trashing—so stupid. Did you actually think you could frame me for your crimes? That you'd get Isabella and the boy back and take over the community?" Mark laughed. Cooter joined in.

Cain grimaced. With a last-ditch effort to escape, he elbowed Cooter hard in the ribs. Cooter grunted and tightened his grip. The knife drew blood again.

"You piece of shit," Cain roared. His gaze locking on Mark. "You're the fucking snake, Wenter. You'll never get that ranch. Your two-bit ministry with your harem of zero self-esteem women, clueless children, and sad old men—you'll all live and die in this same hellhole camp. Your delusions of being some rich TV pastor are pure bullshit fantasies."

Mark sneered and nodded. Cooter dangled Cain above the dark hole. The kid's legs pumped, and his toes reached for the edge of the well. With a final bout of curses and shrieks, Cain plunged twenty feet down into the pit of vipers. His body sounded like a watermelon splitting open as it hit the bottom.

The rattling accelerated to a frenzy. The screaming peaked and then began to die.

Cooter backed up to the door, rubbing his gut where Cain's sharp elbows had connected. But Mark remained on the edge of the hole, watching the mayhem below with dispassionate fascination. Finally, a last keening wail, and Cain stopped fighting.

Mark closed his eyes. "The Lord sent fiery serpents upon the people," he whispered, offering a final invocation for Cain. "They were bitten and many died, until they admitted their sin." He opened his eyes and stared into the abyss. "You never admitted your sin."

The two men left the bomb shelter as the sun broke over the horizon. Mark stretched his arms high. As the orb would make its flight across the sky and begin to dip to the west, Mark was certain Lucy's days at the ranch would be counting down. He was anxious to get back to Jaime and give her final instructions before she left for Malibu. He and Cooter would drop Tanya Lee off at the airport, then return to the Vega ranch for Lucy's final goodbye.

Mark's heart pounded with anticipation and his loins screamed for an epic send-off from Tanya. Mixed feelings remained about her dependability, but he had to have faith and trust in His plan, and Tanya Lee was part of it. After all, even Jesus had faith in a few fallen women.

CHAPTER FIFTY-TWO

From behind a dense clump of bushes, Isabella, a bicycle at her side, watched Mark and Cooter leave the bomb shelter. Was Cain in there? Had they confronted him? If he was there, had he been able to hide? Was he okay? Or was he dead? Her chest tightened with the anxiety of too many unknowns.

Cain had managed to send her a note by paying off the elderly guard at the camp's front gate with money stolen from a clueless tourist in the parking lot of the Ronald Reagan Library a few miles away. The old man had slipped the communication to her yesterday while she was overseeing the children's lunch.

She and Cain plotted to secretly meet for the first time since before the Leo Carrillo murders. Once the love of her life, now driven to desperation by Wenter, Isabella prayed she'd be able to help him get back on a righteous path. But it wouldn't be at Eden's Gate. Without resources and with Cain now on the run from the law, they would grab their son and escape. Somehow.

After the truck retreated toward camp with Mark and Cooter, Isabella jogged across the trail and hiked up the rocky scree to the shelter entry. She had a bag of day-old pastries lifted from the kitchen to surprise Cain. She worried that he was starving.

But Isabella didn't have much time. Dawn had just broken, and she had to be back with the children when they awoke.

Wrenching open the rusty hatch door, she clambered inside. A draught of cold air whooshed into the entry from the hall before her. She shivered and turned on her flashlight.

"Cain?" she called. No response. "Cain? It's me."

Isabella took a deep, steadying breath and stepped carefully down the shadowy hallway. She came to a dimly lit room with a kitchen, several picnic tables, and a row of bunk beds.

"Cain?" She walked over to the beds and spotted an empty sleeping bag. Her hand slid inside it; a bit of warmth remained. Examining it more closely, she gasped. She touched a dark blot with her fingers. Took a sniff. Blood. Her hand began to shake.

"Cain! Where are you?"

Isabella searched frantically amid old boxes of canned goods and random moldering supplies but there was no place he could have hidden. Was there a secret exit, out to the hills, where he could have fled? Or one to take inhabitants further into the earth for additional protection from nuclear mayhem? The only door she saw was standing half open into what appeared to be a small dark closet. Maybe for additional storage? Or a bathroom? It smelled of kerosene. She went inside.

Isabella examined the tight, dank space with her flashlight. In the center was a covered hole, about three feet across. It looked like it could be an old water well. Or maybe there were stairs or a ladder leading down to a different level. "Cain?" she whispered.

Isabella yanked hard to roll the wooden top away. Stooping low and pushing with her shoulder against the rim, it took several tries, but the heavy lid moved enough so she could peek inside with her flashlight.

There wasn't a ladder, just a tangle of ropes at the bottom.

But they were moving. She looked again. Writhing, twisting—
they were not ropes. She felt her heart almost stop as snakes
slithered and squirmed. "Oh, God!"

Then, a foot, an arm, and a head frozen in death. White
teeth grimaced between swollen bluish lips. A small snake
darted into his mouth. Another slowly exited his nostril.

"Cain!" Overcome with horror, Isabella's keening wails
filled the room and rolled out into the desert.

—

Shaken to her core and weeping, Isabella rushed from the
shelter, grabbed her bike and rode back to camp. Despite an
aching heart and swollen eyes, she tried to put on a normal face
as she helped the children dress and get ready for breakfast. She
marched her group of young boys to the mess hall, including her
son, Asher, whom she hugged this morning for way too long.
She couldn't show favoritism, or he'd be moved to another unit,
denying her visitation. That threat always hung over her if she
didn't do whatever Mark ordered.

She almost started weeping again but was able to suck up
the sobs. The effort made her dizzy. What was she going to do?
She had to get out of this place for good, with her child. It was
too late for Cain.

Later that morning as Isabella and her campers crossed the
sports field toward the arts center, she saw Mark, Cooter, and
the new girl Tanya, drive through the front gate in the truck.
Jaime had headed out earlier for her childcare job in Malibu,
where Isabella thought something weird was definitely going
on. Why else would Mark have allowed his Chosen One to work
outside of the community and be exposed to everything that
could make her begin to doubt his God-like authority? What
dangerous game was he playing?

And then there was Tanya Lee Riggs, throwing her sexuality
around like she was passing out hundred-dollar bills to an eager
audience. Clearly, the conniving, no-class, hillbilly stripper was

the up-and-coming Chosen One because Jaime was on the skids. What had Jaime done to displease Mark and May Lou? Maybe surviving the ectopic pregnancy was crime enough.

Isabella felt her tears begin to boil into dangerous rage. Recently, she'd caught glimpses of that anger in Jaime's attitude, too. Rumor was, she'd found Mark having sex with Tanya Lee. No surprise there. Isabella wondered if Jaime could somehow help her get away from Eden's Gate, or if she was still under the thrall of that murdering monster, despite near death from May Lou's incompetence and Mark's inability to keep his snake in the basket, as he described it. She'd have to figure out a way to approach Jaime without putting them all in danger.

—

Back at the ranch, Lucy called to check on Bea, amazed that the woman had only suffered a broken wrist, minor burns, and contusions from the bomb blast.

Bea had interesting news. "The crime scene folks called Pete and told him the explosive device was similar to what Timothy McVeigh used in the Kansas City bombing thirty years ago. Simple, cheap, and deadly. How to build homemade bombs, of course, was all over the internet. Fortunately, the perp didn't have the wiring quite right so it didn't blow like it could have."

"Wow, so it might have been worse. Gratitude for every moment, right?" Lucy said. "You going to stay with Pete for a few more days? Relax and recover?"

"I'm already home. But while I was at his place, we talked about maybe moving in together."

"What?" Lucy steadied herself to keep from falling out of her chair in surprise.

"Yeah, I know it's a shocker. I'd rent out my bungalow, could make a bunch on a cute casa like mine in a prime Santa Monica neighborhood. Lucky I made that investment twenty years ago."

"No kidding."

"Anyhow, we'd stay in the valley at his bigger house until the kids moved out and then we'd come back here, near the beach, to grow old and gray together. We're going to meet with our offspring to see how they feel about it before we make any big decisions."

"Wow. Sounds like some planning's going on. This is serious. I'm reeling—never thought you'd do it again, move in with a man. Fantastic."

"Third time's the charm. Right?"

"Totally cool, girlfriend. Love you both so much."

"Aw, thanks, Luce. You think I'm crazy to do this? Tell it to me straight."

"Are you kidding? I think you'd be crazy not to go for it. I have every confidence in you guys. And with your time apart, seems like you're much more patient with each other, more accepting and willing to compromise. It's very cool, Beebs."

"I'm so relieved to hear you say that, because that's what we're feeling, too. And speaking of my favorite bad boy, he just texted me that the blood on the glass in the gallery belongs to Cain Hensley. He's in the system, picked up for petty theft of some sound equipment a couple months back but the grievance was withdrawn to avoid going to court. The complainant was, get this, Mark Wenter and Eden's Gate Camp Community."

CHAPTER FIFTY-THREE

"Whoa." Lucy gasped. "Mark said he hadn't seen Hensley for a couple years and just a few months ago they were pressing charges against him?"

"Guy's a compulsive liar, but we knew that already," Bea said.

"I want him and his crazy cult out of my life. Like now. Sadly, that means Jaime, too. After the bloody mattress and the barn explosion, it's a done deal." Lucy glanced at her watch. "She should be here any minute and we'll finally have *the talk*. Jaime doesn't know it, but Henry's at day camp this afternoon, so she and I will have some time to get this sorted."

Lucy heard the gravel crunch on the drive. "Gotta run, Bea, I think she just arrived. I'll call you later."

"Okay, good luck, sweet pea."

"Thanks, and I'm so glad that you and Pete are gonna go for it. Gotta grab all the good things we can."

Finishing the phone call with Bea just as Jaime walked into the kitchen, Lucy took a deep breath and released it slowly. It was going to be tough firing someone she liked, someone now part of her family. "Can I pour you a cup of coffee?" she asked. "Half-and-half with no sugar?"

"Sure, thanks." Jaime sat on a bar stool across the kitchen island from Lucy. "Where's the little man?"

"He's at camp from noon until three." Lucy had put off this meeting for too long. As nervous as she was about the confrontation, it was past time to put it all out there. "You and I need to talk."

Jaime gulped and hesitantly accepted the steaming mug. "About what?" Her mouth tightened. "You're letting me go, aren't you. Is it the money? You don't have to pay me at all."

"It's not the money, and you do a great job with your brother."

"Then what is it?" Jaime set the coffee down and pressed her hands together prayerfully. It was her go-to stress tell.

"It's Mark Wenter and his cult." Lucy shifted on her bar stool, unable to find a comfortable position for this conversation.

"Cult? No, it's just a conservative religious community."

"Led by a charming sociopath with little conscience, who demands total loyalty, hates questions because he's always right, gaslights like hell, and isolates you. Any of this sound familiar?"

Jaime chewed on her lip. The prayerful hands shifted to hand wringing.

"That's what I thought," Lucy said. "When you're part of it, you usually don't even see what's going on. I can't have that kind of belief system impacting my life, our lives. It makes me very sad, but yes, Jaime, I'm going to let you go."

She gasped. "But my brother! I'll miss him so much and he'll miss me." Tears pooled in her disbelieving eyes. "You can't do this, Lucy."

"You can still see each other. I don't want to ruin the relationship you two are building, but the meetings will be under my supervision. Without Mark Wenter. Ever."

"This isn't fair." She glanced away, pulling at a loose strand of hair.

"Jaime, look at me," Lucy demanded.

Jaime slowly turned back to Lucy. Her shoulders sagged.

Lucy leaned her way. "I need brutal honesty from you. Do you think you can give us both that?"

Jaime was quiet for a long moment, chewing at her already bitten nails, then she nodded.

"Are you in love with Mark Wenter?" Lucy asked.

There was a long silence.

"I thought..." She gulped again, hard. "I thought I was, thought he adored me, but after the ectopic pregnancy disaster, it was like I woke up from this blur of a fantasy romance novel." Jaime pressed her fingers on the space between her eyes. "And now, to be honest as you asked, I don't know how to get out of it. Mark doesn't have the ability to love anybody but himself."

Jaime paused, tears dripping down her cheeks. "And you're right. Mark shouldn't be around my brother. He and May Lou, who I'm pretty sure is his older sister, are out to be the next proselytizing, prosperity-gospel zillionaires. Would Jesus be striving for a closet full of designer clothes and a private jet? Hell, no. But that's what he wants, thinks he deserves. Mark's not interested in saving souls. But you can trust me with Henry, I swear you can." Her voice was pleading. "Having him in my life is one of the best things that has happened to me."

Lucy sighed. "I can't have him influenced by Eden's Gate thinking. It's obscene. If you want to get away from them, I can help you." Lucy reached out and took Jaime's hand. "If you want to cut ties, you don't have to be alone in this." Jaime pulled away and Lucy leaned back, examining the young woman's beautiful, pained face. "I have a bit of experience about how these things go. I hung on too tight for too long to the relationship with your father," Lucy said. "I wanted my fantasy family so badly I looked the other way, kept thinking things would change, ignoring the now obvious signs out of my own neediness. Can you see yourself doing the same thing?"

Jaime chewed hard at her lip, then nodded.

"And as someone struggling with addiction, giving him up must be incredibly difficult. You know he can bring you only heartache. You're used to that, but there is so much more, Jaime. Cut the creep loose. Take the relationship as a hard lesson and move on. "I'll be there for you. I promise."

Jaime reached across and took Lucy's hand.

There was a knock at the door.

"Who could that be?" Lucy checked the Ring cam on her phone. "It's Mark and another man, a big guy."

"It must be Cooter, his security chief," Jaime said, looking confused.

Or was it afraid? "Did you invite them up here?" Lucy asked, heading to the entry.

Jaime was right behind her. "No, but I knew they were coming. I'm so sorry, Lucy."

"I'm going to make it crystal clear to Mark that he's not welcome here."

As Lucy opened the front door, Jaime cried out and tried to block the way. "Don't let them in!"

Lucy gasped and struggled to engage the screen door lock, but Jaime's warning came seconds too late.

Cooter, the size of a pro linebacker, almost ripped the screen door off its hinges and lunged at Lucy, knocking her down. Jaime tried to stop him, but he shoved her so hard against the wall she lost her breath.

Mark and Cooter had Lucy subdued in seconds. She slumped on the floor by the open door, her arms and ankles zip tied. Duct tape was slapped across her mouth.

Jaime stood back, shaking.

Mark paced, clearly furious. "What the hell was that, Jaime? Saying not to let us in?"

Lucy saw Jaime clenched her fists again and step further away. "I don't want to do this anymore. I don't want Lucy hurt.

She's a good person; I want to be like her. You never loved me; you're just using me to get her ranch and I'm sick of it. I'm done, Mark."

"I knew you were too weak for this." He sneered in disgust, grabbing her roughly by the arms. She winced in pain as he pulled her face inches from his. "You *will* help me if you want to see Vega and your little brother continue to draw breath. But we'll start with the animals. That'll loosen you up. A tough thing for a kid to watch."

Lucy yelped in horror.

CHAPTER FIFTY-FOUR

"You're insane, you wouldn't..." Jaime coughed hard, wheezing like she was breathing brimstone. Maybe she was. Shuddering, Lucy pressed her back against the wall.

Wenter snarled. "I'm on God's sacred mission, Jaime. Don't test me. I'll do whatever it takes to serve His will."

"*His* will? Only the devil himself would do what you're talking about, you Godless piece of shit."

Mark slapped her hard across the face. She fell to the floor, a nose bleed exploding onto the tiles.

Horrified, Lucy struggled with her bonds, but it was futile.

Mark loomed over them both. "Now, my sweet wife, I need assurance you'll be here with the boy. We'll get custody, and you'll get me this property, or I'll start with Odin first." He aimed a demonic grin at Lucy.

Cooter pulled out a 9mm pistol. She gasped.

Her hands bloody, Jaime covered her mouth like she was about to vomit. Then her rebellion began to deflate. "Okay, okay, I'll do whatever you want," she said. "But my brother is left out of this, and you don't hurt Lucy."

Lucy guessed that for the first time, the reality of the situation was hitting Jaime like a sledgehammer. They could all die. And Mark, her lover, was the devil, no longer under any pretense of disguise.

Jaime's crying stopped and her eyes narrowed.

"Agreed, no one gets hurt," Mark said. "You're in charge of the kid as planned, but we're going to take Lucy off the grid for a few days until we get this all back on track. Cooter, get the whore to the truck."

Jaime flinched at the degrading word as Cooter roughly yanked Lucy up from the floor. Her gaze locked with Jaime's for an instant. The girl had to step up, there was no one else. Lucy had welcomed her into her home and allowed her to bond with Henry, and Heath had saved her life. Would Jaime come through for them? Or would she make decisions she'd regret forever. It was reckoning time, and Lucy was unsure as to the outcome.

"I'll delete the security footage of this." Mark tapped a few keys on his phone, and it was done.

Lucy realized that when Mark had helped program her cameras after Odin had been bitten, he'd also installed the controls onto his own system.

Mark stepped to the door and turned, glaring at Jaime. Blood from her smashed nose dripped red onto her shirt. "It will be your fault if anything happens to Lucy or your brother, or to the animals. Their fate is in your hands, sweetheart. Don't make me do something desperate." His face softened. "Realize that I do love you and the Lord will give you another chance to love me back and even bear my child."

Disgust shown dark on Jaime's damaged face.

He continued. "As is said in Jeremiah 8, *When people fall down, do they not get up? When someone turns away, do they not return?*" He licked his lips. "I'm praying you will return, beautiful Jaime, because I am the only man who truly loves you."

Lucy sneered beneath the duct tape.

Cooter twisted her arm hard, waving the 9mm.

Jaime wiped her face on her sleeve and stood up straight. Her fingers twitched as if she were pulling a trigger. "In Jeremiah," she admonished, "the Lord also says, *They make ready their tongue like a bow, to shoot lies; it is not by truth that they triumph in the land. They go from one sin to another.*"

Jaime looked at the handgun and shook her head. "For all your Bible quoting bullshit and supposed adoration of the Lord," she said, "I've realized that you have no idea what love is, Mark. I have no choice but to do what you ask," her eyes were angry slits, "but never, ever, touch me again."

And yes, Lucy thought, given the opportunity, Jaime could pull the trigger.

—

Tanya Lee let out a sigh of relief. So far, so good. She was really glad she'd watched the cultural and travel videos Mark had hassled her about. She survived the LAX security screening— she'd been body scanned, her documents okayed, and her bags X-rayed. Looking around at her fellow travelers, she felt at once scared and exhilarated. There was a whole world of opportunity out there, and the doors to it all were cracking open.

There were plenty of women in line at the gate who were wearing Western clothing, but she'd agreed to the traditional Middle Eastern look. This was the LAX to JFK leg of the journey, so dressing like a religious woman was not as important. The JFK overnight flight to Baghdad on Quatar Airlines, however, would be different. She would have to engage her acting chops. It would be great practice.

Slipping the dark navy scarf off her head, she stuffed it into her carry-on, pulled the hot pink scrunchie from her ponytail and shook out her freshly washed curls. While side-eyeing several of the younger male passengers nearby, Mark's voice rasped in her head from between sharp, rattlesnake fangs, "*Be bland, innocent, low profile. Do you know what unobtrusive means, Tanya Lee?"*

Despite her acting skills, this was not going to be easy. Every piece of control in Tanya's life had come from using her sexuality to leverage her survival. What was she going to do when she was covered up like a Ferrari under a canvas car cover? She'd have to figure it out without getting stoned to death in the process.

Tanya Lee took a long slurp of Diet Cola and gazed out the huge window as a British Airways jet touched down across the runway. She lifted the Big Mac from its carton and took a bite. Only a month ago she'd been a stripper at the Klapperville Honeysuckle Club. Today, she was jetting off to New York and the Middle East.

She smiled as she chewed. Anything was possible.

CHAPTER FIFTY-FIVE

Jaime sat with Henry at the kitchen island, his fruit salad and chicken fingers untouched. He yelped and threw his beloved stuffed T-Rex across the room.

"Why didn't she take me with her?" he demanded, face in a frown and ready to cry. "I want my momma. And I want to see my daddy. We FaceTime tonight on Zoom." He pointed at the clock over the stove which read almost 6:00 p.m. "Come on." He grabbed his sister's hand and pulled her off the stool toward the office. "You have to sign us in."

Jaime wasn't having much luck comforting the child, maybe because she was in deep need of comfort herself. For them both to survive, she had to get it together, fast. And she didn't want to talk to her father. "I know we scheduled it, but we're not going to Zoom with Dad tonight, Hen. Maybe tomorrow."

"Yes, tonight." He ran through the doorway and climbed onto Lucy's office chair. "Tonight! Hurry."

"Another time, kiddo," she insisted.

"No, now! Now! I want daddy, now!"

Henry screamed, cried, and threw himself on the floor,

taking a mug of pens and the desk lamp with him. The dogs started barking then dashed from the room. Having never experienced a four-year-old's meltdown before, Jaime froze, at a complete loss. The child was inconsolable.

Shaken, she gave in. "Okay, okay, you can have your Zoom meeting." Jaime slid onto the desk chair, overwhelmed, with Henry sprawled at her feet, kicking. This was a new aspect of caring for a child she knew she wasn't ready for. Childcare with Henry usually consisted of swimming, feeding the animals, goodie-making, and Legos. "Calm down, Henry. You can talk. Let me get it set up." She had no idea how to set up a Zoom meeting.

"Daddy sends a Zoom link," he hiccupped, beginning to calm down. Maddie slinked into the office and licked Henry's tears.

Henry crawled from under the desk and edged onto the corner of Jaime's chair. He let her put her arm around him and give him a hug just as the Zoom icon showed up on the laptop screen. She'd watched Lucy key in her password and made a point to remember it—HenryChickinMan1. Jaime was totally dreading seeing her father and having to bald-faced lie to him. It was going to be mortifying. How could she bring off this total deception? She had to do it to keep her brother alive.

When her father's face materialized on the screen, Henry crawled onto her lap and positioned himself in front of the camera, rubbing his red eyes. Michael could see them both.

"Wow, this is a nice surprise," he said. "Hi, Henry, and good to see you, Jaime. It's been too long. How's everything in California?"

At four in the morning Fallujah time, his smile looked tired, but he seemed sincerely happy to be with them. Lucy's kind words to her dad about how responsible she was being with Henry had helped to unthaw their contentious relationship a bit.

"Is Mommy there?" Henry asked. "I've been crying."

"What? No. Mommy is in California with you, little man."
Questioningly, Michael looked at his daughter. "Isn't she?"

Henry persisted. "Jaime said she went to see you today. But
she didn't take me." He sniffed, tears threatened to come again.

"I don't know what you're talking about, buddy. Jaime,
what's up?" he asked, eyes dark and unreadable under the tepid
overhead fluorescents.

She took a deep breath. What was she supposed to say?
Unspoken words nearly clogged her throat. "Lucy called me
around noon to come and take care of Henry for a couple of
days." Jaime gulped hard. "Said she had a change of heart and
wanted to talk with you in person. She's on her way to Iraq. I
can't believe she didn't tell you."

An uneasy silence hung between them. Michael finally said,
"She's always been impulsive, but this is strange. I thought we'd
talked things through pretty well last weekend." He rubbed at
his chin. "What else did she say?"

"Nothing. That's it."

"Would you text me her flight and hotel information?"

"Okay, sure." Jaime would have to conveniently forget to do
it and would look like a total slacker in his eyes once again. She
despised this charade.

After checking his phone, he let out an uneasy sigh.
"Nothing from her. Okay, well, I guess I'll just have to wait. Let
me know if you hear anything, okay?"

"Of course."

Henry and his father chatted for another half hour. Jaime
barely heard any of it. Bea was going to freak out when she
learned Lucy had taken off for the Middle East without telling
her. Mark hadn't considered Lucy's small but strong social
network, particularly an L.A. County Sheriff and the head of a
growing online news outlet.

"I'm really proud of you, honey, for stepping up with your
brother," Michael said.

When Jaime heard her name, she whiplashed her focus

back on the screen. Her father was actually complimenting her for something she'd done right. Except she hadn't.

"Thank you," Jaime replied. "I love this kiddo so much and I know I'm super lucky Lucy gave me a chance."

"I admit, I was more than skeptical, given our past experience, but she made the right decision."

Jaime snuggled with Henry, awash in the shame of betraying him, betraying all of them. How could she be part of keeping this child from his adoring mother? Mark's evil had poisoned her.

"What happened to your face, Kiddo?" Michael asked. "Looks like you've been hurt."

"I, uh, took a fall by the pool. Was running in front of the sign that says, *No Running*. Duh."

On the screen from thousands of miles away, he regarded her carefully. "Doesn't have anything to do with your husband, does it? I know Lucy isn't a fan."

"Oh, no, he'd never lay a hand on me. All is well on that front." She was pretty sure he didn't buy it. He'd spent his whole career digging for truth.

"Good to hear." His eyes still studied her face. She turned away.

After goodnights and I love yous were said, the Zoom meeting ended. Jaime and her little brother returned to the kitchen and finished dinner. They played dinosaur games on the porch, and finally it was bedtime. He had relaxed considerably. On the other hand, Jaime had become even more anxious and distressed. She needed to figure a way out of this disaster.

Her cellphone sounded. It was Mark.

CHAPTER FIFTY-SIX

Isabella perched on a bench outside the dining hall, yearning for a fix, or even a cigarette, for the first time in a very long while. Jangled nerves made her so nauseous she didn't want dinner. Even the familiar sounds of silverware clinking against plates and kids laughing as they enjoyed pizza night wasn't reassuring. Just the opposite. Where she had once convinced herself as to the safety and security at Eden's Gate, now she saw only a haven for murder and sexual assault. Awash in shame for allowing herself to be preyed upon so foolishly, she implored God, the real God, not the one of Mark Wenter's egomania, to provide guidance.

The camp truck caught her eye once again. It was heading unusually fast past the playing fields toward the burned-out barn and the bomb shelter. What was Mark up to now? Why was he going out there again? Maybe to retrieve Caine's body and bury it or grab a few more snakes for his worship services. Whatever he planned, it would be unholy and obscene.

"Where is Isabella?" a voice from inside the dining hall asked. "I need help passing out these ice cream bars."

Isabella put aside her traitorous thoughts and hurried back to work.

—

Visions of being crowded into another tight row of seats with random passengers for nineteen more hours was almost too much for Tanya to bear. The flight from LAX to New York was basically uneventful except for a half hour of turbulence flying over the Great Plains. It was scary but a kind flight attendant was patient and explained that it wasn't dangerous.

Hijab and Abaya in place, it was late as she walked down the dimly lit jetway into the Qatar Airlines Boeing 777. The scent of jet fuel tinged the air. At midnight, the passengers' energy was subdued. Most were dressed in casual clothing, including several women in comfortable upscale sweatsuits for the long flight. Tanya was the most conservative-looking person in line. Mark didn't know what he was talking about when he made her dress like the pictures she'd seen of grandmothers in rural villages. Thank heavens she'd packed alternate outfits. She already had the pink leggings on beneath her black skirt.

Tanya was welcomed onboard by a professional-looking team of smiling flight attendants. The women, in fashionable burgundy suits and stylish hats, with their male counterparts in striped ties and high-end navy blazers, inspired confidence.

Feeling grubby by comparison, she trudged down the long center aisle through the luxurious business class into a packed economy class with its dense, three-four-three seating arrangement. Twelve rows passed the end of business class, Tanya struggled into the middle group of seats and found herself second in from the aisle. Flanked by extremely overweight businessmen pressing on each side, one sweated profusely and the other had a large bag of food spread out on his lap and tray. The smell of unfamiliar spices turned her stomach.

Action had to be taken, or Tanya wasn't going to make nineteen hours trapped in this flying bus without melting down.

Grabbing her purse and carry-on, she rose and rushed back toward business class. She approached a young male flight attendant who wasn't hiding his irritation as he banged on overhead bins trying to get them shut.

Pulling off her headscarf, Tanya primped her hair. "I'm so sorry to bother y'all, sir," she said, leaning in to whisper her secret. "I'm extremely claustrophobic and afraid I'm going to have to get off the plane unless I can sit in business class where I can breathe." Oscar-worthy tears welled in her eyes, and she slowly licked her full lips, which she considered her second most alluring feature. "I've never been in economy; I don't know what I was thinking." She brushed his arm. His gleaming gold nameplate said Hamid.

He studied her mouth. "I'm so sorry ma'am, but unless you already booked business class, it's too late."

Tanya pulled out one of the $500 Visa cards Mark had told her to use only in an emergency. This was definitely an emergency. She held it low where others could not see. "Please. It's five hundred American."

He took a quick glance then pursed his thin lips as if he'd bitten into a lemon. "Business class is about $5000 per seat."

Tanya pulled out a second card. "This is all I have. A thousand, total," she whispered. She needed to reserve the last of the three cards, just in case. "I see there are a couple empty seats up there."

He paused, glanced around the cabin then took the cards, slipping them into his pocket. "Okay, follow me."

"A little misunderstanding," he said to one of the attendants staring at him questioningly as she passed. "I'm taking care of it. No worries."

The attendant rolled her eyes and went about her business taking drink orders.

"There are two empty spots," Hamid said as they stood at the back of business class, taking in the spacious rows of a two-by-two seat set up before them. "Both last minute cancelations.

He took a quick glance at his electronic notebook with the seating chart. I'm sure you'd rather be next to the businesswoman in row five." His fingers massaged his gold nameplate.

Tanya's eyes quickly skidded over the woman and landed on a middle-aged man wearing a long white robe with a red-and-white checked headscarf. He turned her way with interest.

They made eye contact. Tanya felt the thrill of adventure. Was he an actual a sheik? Oil rich, repressed, he was moderately attractive. "How about next to the gentleman in row three?" she said, beelining in his direction.

"Very well." Hamid and the sheik helped her get settled.

In what seemed like seconds, an attendant was there to present her with a lovely tray of snacks and pour a glass of champagne. Tanja smiled, thrilled. She stretched and unbuttoned her abaya.

CHAPTER FIFTY-SEVEN

The next morning, after dropping a sad-looking Henry off at day camp, Jaime headed back to Eden's Gate feeling despondent. She had become her worst self, thinking she was doing the opposite in turning her life over to Mark and his blind followers. If anything happened to her little brother or to Lucy, she would be to blame. She had spent years being a victim—it had been her go-to behavior. It kept her from taking responsibility for herself. But she couldn't do it anymore. For the first time, people she loved depended on her. She couldn't fail them.

When Jaime stepped into the cottage, she walked past May Lou and straight to the bedroom without a word. Thankfully, Mark was gone. She threw clothes and toiletries into a bag to take back to the ranch.

"Sounds like all went well, yesterday," May Lou said, leaning on the doorframe and scrutinizing Jaime through narrowing eyes. "But what are you doing back here at camp? Aren't you supposed to be with the boy?"

"My brother's at pre-school this morning. I need my stuff."

"Mark said you tried to keep him and Cooter out of the Vega house in defiance of His ministry and His mission."

Jaime's hand grazed her cheek where she knew a purple welt colored her skin.

The woman crossed her arms on her bony chest. "You deserved what you got." Her lips curved into a crescent slash. "Actually, you got off very lightly."

Bristling, Jaime thought the old witch looked like a Nazi women's prison warden she'd seen in a World War II movie. Throwing a handful of underwear into the bag, she zipped it shut, then asked, "where's my loving husband?"

"Picking up supplies in Simi."

"Yeah? Or maybe banging some clueless new sycophant."

May Lou frowned. "Watch how you're talking about your husband, our pastor, and leader."

"Our marriage is over." She pushed by May Lou, almost knocking her down. It felt great.

"Your marriage is over when we say it's over," the woman snarled. "First Corinthians tells us that *a wife is bound to her husband as long as he lives.*"

"According to the study guide you gave me, first Corinthians also says—*if her husband dies, she is free to be married to whom she wishes.*" Jaime smiled and slammed the screen door behind her, went to her car and tossed the bag onto the passenger's seat. She felt a pang of dizziness and slumped against the hood. She'd been so completely focused on amping up the emotional energy to appear normal to Henry, she hadn't even had a cup of coffee. She decided to walk over to the dining hall and grab something to eat before driving back to Malibu. As she passed the pool's utility shed, she heard her name quietly called.

"Jaime, we have to talk. It's very important."

It was Isabella. Jaime paused at the door where the woman stood in front of a shelf of pool toys. The building smelled of chlorine.

"What is it? What's wrong?" Other than everything.

Chewing at her thumbnail, Isabella stepped further back into the shed. "If I talk to you, my life and my son's life are in your hands. You can't betray us." Her face anxious and weary, she opened her arms in supplication.

The little hairs on Jaime's arms stirred. "Of course you can trust me. We've never really had the opportunity to become friends, but your presence in this community, even at a distance, has brought me comfort."

"I'm glad of that." A smile flickered and extinguished like a blown-out match. She paused then said, "I'm leaving tomorrow night with my boy."

"What?" Jaime's head spun.

"It's now or never. Mark's sending us all to somewhere in Tennessee the day after tomorrow. This may be my last opportunity to escape. He controls us women 'cause he fathered almost every kid here. Few would abandon their babies to this monster. You must have sensed that. He tosses the male children out as soon as they reach sexual maturity so he can eliminate the competition. Mothers are forbidden contact with their sons after that."

Thinking of Cain and all the abandoned boys and heart-broken mothers, Jaime winced, then asked, "A lot of the women have been Chosen Ones?"

"Afraid so or Chosen One wannabes. They're the most dangerous." Isabella peeked out of the shed.

Jaime had been a fool to once think she was special to him. Now he was planning to take them all away? "Why Tennessee?" she asked.

"His cousin Clement's there. He's done a lot to help Mark with the ministry. Financed this place through prostitution, drugs, running illegal firearms, I don't know all what, I can only imagine." Isabella's next words came fast. "And I was snooping around outside your cottage looking for you yesterday when I overhead May Lou say that Mark sold this place to a developer for millions of dollars. He thinks he's on the doorstep of his prosperity ministry."

"What?" Jaime felt her mouth drop open.

"You heard me right. He's counting his money and taking most of the community members, except for selected disciples, back East where he has some kind of primitive camp somewhere in the mountains."

Children cheered in the distance. Isabella flinched nervously.

"How can he move so quickly?" Jaime asked.

"Snakes can do that." Anger lit sparks in Isabella's brown eyes. "We load into school buses early in the morning and head out. If we go to Tennessee, I swear to God, no one will ever find us. I won't do it. With the big bucks Mark supposedly has now, he's already in escrow on a piece of land near the ranch you work at. He has this weird lawyer friend who did the transaction."

"Probably the same creep who re-did Lucy's Will and custody arrangements." Jaime paused, then said, "They abducted Lucy yesterday afternoon. They're probably taking her with them."

Isabella shrugged. "Or they'll kill her."

Jaime gasped for breath and grabbed the door jamb. Her worst fears were rising fast.

Isabella peeped out again. Her eyes scanned the area looking for anyone who might be within earshot. "May Lou and Cooter just left the dining hall. They're walking toward us."

As the two approached, Isabella and Jaime pretended to be organizing the pool toy shelves. "But before I disappear," Isabella whispered, "If she's not already dead, I think I know where your friend is being held. But you'd better hurry."

Jaime swallowed a frightened cry.

CHAPTER FIFTY-EIGHT

Jaime trudged back to her car, stunned and confused. What the hell was she going to do? This phantom bomb shelter out in the desert somewhere—was it for real? How would she find it? Isabella couldn't give any understandable directions.

When Jaime returned to the ranch after picking Henry up at school, her mood sank further. On the terrace, Mark sat in a rocking chair looking like he already owned the place, sipping a cold drink and petting Howard the cat.

Jaime helped Henry from his car seat. When the boy finally jumped out, he skipped toward Mark.

"It's the Fourth of July and I'm going to the fireworks tonight," the child announced.

Mark feigned interest while continuing to stroke the cat. Jaime had a horrifying flash of him snapping the animal's neck. She frowned and steadied herself.

Henry turned to Jaime. "Can I have a juice pop? I had my lunch already. Puleeeze."

"We just stopped for frozen yogurt, young man. Enough sugar."

Henry groaned, scowling. "You're so mean."

Jaime knew he was frustrated and angry that his mother was travelling far away again without him. "Grab some carrots and hummus. You know where they are," Jaime said. "But I don't remember anything about fireworks tonight. I heard they're cancelled because of possible fire danger."

"They're not cancelled. I'm going. I don't care what you say." Henry left Jaime and Mark behind and stomped into the house.

Jaime stood by Mark, her stomach in a knot. She would never forgive him for hitting her and ripping Lucy away. The last days had been the ultimate wake-up call. "What are you doing here? What if one of Lucy's friends stops by? In case you didn't know, they don't like you." The Paw Patrol TV show sounded from inside.

Mark chuckled. "They don't have to like me. They have to like you. And I'll stop by whenever I want. Gotta make sure you're honoring God and doing your job."

Jaime seethed. Hands on her hips, her gaze crossed the meadow toward Kanan Road. A silver vehicle turned in at the bottom of their drive. "Oh Goodness, it's Bea. You'd better get out of here."

"Okay, okay." Mark's twitchy body language said he didn't have any interest in a conversation with the black woman Jaime knew he found intimidating. She smiled. There was nothing in Bea's demeanor that smacked of victimhood, which was the only type of woman Mark could relate to and control. "I better get back to camp anyway," he said. "I have a couple buses of my good ol' boys coming to help defend the community tonight."

She scowled. "What do you mean, *defend the community?* From what?"

"Don't worry your pretty head." He kissed Jaime's cheek. She recoiled, now sickened by his touch, one she used to find irresistible. And what was he talking about—his boys? Was he setting up another Ruby Ridge or Branch Davidian type of bloody confrontation with authorities? Made no sense. Jaime's throat tightened. The one thing she did know for sure, she had to find Lucy.

"See you soon, my love." Mark jumped into his truck and sped away before Bea could finish parking.

—

Bea slammed the car door then strode toward Jaime who stood on the flagstone terrace between the front door and an empty rocking chair. Face pale as a dim light, hair disheveled, the girl wore a faded orange sundress and old flip-flops.

"Where's Henry?" Bea demanded.

"He's inside having a snack. He's fine."

Bea pointed down the drive, frowning. "Mark just zoomed past me like he was in the Indy 500 or something. What the hell is going on here, girl? Your father just called me and said you told him Lucy jetted off to visit him in Iraq—supposedly to try for some kind of last-ditch reconciliation." Hands on her hips, Bea drew herself up to her nearly six-foot height. "I don't buy it for a second. Lucy is closer to me than a sister—she would never, ever take off like this without telling me. So, I don't buy the Iraq story. Neither does Michael." She raised her chin and peered threateningly down at the girl. "So, start talking."

Jaime stuttered, "I, uh, uh..." She pressed her back against the door jamb as if trying to block Bea from entry.

Bea's patience was non-existent at this point. "Let me see her flight information. Now." She stepped toward the front door giving Jaime no choice but to hustle out of the way and let her into the house.

"I, uh, she didn't give it to me."

Bea sneered. "You're taking care of her son, and she didn't give you her itinerary? That's bullshit." She shook her head. "So, when did she leave? You at least have that much?"

Jaime shoved her hands deep into the pockets of her loose dress. "Yesterday around 3:30, to New York, I think, then on to wherever the Iraq airport is. That's all I know, I swear. She was gonna text me." Jaime's flushed skin began to film with perspiration. Her shoulders shook.

Bea could smell the lies, but as she became increasingly aware of Jaime's stressed body language, she paused her barrage. She didn't want the girl to dig in her heels and stonewall. Bea needed another strategy and called on her mama bear skills. The young woman was about the age of her son Dexter, and not much older than Allicia. Clearly, Jaime was in way over her head. She had to handle her with a bit more empathy in order to squeeze out the truth. Nevertheless, Bea began to pace again, giving off vibes of someone who couldn't be manipulated.

Then she paused and pulled out her phone. Pressed speed-dial.

Jaime looked paralyzed, scared, and unsure as to what to do next. Bea was glad she was rattled. Empathy was going to be hard to conjure with Lucy at risk.

"Pete," Bea said, "Lucy supposedly left LAX for Iraq to visit Michael around 3:30 yesterday afternoon. Can you have your people find out if she's on any boarding lists?" While listening to Pete's animated response, she glared at Jaime, who plucked at a speck of imaginary lint on her skirt. Then Bea continued her conversation with the detective. "Yeah, babe, Michael and I don't believe it either. And I'm sure they have CCTV at the flight gates." She listened for a moment more, then thanked Pete. "Get back to me ASAP."

She disconnected and stepped directly into Jaime's personal space. "Seems like working here at the ranch, you were just starting to get your life together. Would be a damned shame if you landed in jail as an accessory to murder and kidnapping, barred from any further contact with your brother." Bea wanted to make the consequences sound as ominous as possible.

Jaime gulped hard.

Bea gave the girl a long, appraising look. "Incarceration would be a drag. And orange is not your best color."

CHAPTER FIFTY-NINE

Jaime gripped a fistful of her dress then let it go. Her breath was shallow and rapid. Appearing to weigh her options, she seemed on the verge of a panic attack. Then she spoke to Bea.

"Mark's like, insanely driven to make his idea of God's plan for himself and his followers come true." She wiped her eyes. "It's a losing battle to try and go up against—what do they call it—a zealot."

"Fuck zealots," Bea said, then took a beat. "Okay, girl, let's calm down." Then, something on the floor by the doorway where they stood caught her attention. "Whose blood is on the tile? I know blood when I see it. My God, was Lucy hurt?"

Seeing the dried pool of blood spatter, Jaime shuddered. Her fingers grazed her cheek.

Bea's eyes narrowed. She looked closely at Jaime and became aware of pale purple bruises beneath the girl's eyes and across her nose, all poorly concealed by makeup. "Mark hit you." Jaime had to be under serious pressure from Wenter. "Blackmail? What?"

A recording of The Lion King sounded from upstairs. Bea

hoped Henry hadn't heard the angry confrontation. "Come on. Let's sit down." She guided Jaime into the living room to a small couch. When Jaime sat, Bea planted herself next to the girl.

Edging as far away from Bea as she could, Jaime grabbed a throw pillow and clutched it to her chest like a shield.

"You've been through a lot of shit, I know that," Bea said, softening her approach. "But you're alive because of Lucy and Heath. You have a relationship with your little bro because of Lucy. You know that, right?"

Wiping her forehead with her hand, Jaime sniffed, nodded, and swallowed hard.

Bea continued. "Right now, this moment, you have to decide to do the right thing or live with some very nasty consequences. You have your whole life in front of you, Jaime. You're smart, beautiful, kind, but naïve. You're at a crisis point. Things could go in either direction."

Jaime looked away and rubbed her bruised face.

"Listen, I know a fair amount about what you're going through. When I was a little younger than you, like in high school, I got involved with this beautiful young man with some pretty fringe beliefs. I was sure he loved me. There were so many red flags telling me he was a total predatory con, but I ignored them. And then he almost killed me. I think you're on the same road."

Bea touched Jaime's arm and immediately withdrew when she winced. But it was come-to-Jesus time, as Bea's Baptist minister father would say. "The clock is ticking, Jaime, and my dearest friend is gone. I want answers." She had to get through to the girl because Lucy's life depended on it.

Bea took a moment to consider her words.

"Okay, Jaime, you have to trust your gut, not your brain. Or even your heart on this one. You listening?"

She nodded. "Yes."

Bea continued what she knew sounded like a homily, but Jaime was part of that world. And as a minister's daughter, Bea had listened to a lifetime of sermons. "Your brain will intellectualize and tell you the smart thing to do," she said. "Your heart will tell you what you yearn to do, but your gut, it'll tell you the down and dirty truth of what you have to do to be true to yourself. Make sense?"

Finally, the girl spoke. "I've known what I have to do for a while now." Her voice came low and raspy. She swiped away tears. "But I've been too scared."

"Jaime, if you tell me the truth, I've got your back, completely. Understand?"

The girl cleared her throat, then looked directly at Bea for the first time.

Bea felt a trill of hope. Maybe she'd gotten through.

Leaning back, Jaime rubbed her temples. "I have to protect my brother."

"What do you mean?" Bea felt her chest tighten.

"Mark threatened to kill Henry and me if I said anything." Jaime inhaled deeply. "And said he'll murder the animals and make us watch." A strangled scream escaped from her throat. "Mark Wenter needs to be stopped, even if it means I'll go down in flames."

Bea frowned. "You think I'd let that snake-kissing psychopath touch any of you?"

Wiping her eyes again, Jaime said, "I don't care about myself anymore. I deserve whatever I get. But Lucy, and Henry—you have to make sure nothing happens to them."

"I helped him enter into this world. I love him like my own and won't be part of his exit, or yours either. And I sure as hell am not going to let Lucy down." Bea edged back a bit to give the young woman the room she needed to talk. "No time to waste, Jaime. I'm worried sick about Lucy. Tell me everything."

Jaime chewed at the inside of her cheek, then gulped and sat up straighter. "Mark and Cooter did it. They took Lucy." The story gushed out. "I think they have her in a bomb shelter out beyond some barn that burned down. My friend, Isabella, told me. She's going to try and escape with her son, like tonight." Jaime paused for a shaky breath. "Mark's bringing in a bunch of men soon and they're taking almost all the Eden's Gate residents away."

Bea let out a low whistle. "Whoa. Moving everybody out? Why? To where?" She wondered how abducting Lucy tied in?

"My friend Isabella says they're taking people to some way off-the-grid camp in the Tennessee mountains," Jaime said. "She says it's a place you could never escape from. She also overheard that he just sold Eden's Gate for millions to a developer."

Bea groaned. "Of course he did. California gold. Now what are these good ol' boys from the hills supposed to be doing? Help pack up the community? Sort through the choir robes and boxes of frickin' pancake mix?" Her tone oozed contempt.

"I have no idea. But I know they love their guns and moonshine."

"A bad combination," Bea said.

Jaime continued. "If anything happens to Lucy, then Mark and his weird lawyer have changed all the paperwork, like her Will and stuff. The new Will leaves everything to Henry, with me, his sister, as the executor."

"Oh, shit. And with Mark as your husband, he has his hands in all of it. He'll try to take Lucy's ranch for his ministry, or whatever he calls this wacko sect."

"Right. But I don't know if we're actually legally married. He just takes women and pretends to be their husband until he's ready for a new one." Her lips quivered.

An illegal marriage could put a crack in Wenter's plans. But the lawyer would have filed a marriage license. "You know this lawyer's name?" Bea asked.

"No, but it's probably on the paperwork in Lucy's filing cabinet."

"Let's go check," Bea said, standing.

"I have her laptop password, too."

"The fact that her laptop is still here speaks volumes. She'd never leave it."

The sound of the dogs barking filled the yard outside the window. Jaime rose and looked out. "Heath just drove in." She groaned. "He'll have to know all this, too, won't he?"

"Of course."

"I've been trying to avoid him." She hung her head in shame. Her straight blond hair curtained her face.

"But you're stepping up now. You're done being a victim." Bea pushed the hair out of Jaime's eyes and gave her a hug. The girl tensed, then her body softened, accepting the contact. "It's high time for Mark Wenter to be the victim. Don't you agree?" Bea asked, letting her go and moving toward the office.

"Absolutely." A smile flickered across Jaime's lips.

CHAPTER SIXTY

Lucy woke with a brutal headache from hours hogtied in the back of Wenter's truck, sucking in gas fumes and roasting from the heat like meat on a grill. Where the hell was she? The dark, concrete entombment she found herself lying in, felt like a hardcore survivalist's man cave.

Thrust into a grinder of pain and anxiety, her first thought was of Henry. She couldn't imagine life without the child she never thought she'd be able to have with her body wounded from the accident that claimed her family so many years ago. For her son to suffer the empty hole of growing up without a mother, and with a father largely absent like Jaime experienced—the thoughts drove her to a familiar dark place. It was a place she'd hoped to avoid for her only child. And she knew that children would always take a parent's absence personally. *Why don't they love me? I'm not good enough. Is this my fault?* And in Lucy's case—*why didn't I die, too?*

Screaming and screaming until there was nothing left but exhaustion and a raw throat, Lucy knew she couldn't give in to despair. She had to survive.

Hands zip-tied behind her and feet bound with the same unyielding plastic, she pushed herself up against a wall and carefully surveyed the dimly lit space. As her eyes acclimated to the gloom, she found herself in what she looked like a high-end 1950s concrete bomb shelter. She'd seen pictures in one of her grandmother's yellowed Time magazines. It was a monument to terror and paranoia. Her own matched that of the people who built it, anticipating something horrible. But with cartons marked as supplies still on storage shelves, she had a sense that maybe Mark didn't want to kill her. Yet. That delay could give her the chance to destroy him first.

Although restrained, Lucy was able to crawl. Painfully on her elbows and knees, she struggled along the ten-foot-long hallway leading to the bunker's entry. Could she pry it open?

The way was lit with dim LED lights at the base of the wall, like what one might find flanking the aisles of a movie theater or an airplane. At the end was the hatch. Not a glimmer of light leaked around the edges. She managed to stand and threw herself several times against the metal door. Meant for permanence, it was sealed tight and didn't budge. Lucy's shoulder soon throbbed from the effort.

Leaning near the hatch was a motorbike. The key was in the ignition. Lucy smiled. Hope began to glimmer. She'd ridden everything from Vespa's in Europe to a Harley down in Georgia with Rio. This would be her escape—probably the very bike Cain had been riding when he blasted out of the barn and almost ran her over. Turning and leaning backwards so her hands bound behind her could reach the key, she tried to twist it. On the second try, the bike sprung to life. Groaning with relief, Lucy turned it off immediately so as not to asphyxiate herself in the closed space.

She would camp here on the floor next to the bike, waiting and hoping for a break. The instant she heard the entry hatch lock being keyed, she planned to explode through the door on the motorcycle, just like Cain had, with all the propulsion she could muster. But first she had to get her hands free.

She hopped, fell painfully, then inch-wormed back to the main living area where she discovered the door to a single dank room. The smell in the enclosure was ripe. Lucy shivered; she didn't want to recognize the scent. But she did. Chills of dread sent icy ants down her spine. She crawled inside the room.

A whispery sound like wind, emanating from the covered cistern, caught her attention. What the heck is that? A gust from a secret passage that was an exit? One could only hope. A ventilation source deep below the ground?

Lucy sat next to the heavy round lid. She pushed it with her feet a few inches aside, scraping the rough cement lip surrounding the hole below. That was when the mysterious sound became unmistakable. She sucked in a sharp breath.

No air source or escape route.

Snakes.

Falling backwards, her heart battered her ribs. Could the snakes get out? Could they attack her? Ordinarily she didn't have a great fear of rattlers, encountering them in the meadow and along the trail at her ranch, but there was something about Mark Wenter's snakes that made them terrifying. Maybe because he used his serpents both as instruments of divination in his sick cult, and as instruments of murder.

Taking a moment to calm down, Lucy noticed a camp lantern near the door behind her. With much effort, she rolled over to it and found the on button. She pressed it. The lantern batteries were strong. It must have been used fairly recently. Maneuvering the light close to the hole, Lucy held her breath at the smell rising from below and peeped through the narrow crack between the well cover and the lip of the pit. Pale light filtering from the lantern revealed a body. Bruise-purple and rotting, it was frozen in a posture of terror. Cain.

In near panic mode but realizing the rattlers were secure at the bottom of the well, Lucy began to desperately saw at her wrist bindings, moving them across the rough, concrete edge of the pit. Sweating with effort, the plastic tie began to fray but also ripped her skin until it bled like fresh hamburger.

At last, the zip tie popped open. Gasping, she filed off her ankle bindings the same way.

Despite the dead body and the snarl of snakes hissing and rattling at the bottom of the blackness, Lucy was energized by the victory. She rubbed life back into her aching hands and feet.

Pulling the lid closed, she sure as hell wasn't going to let Mark throw her in that hellhole to die. Her brain hummed with anger and resentment. How dare he think he could destroy her life. Instead, she would be the viper who would take him down. But how?

As Lucy stood and grabbed the lantern to bring it into the main area, something shiny caught her eye. In the far corner of the room—a piece of metal? Could she use it somehow? Bending to pick it up, she discovered an old school can opener, the type called a church key for opening beer bottles and aluminum cans. Maybe for opening Mark Wenter's face as well. She smiled and stowed it in her jeans pocket. Small advantages could add up.

Back in the living space, from behind a bunkbed, Lucy pulled out a cardboard container smelling of mildew, marked BIBLES. Inside, she didn't find Bibles but moldering hymnals and church bulletins for an Easter service decades ago. Not much utility in those things, at least for now.

She yanked a cardboard box marked CANNED GOODS from a low shelf and discovered a dozen cans of baked beans and one of tomato soup. She checked the expiration dates—five years beyond the suggestion use date. But Lucy went for the soup anyway, poking holes in the top with her new tool. The contents still smelled tomatoey, not rancid. In her hunger it tasted like heaven. Her queasy stomach settled, and her spirits rose because now, she had food and some minimal weaponry— the jagged soup can lid and the church key. How ironic.

Her work wasn't yet done to optimize her chances for

survival. Lucy had no idea how long it took her, but she dragged all four heavy steel bunkbeds in front of the well room door to block it. If the assholes tried to throw her in, pulling away the heavy bunks could buy her time. She wiped perspiration from her face.

Returning to the entry where she planned to camp, Lucy reexamined the bike and discovered a small saddle bag attached to the rear fender. She squatted next to one of the strip lights and unzipped the nylon bag. It contained seventy dollars in fives and singles, a driver's license for Cain Wentworth, a melted half of an energy bar which she downed immediately, and a burner phone. The battery was dead.

Her rising spirits plunged downward like a broken elevator. Tormented again with thoughts of Henry and terror for his safety, she wondered—if she was murdered here—who would love and take care of her son? Keep his grief from turning to anger and powerlessness?

It would be Bea.

Had she discovered Lucy had been abducted? What deceit would Wenter and his sycophants be orchestrating? Had Jaime been intimidated into silence? What would Bea and Pete be thinking? And Heath? Unrelenting questions. Her psychic electrons could easily spin out of control. She had to stay cool.

Exhausted, Lucy fought back tears and returned to the front of the shelter where she positioned the bike to point outward toward escape. She'd fly through the hatch, Hell on Wheels, like Cain had done at the barn, knocking her down. This time, it was Wenter's turn to go down.

CHAPTER SXTY-ONE

Heath rang the doorbell. Jaime could hear Gracie talking to Howard who'd been lurking behind the pot of geraniums next to the porch swing. She took a nervous breath, then opened the door.

"Hey, Jaime," Heath said, smiling. "We're here to pick up Lucy and Henry for dinner and the fireworks. I haven't been able to get hold of her."

Ginger hair freshly cut and handsome, he wore a black T-shirt with a patriotic Willie Nelson graphic. His work khakis and muddy boots had been replaced by tight jeans and shining cowboy boots. Gracie proudly strutted in a sparkly dress exploding with red, white, and blue. Her headband lit up with battery-powered stars to match the dress. It was clear to Jaime that the party had started, and Henry was going to the fireworks after all.

"Come on in." Jaime dropped her voice and turned to Heath. "Bea and I have something we need to talk with you about. Lucy's not here."

"What?" Heath's forehead creased with concern. "Where is

she? At the gallery?"

"I'll explain in a minute." Jaime turned to Grace as they all walked into the kitchen. "Gracie, would you like to go upstairs and see if Henry's ready?"

"Sure. And I have glow sticks for us." She grinned and flashed two packages of glow light sabers.

"Ah, fabulous," Jaime said. They watched Grace run up the stairs.

The instant the child was out of earshot, Heath demanded, "Jaime, what is going on? Is Lucy okay?"

"She's been kidnapped."

"What the..." He paused, looking skyward. "Wenter?"

She nodded. At the kitchen counter, Jaime nervously steepled her hands and told him the story. Taking responsibility for her part in it, she begged for his forgiveness.

Heath nodded, too overwhelmed to bother pointing fingers. "This in insane. We gotta find her, like now,"

"Let's go to the study," Jaime said. "Bea's in there trying to find information we need about Mark's lawyer. That could give us a clue."

Face bleak, Heath followed her down the hallway into the office where Bea pored over a document folder.

She looked up when they came in, a confused frown on her intense dark face, reading glasses perched low on her nose.

"What are we going to do?" Heath demanded.

Jaime could feel him humming with a physical need to act immediately.

"You call Pete?" he asked, beginning to pace.

"Doctor Sinclair, take a breath." Bea nodded to a chair, but he didn't sit. "The Sheriffs are on it. But let me ask you something that might be pertinent." She drummed a pen on the desktop.

"Okay. Like what?"

"Have you ever heard of someone by the name of Sean Sinclair?"

"My last name."

"Yes."

Heath chewed at his lip and thought for a moment. "That's a common name in Scottish circles." He squinted as if trying to bring something into focus. "Okay, I have, like, a third or fourth cousin named Sean Sinclair. I remember that he worked with my grandparents decades ago on our family lodge up near Mammoth. They used to complain about him."

"Lucy and Henry were up there with you when Jaime had the hemorrhage, right?"

Jaime grimaced and pressed her hands against her abdomen. She would always be traumatized by what had happened. And grateful that Heath had saved her.

"That's the place," Heath confirmed. "I also remember hearing that my grandparents had a big falling out with a cousin Sean because he wanted the lodge to be used for a fringe religious community of some sort. As good Presbyterians, they would have none of it, so they cut ties."

Bea nodded. "Sound a bit similar to Eden's Gate? A religious group?"

"My God." Heath scrubbed at his head, as if trying to make sense of a crazy puzzle. "I was too young to have known the guy but now I remember the grown-ups talking. My dad might have met him, but I think the dude died years ago. Why are you asking? What connection could he possibly have to Lucy?"

"The Conejo Valley was a small community back in the old days, wasn't it?" Bea asked.

Heath nodded.

She raised her eyebrows and looked from Jaime to Heath. "I'm asking because I think your ancient cousin, Sean Sinclair, might be Mark Wenter's lawyer."

"What?" Heath looked at Bea in disbelief.

Her phone pinged. She held up a finger to pause the torrent of questions he was about to zing her way. "Hold on a minute, Doc." She checked her caller ID. "It's Pete. He must have info about Lucy's flights."

Heath folded his arms impatiently across his chest.

"Hey, love," Bea said to Pete. "I'm here with Heath and Jaime. Putting you on speaker." She leaned forward and placed her phone on the desktop.

After Bea caught him up on Jaime's disclosures, Pete started in. "Okay, my FBI friends found passenger Lucia Vega through automated customer tracking," he said. "The Fibbies have access to facial recognition, biometrics, and stuff like that to track folks from check-in through ass-in-narrow-miserable seat."

"Good to know, hon, but did she frickin' board?" Bea was impatient to cut to the chase.

"She first boarded at LAX to JFK, then changed planes in New York onto a Qatar Airlines flight non-stop to Baghdad. It's still in the air. However," he paused, "I got the passenger photo of her from the airline surveillance cameras. It's not Lucy."

"What? Who is it?" Heath and Bea demanded, almost in unison.

Pete continued. "Alright kiddies, I just sent the photo to you, Bea. Pass it around. Maybe one of you'll recognize the woman."

"I know who it is." Jaime's head bowed. She responded before even looking. "It's Tanya Lee Riggs, a stripper from Klapperville, Tennessee. I heard she was accused of murdering a man there. Mark's been having an affair with her."

Bea side-eyed Jaime. "His Godly behavior never ceases to amaze."

"Jaime, would you look at the photo and confirm it's Riggs?" Pete asked.

Jaime flushed, she took the phone from Bea, her hands shaking. "That's her."

"For sure?" Pete asked.

"For sure." She gave the phone back, almost dropping it. "Tanya's been an Eden's Gate Community member for about a month. Mark got her a passport in Lucy's name. The lawyer arranged for it."

"But what's the point in sending Lucy, or fake Lucy, to Iraq?" Bea asked.

Jaime licked her dry lips. "Tanya will make it look like Lucy disappeared in Iraq, then she'll return to the U.S. under another name and passport. It'll look like Lucy arrived but never returned to the states."

Heath groaned and began pacing.

"What's the return name?" Pete asked.

"I don't know. Probably some version of Wente, Wenter, or Wentworth."

"Okay, we'll start with that."

Jaime continued. "Mark thinks some kind of international police will go after my dad and blame him for Lucy's disappearance."

"Snake man thinks this off-the-wall plan is brilliant?" scoffed Pete.

"He has dreams, or so-called visions from God, about building a world-wide prosperity gospel empire. What a joke." Jaime wiped fresh tears. "He swore he wouldn't hurt Lucy, but now I see he totally plans to get rid of her. This is all my fault."

"Hell, she could even be dead already," Heath growled.

Jaime winced.

"We have to go with the belief that she's alive." Bea's voice crackled with exasperation. "Focus everything on finding Lucy. Clearly, she's not in Iraq. Probably in that abandoned bomb shelter you heard about. On the edge of Eden's Gate property, right?"

Jaime nodded.

"Okay, let's get moving. It's the only lead we got." Bea stood up from the desk chair, eyes fixed on Jaime, fists clenching and unclenching.

Jaime slumped down on the couch, her shoulders raised to her ears as if she were awaiting a physical thrashing.

"Very original scheme Wenter has going," Pete said. "Gotta

give him that much. Too bad we're gonna fuck it up." He chuckled without humor. "Okay, peeps, I'm getting warrants to search the camp and get police back-up ready to go. Will be in touch ASAP as to timing. Hold your horses until you hear from me. Got that, Beatrice? No Lone Ranger shit, okay my beauty?"

"Uh huh. Later, hon." Bea signed off on the call and turned to Heath. "If we wait for the sheriffs, it could be too late."

He nodded.

"Let's roll," Her resolve hardened.

THE SNAKE HANDLER'S WIFE | 265

CHAPTER SIXTY-TWO

Tanya Lee snuggled into her fancy leather seat, had a second glass of bubbly, and ordered the filet mignon. The husky, middle-aged sheik, unable to take his eyes from her open abaya, complimented her menu choice.

"Are y'all on your way home to Iraq?" she asked conversationally.

He smoothed his moustache. "On my way to visit my mother, ex-wife, and children. But we live very separate lives. I have an apartment in New York, and houses in Ibiza, Barcelona, and Erbil."

Tanya's attention perked up. "Y'all must be a very successful man. I admire that." She crossed and uncrossed her legs, flashing her hot pink tights. A sharp puff of air escaped the man's mouth. He smiled. Nice Hollywood white teeth. She liked good teeth. So many of the Klapperville fools she'd danced for looked like they'd been kicked in the mouth by a mule.

"I guess you're not as traditional as you first looked," he said, appreciatively glancing at her leggings. "You must be an actress, or a singer."

"How perceptive." A little shake of her shoulders. "I'm an actress. From L.A. Doing a quick smidge of business abroad then heading right back to the city."

"Unfortunate that you are on such a tight schedule," he said as the meals were served. "I'd like to show you Baghdad. It's nothing like the Western media portrays. It's a very nice place. The Port of Basra on the Persian Gulf is spectacular. The mall in Al-Mansour is first rate—Tiffany, Dior, Prada."

Malls. Designer brands. Tanya's pulse quickened. She smiled and took her time making sure every bite of the succulent meal looked even better going into her mouth than it did on the plate.

As the dinner chat progressed, the sheik asked, "Have you been in any movies or TV shows I've seen?"

She languidly wiped her mouth with a white linen napkin. "I'm in kind of uh—what do they call it—a niche market."

"Niche?"

"Adult entertainment." She popped a purple, parmesan encrusted fingerling potato into her mouth. First class was the only way to go.

Tanya saw the man's eyes widen, glowing like the shiny silver dollar a blotto dude once stuffed into her thong. She'd sold the coin for twenty cash.

"I know ya'll are a very, uh, conservative culture. I don't want to get stoned or anything." Visions of stoning had haunted her previous night's sleep.

He laughed, genuinely amused. "Because we're such a conservative country, we have more online porn sites than any other place on Earth. Between you and me," he leaned across the armrest, "it's an area of business I've long been looking to expand into. And nobody's going to stone you, my dear. Quite the opposite, we love our beautiful actresses."

Tanya let out a sigh of relief. She primped her hair and smiled. "If y'all ever need a consultant from Hollywood, just shoot me a text." She took a pen from her bag and wrote her contact information in pink on the back of the wine list, and pushed it his way. His six o'clock shadow of a beard was kind of sexy. Maybe it was the booze talking, but who cared.

He studied her information and nodded. "I know very little about the adult industry in Los Angeles, I'm just breaking in. But you sound very experienced." He took a big gulp of wine. His hand grazed Tanya's wrist. His gold watch was brighter than the silver dollar.

"You must spend a few extra days in Baghdad with me. I do legitimate movies, too. You can see my studio in Erbil. I have a car coming to the airport, I own a lovely hotel, I'll take care of everything, it would be my honor." He poured them each another glass of the premium red.

"Studio?" She was getting seriously hot. Managing an upgrade to first class was an incredible use of her two emergency expense Visa cards. It was God's plan that the sheik was next to her on this plane—it also proved that her financial investment instincts were solid.

But should she go with him? Did it really matter if she decided to spend a few more days in the Middle East? Maybe it could help her and Mark launch their series. Mark Wenter, however, was becoming less interesting with every sip of Merlot. This Iraqi dude, obviously dripping with bucks, could potentially come up with major funding. She was an entrepreneur, a businesswoman at heart.

"I supposed I could arrange a few more days to help you out." She tried to sound as if she was doing him a major favor, then reapplied Barbie pink lipstick

He giggled like a schoolboy. "Thank you, beautiful, stunning woman, adult entertainment consultant. I assure you, you'll have an amazing visit to my country. Now, how can I make the rest of this long flight more pleasurable for you? More wine? Kunafa? Baklava?"

She licked her lips. The sheik was a willing score. "Have you ever heard of the Mile High Club?"

CHAPTER SIXTY-THREE

Heath scanned the freeway for patrol cars as he sped too fast, lead-footing it toward Thousand Oaks. He glanced into the rearview mirror—Bea was right behind him in her BMW. They raced down the 101 on their way to drop the kids off at the Santa Monica Mountains Veterinary Clinic where their annual Fourth of July staff, family, and friends, picnic would be in full swing.

Passing the Thousand Oaks Mall, just below the hill where the Fire Department readied the fireworks, traffic clogged the streets as area residents packed the shopping center parking lots to grab prime spots for viewing the holiday extravaganza. The place was already mobbed with tailgaters set up with campers, barbeques, and yard games. Heath ground his teeth as they crawled down the surface streets.

Several blocks from the show's biggest crowds, the clinic employees and their families gathered every year for a parking lot picnic and fireworks. Heath pulled the truck to the rear of the clinic. Bea's car slid in beside his. As they hopped from their vehicles, the sound of illegal fireworks popped and sizzled from nearby neighborhoods. People started igniting their explosives early in this part of town. The smell of burned black powder hung in the air. A lick of terror accompanied the scent as brushfires routinely threatened the area.

"Are you scared of the fireworks?" Grace asked Henry while Heath helped them unbuckle their car seats.

"I didn't get to see them last year. I was only three," he held up his fingers. "I'm four now, though."

"I'm kinda scared," Grace confessed, picking at the glitter on her skirt.

"Yeah, I'm a little scared, too." Henry wrinkled his nose.

"I'll be with you," Jaime promised. "And I bet there'll be drones, too. They're pretty quiet."

"I want noise," Henry declared. Both kids clutched their glow saber packages, impatiently waiting for darkness to fall before tearing them open.

"Me, too." Grace made an explosive sound.

Laughing loudly, both children seemed to think it was hilarious.

The children's conversations were funny and innocent, but Heath's patience was strained almost to the breaking point. There was nothing funny or innocent about what was going on at Eden's Gate. He waited for Bea, then followed the kids, hand-in-hand with Jaime, toward his parents. Outside the clinic's front door, Old Doc Sinclair was aproned-up and flipping burgers. Heath saw his energetic, gray-haired Mom uncover a pile of hot corn-on-the-cob at the buffet table. The food looked great as usual, but Heath had no appetite. All he could think about was Lucy. He chewed on his lip. Was she dead? Or, alive?

Children shrieked from a bouncy castle, a new addition to this year's celebration. Henry and Grace beelined in that direction with Jaime closely trailing. A loudspeaker was linked to a local radio station which rang out patriotic country songs.

Heath could feel Bea's impatience buzzing on the same wavelength as his own. "On the way over, I called one of our veterinary techs," he told her. "He's former Marine Special Ops.

Works at the clinic with dad while he's applying to vet school. I asked him to keep an eye on Jaime and the kiddos at all times." The children's safety was paramount.

Bea nodded, moving fast at Heath's side.

"Come on, let's touch bases with my folks, see what they know about Sean Sinclair, and then let's get the hell outta here." He lost his breath for a moment at the thought of what could be happening to the woman he'd fallen hard for.

Hot air from the grill smelled of burgers, fried chicken, and tangy barbeque sauce. Hungry guests lined up with paper plates ready to load with picnic fare. Heath knew most of them and usually schmoozed with the partyers, but not this time. He pushed toward his father.

"Hi, Dad. We're on the run but this is Bea Jackson, she's a journalist and Lucy Vega's best friend. We need to know about Sean Sinclair. Did you find anything?"

Heath's mom moved up next to her son.

Old Doc's face clouded. "We have a cousin who might fit the bill," he said, then handed the spatula to a young man wearing an *I Love Malinois* T-shirt. "I thought Sean was long gone. I rummaged through my old file cabinets and found a forty-year-old address. If he's among the living, he's probably still out at his place in Santa Paula. I emailed you the address a few minutes ago."

Heath checked his phone. "Got it. Thanks." He forwarded the address to Bea. "We gotta go. Will be in touch. Love you guys. Thanks for keeping the kids."

Bea touched Old Doc's arm and added, "I just texted you both a direct line to Detective Sargent Pete Anthony with the county sheriffs. If you sense anything wonky going on here, text him immediately. He'll get right back to you. Okay?"

"Yes, thank you." The vet smiled at Bea. "But I'm sure we'll be fine."

She nodded. "Yes, I'm sure you will be."

Heath picked up the tentativeness in her agreement.

Mom wiped her hands on her red-white-and blue apron. "Be careful, sweethearts." Deep concern shadowed her face.

They hugged goodbye. As Bea and Heath hustled away, Old Doc caught up with them. Heath winced, not wanting to be slowed down.

"Wait a sec," Old Doc said. "Just thought of something I remember as a kid when we met Sean one time at the lodge. May have no bearing whatsoever on what you're dealing with, but he may have come from a branch of the family who were into weird stuff in their church."

"I had a vague recollection of grandma and grandpa talking about that. Anything specific stand out?" Heath asked.

"Yeah, animal sacrifices. And lots of talk of serpents. My folks thought it was all sacriligious, so not much was mentioned."

Heath felt the small hairs on his arms stir. He and Bea's eyes met, mirroring their unspoken fears.

Bea said, "In the Bible the Lord spoke to Moses and said, Make a snake and put it up on a pole; anyone who is bitten can look at it and live."

Old Doc's eyes widened.

A small smile flashed and disappeared from Bea's face. "I've been studying up on my Biblical serpent references."

The man with the Malinois T-shirt handed the spatula back to Old Doc and picked up a crying toddler at his feet. Old Doc returned to grill duty.

After a quick *love you* to the kids, who were already sweaty from non-stop castle bouncing, Heath and Bea jumped into her car and sped toward Eden's Gate.

CHAPTER SIXTY-FOUR

Heart pounding and breath coming fast, Isabella stood in the shadow of an olive tree, looking out across the sports field, hopefully for the last time. A shimmer of wildness rent the air around the community while men disgorged from a dark panel van and three school buses with the Klapperville, Tennessee congregation's logo on the side.

Its stumbling passengers were guided to the dining hall. By the sound of the hootin' and hollerin' most had probably been drinking throughout the thirty-hour road trip. Several of the new arrivals tossed firecrackers into the pool, and others appeared to be setting up for something bigger. The acrid scent of flash powder wafted in the air.

Isabella cringed, vividly remembering when the Tennessee assholes had been at the camp three years ago to help build several new cottages. She'd barely escaped being raped. Others weren't as lucky.

Now was the time, while the men were rowdy and disorganized, to make her break. Dressed in dark clothing, she was off to grab her son. They'd ride out to the bunker on her bicycle, free the padlock with the heavy-duty hammer she'd stolen from the maintenance shed, and ride as fast and as far away as they could go on Cain's dirt bike.

She wondered if Jaime's friend Lucy was in that bomb shelter and if she was alive.

Moving quickly, she turned toward the cottages and tried to will herself into being a ghost. But very bad people often stalked the ghostly world of phantoms and ghouls.

As Isabella scurried beneath the live oak sheltering the outdoor arts and crafts classroom, a hand reached out and grabbed her by the hair. She gasped at the pain. The man pulled her tight, pressing her into the rough bark of the big tree. His breath stunk of booze and his clothing reeked of an unwashed body. His erection was hard against her stomach.

"You the one I didn't git last time," he hissed hot into her ear. "Looked for you the minute I got off the bus. Been thinkin' 'bout those soft titties for two thousand fuckin' miles."

Isabella cringed, terrified and unable to move. Could she talk her way out of this? "No, please. Some are totally willing. And prettier. Stop, I'm begging you. You don't have to do it this way. This is not how real men have women."

"You plenty pretty. An' I don' like willing. And I one helluva real man." His laugh was pure evil. "Not gonna let you off this time, bitch. Comin' for 'ya sweetheart, and gonna bury my thang in dat sweet place a yours the pastor used to like so much. His discards're good 'nough for this ol' boy. Uh-huh."

Isabella struggled to escape his grasp. He wasn't a big man but his arms were like rough metal cords, abrading her skin.

Grinding against her, he stuffed his tongue down her throat. She gagged. Visions of her child, the motorcycle, of freedom, flashed-banged through Isabella's mind, igniting like a dreaded wildfire. No, she would not let this happen.

Pinned tight, she took an awful breath of his stink and managed to sink down just enough to slide the ball-peen hammer from the pocket of her cargo pants. The recollection of

Mark sneering above her as he took her again and again, turned her vision blood red with hatred. A physical strength she didn't know she had lit her determination. Long-repressed rage and resentment welled in her diaphragm. She would not be raped again. She was done. She would die first.

She gripped the tool, the instrument of her salvation. In a fast, determined stroke, she pounded him in the groin, then bashed his fucking brains in.

The man groaned, released her, and slid down the tree trunk. With a look of surprise on his evil face, he lay crumpled, unmoving on the ground. A dark pool around islands of pale brain matter, spread in the dirt. Isabella shuddered. Now, there was no going back for sure.

In the growing darkness, both horrified and exhilarated, she bounded toward her son's cottage, holding the bloody hammer like the Olympic torch being run through the streets.

CHAPTER SIXTY-FIVE

As dusk turned to night, Bea and Heath arrived at the low mesa above the burned-out barn where she and Lucy had previously parked. Stepping out of the car, Bea gazed across the distant hills, feeling agitated and impatient. She knew all too well that minutes, even seconds, could be the difference between life and death.

"So, where is this place?" Heath pulled out his Glock and popped in a magazine before re-holstering.

"According to Jaime, who heard it from a woman at the camp, the bomb shelter is beyond the barn, like a half-mile or so. Maybe. It's a crap shoot. Not sure Jaime's a reliable source, but it's all we got." Dressed in black jeans and T-shirt, Bea carried a flashlight, water, and her 9mm handgun in a fanny pack. "Okay, we ready to roll?"

"You okay for this?" Heath asked. He looked at her wrist, still wrapped in a bandage. "I know you were hurt in the explosion."

"Hell, I'm locked and loaded. And very pissed off. Follow me." She headed up the rise at a good pace.

"If we see any lights in the area, we go dark immediately."

"Agreed," she said.

Twenty minutes later they stood before the still smoldering remains of the barn. The acrid stench of smoke tinged the air.

"What a mess. Lucky you didn't get killed," Heath said.

Bea gently pressed her ribs. "Yeah, it was quite the boom. My body still aches. Hard to believe Cain rigged it."

"Why do you say that?"

"When the bomb squad did their forensics, they told Pete it was a more sophisticated setup than they first thought."

"You thinking Wenter's responsible?" Heath's eyes continued to scan the huge black scar where the wreckage stained the grayish, rocky sand.

Bea shrugged. "Seems more likely. To take out Pete, me, and Lucy, all at once—that would've solved a lot of his problems. Cain is young, probably not thinking as strategically or have as much bomb-making knowledge."

They paused for a moment, suddenly aware of a group of ATV headlights in the distance, swarming like dizzy fireflies.

"The Tennessee boys just arrived in school buses, right? Think that could be them roaring around already?" Heath wondered.

"Maybe, or just local ATV enthusiasts out for a holiday bash." Bea's pulse accelerated. "But we better be prepared for anything.

Off to the east, with a spray of illumination above the hills, the Simi Valley fireworks began. Bea hoped to God that Grace, Henry, and Jaime were safely watching the Thousand Oaks show from the clinic's parking lot.

As coyotes sang in the distance, Heath and Bea hiked north, stopping to check every dark place shrouded in rocks, cacti, and yucca for evidence of a hidden bunker. If the place didn't exist, Bea had no idea what to do next.

—

At Eden's Gate, Cooter, breathing hard, rushed up to Mark who was holding court with a bunch of the rowdies. They were gearing up to help take down the camp and move it to God's southern wilderness.

"Pastor, we have a problem." A film of shiny perspiration slicked the big man's face.

Mark ignored him. Cooter always had a problem. Coot was an effective, reliable operative but often an alarmist. Mark continued to hand out ATV fobs to his happy, drunken minions. Payment for thirty hours in the back of a bus and a week of hard work, the acolytes were promised good grub, booze, women, and ATVs to ring in the Fourth of July. With Mark's big real estate score, he was going all out to entertain. After steak dinners, the kegs opened, and bottles of Tennessee's best Pappy Van Winkle whiskey were passed out like party favors. Engines roared, the men whooped, and the women cowered in their cottages, readying for the inevitable.

"Pastor," Cooter panted. "This is important,"

"Sweet Lord, Coot. What is it?"

He leaned in and whispered in Mark's ear. "Clement's son, Clem Junior—he's dead."

"What?" Mark jumped up, almost knocking over a crate of booze.

"Yep. Brains bashed out."

"Oh, Holy Hell. One of the boys beat him down? Those assholes fighting and kicking ass already?" He banged his fist on the table. Whiskey bottles clinked. Glowering, Mark passed the handing out of favors duty to one of his octogenarian deacons and stepped away from the table. He and Cooter hurried outside the dining hall.

"So, what the hell happened?"

"Nobody saw it, found him over by arts and crafts. But his pants was down. I know he ain't no fag, so I think a woman mighta done the deed. You know he's hot for Isabella, shot his mouth off to anybody who'd listen. Didn't get her last time.

Wanted it bad."

"Isabella, trouble from day one." Mark paced. "Cousin Clement's gonna go nuts. We sure as hell don't want his Tennessee money to dry up."

"Clem Junior's always been such an asswipe. Surprised he made it this long without getting murdered."

"Nevertheless, he's Clement's eldest. Grab some men and find Isabella immediately," Mark said. "Do her in and the Vega bitch with her. Both. Now. Should've done it right away. Kept thinking I could use her somehow, like for bargaining, or whatever. Fuck that."

"I tol' you waiting was a mistake." Cooter frowned and wiped sweat from his forehead.

Mark ignored the comment. "Plant 'em in the old graveyard. I leave a shovel out there for emergencies like this. Can you handle it?"

Cooter nodded. The evil snarl of a mean old guard dog finally allowed to bite, twisted his lips.

"But first, check camp for Isabella," Mark directed. "If she's not here, she could be on her way to the bomb shelter. She knows about that place, might head out there like Cain did. You can take care of both women at once, but if my son is with Isabella, bring him back here unharmed. Understood?"

"Yes, pastor. Understood."

"It's time for the boy to begin learning the snakes." Mark blew out a long, slow, contemplative breath. "I'll grab Jaime and the boy. I want them at the lawyer's under lock and key 'til the custody and executor stuff gets settled," he said. Cooter was great with wet work, but retrieving Jaime and Henry would require finesse. He'd have to do it himself. He'd tracked Jaime's movements on her phone and knew right where she was. He turned to Cooter. "There'll be a nice bonus if you take care of things right," Mark said. "I don't want to see those bitches again."

"Shine that bonus up nice and bright, pastor, 'cause I be

gittin' it for sure." Grinning, Cooter jogged off to recruit his posse.

—

While her son, Asher, sat on the handlebars enjoying the big adventure, Isabella pedaled the old bicycle as fast as she could, trying desperately not to scare him. His name meant happiness in ancient Hebrew. Would they ever get to experience that together? She pedaled harder.

The sky was dark and starry, and a cool wind began to pick up, driving against them. Reaching down to touch the hammer in her pants pocket, it was sticky with the man's blood and brains. Isabella winced as she fingered it, wondering if the tool would be strong enough to crack open the padlock. And also, she wondered if Lucy was still alive. So much pain and death for a community that was supposed to believe that God is Love. She pedaled even faster as if trying to outrace judgement.

When they arrived at the bomb shelter, her legs shook from exertion. Asher hopped off the handlebars and together they pushed the bicycle up the hill above the entrance. "Stay right here while Mommy gets the motorcycle." She struggled to keep her voice light.

"Then we'll really have fun and go fast, won't we Mom?" he asked.

"That's right, sweetheart." She wondered if he knew something was up. Of course, he did. Kids had well-honed sensors. After handing him a candy bar and kissing his cheek, she crept down twenty yards to the entry hatch. Pulling out the hammer, she immediately went to work.

The sound of engines thrummed in the distance. Isabella's hands shook as she struggled with the tool. "Hit it again and again on the same spot to disengage the pins," the YouTube video had instructed. Banging the padlock, relentlessly wielding the hammer with both hands, Isabella put her whole weight into it.

The lock's shackle didn't crack or pull out. Fear and frustration singed her synapses. She swallowed an upsurge of despair. Visions of the dead rapist rose in her mind, of the audacity it took to stop him. Praying for strength, she gave the failing lock-breaking challenge another desperate shot.

Then, *crack*. She gasped. The lock sprung.

Isabella wrenched open the hatch. She was about step inside when Cain's motorcycle roared out. A dark figure gunned past, leaving Isabella stunned and disoriented. She tripped, and fell as it zoomed away. "No! Please, no!" Her only source of escape dimmed like a spent cinder.

Asher came running down the hill. "Mommy!"

"Lucy! Lucy!" Isabella screamed, crawling after her. "Don't leave us here!" It had to be Lucy; Cain was dead.

Isabella stood and screamed again, stumbling into the desert after the rider.

CHAPTER SIXTY-SIX

Over the sound of the accelerating engine, Lucy heard a scream, definitely not from Mark or Cooter. Then, a woman's voice cried out her name. Stopping short, the dirt bike skidded in the sand. Lucy looked behind her. In the silvery light of the half-moon, she could see a young, raven-haired woman collapsed onto the ground. A boy, a few years older than Henry, clung to the woman, his arms around her neck. Lucy's heart ached for them and for her own child.

"Isabella?" she called out.

The woman's voice was anguished. "Lucy?"

"Yes. Are you hurt?"

"No, I'm okay."

"Let's go. Gotta get the hell out of here. Jump on."

The woman grabbed her child, hustled to the bike and climbed behind Lucy with the boy sandwiched between them. The engine revved and they barreled up the hill toward the barn, headlights dark, staying off-road to avoid Wenter and the camp truck. The cycle, small and old, strained under the extra weight. Lucy had the throttle full open, but they were hitting less than thirty miles an hour. She spotted a throng of ATVs in the distance weaving back and forth in their direction. How were they going to outrun them?

"Those are men from the camp," Isabella shouted over the engine's whine. Lucy glanced back. Isabella was pressing her fingers to Asher's ears so he couldn't hear what she was about to say. "Drunk fools, very dangerous. And Mark wants to kill both you and me."

Lucy gave a thumbs-up in acknowledgement. So, on one side, Mark and Cooter would be hunting them along the road, and on the other side were the plastered good ol' boys looking for wild times. She and Isabella would have to thread the needle between them. That meant continuing directly toward the barn. Lucy gunned the engine in desperation.

It sputtered.

It sputtered again, wheezed like an asthmatic, then died.

Icy fingers of terror squeezed Lucy's throat. Beyond distressed, she could barely croak the words, "We're out of gas."

Isabella moaned.

"What's wrong, Mommy?" Asher's dark eyebrows drew together. His angelic face was washed pale in the moonlight.

Lucy saw fear in his eyes, and it broke her heart.

"We ran out of gas, honey," Isabella said. "We're going to have to walk." She kissed his cheek.

"So, we're going to play a game of hide and seek from those people on the big ATVs out there," Lucy said. "Then, we'll go to my ranch, and you can play with my son, Henry, and ride a horse, too, if you want."

"A real horse?" he asked. The little boy's brows relaxed.

"Yep, a real one." Lucy smiled, praying she could come through for all of them. She and Isabella stashed the bike behind a mound of boulders so it wouldn't be apparent that they were now on foot, and even more vulnerable.

—

Heath and Bea trekked past the barn, picking up their pace as the all-terrain vehicles grew in number, swarming closer. Along the trail, they came upon a dark thatch of vegetation. As they approached to inspect it, looking for the hidden bunker, they heard groaning, and vomiting.

"What the hell?" Heath whispered.

They pulled their firearms and stalked toward the sound. In the deep shadows behind a cover of creosote bushes was a quad bike, and a man on his hands and knees in the dirt beside it. Bea could smell the stench of stomach acid and booze from yards away.

"Let's grab the ATV," she mouthed.

Heath nodded agreement.

The two bolted to the vehicle. Spotting them, the drunk crawled, then staggered to his feet, waving a whiskey bottle. Bea jumped onto the driver's seat.

"Hey, you muthafookahs. Thaz my rig. Keep 'ya fookin' hanz offa it." He could barely form words. He swigged down the last dregs of booze, then gripped the bottle by the neck like a weapon. About 5'5" and 200 fire-plug pounds, the guy took an off-balance swing at Heath, who countered with a gut punch. The bottle flew into a patch of cacti.

The man, at first, looked unfazed. Then he bent over and puked again. Clumsily, he managed to straighten up and lunge at Heath once more. The doc smacked him hard on the jaw. Disoriented this time, the man turned and stumbled into the thorny creosote bushes with their harsh, stinging spines. He began to shriek. Then, passed out.

Heath hopped into the ATV next to Bea.

"That ol' boy's gonna hurt bad when he crawls out of there. Nice job," she said, firing up the engine but keeping the vehicle dark. "My first ex-husband had one of these."

The crackle of a walkie-talkie sounded from behind them. Heath reached to the rear seat and grabbed the device. A familiar voice shouted out.

"Hey, my brethren," Mark said in his most motivational, preacherly voice. "Pastor Wenter, here. Listen up, my good men. We got us two renegade, apostate women and a boy on the run out there in your vicinity. Whoever can catch the whores and bring me the boy, unharmed, will receive a bounty of ten thousand dollars. Yep, you heard me right. Ten thousand blessed bucks. God rewards those who follow His decree. But hear me, the boy is mine. The women, do what you choose, they're abominations against the Lord. We must smite them down."

Bea could hear excited whoops and cheers from across the chaparral, maybe two football fields in distance away. She shuddered. "That excuse for a human being can make the most despicable of acts sound like one of the Ten Commandments."

"We have to find Lucy now, before those assholes beats us to her." Heath drummed on the dashboard with nervous fingers.

Bea's heart hardened with determination. Her foot pressed the gas pedal to the floor. "If this damn bomb shelter exists, it can't be much farther."

Atop a low ridge, she spotted the Eden's Gate pickup speeding back toward camp. A high-powered spotlight scanned the roadside.

Bea blew out a long breath, trying to cool her adrenaline rush. "Okay, they must be coming from the shelter. Has to be nearby."

"Are we too late?" Heath whispered; his face twisted in pain.

"The bounty announcement said they don't have her, that means she and Isabella are safe, for now."

"I hope you're right."

Cresting another rise, their vehicle moved down onto a narrow, flat mesa. Nearby to the west, a black hole appeared in the rock face.

"There it is," Bea exclaimed, speeding over tooth-rattling terrain. They braked to a stop in a cloud of grit, parked, and jumped out.

An entry hatch door gaped open into blackness. They approached cautiously.

"The padlock's been broken," Bea observed.

"Going in." Heath reached for his pistol. Bea followed, also armed.

They did a careful search of the concrete interior, dimly lit with a ribbon of LED lights along the floor. Their inspection offered no clue as to where the women might have fled.

Calling Lucy's name repeatedly, Bea garnered no response.

With one final, dire possibility before them, Bea and Heath worked to pull heavy bunkbeds away from a blocked door. When they made it inside the small room, they found a covered well. Dragging off the heavy lid, their flashlights probed the contents of the pit.

"Oh, no," Bea gasped, heart hammering. But as she looked more carefully amid the slithering snakes, she realized it wasn't Lucy at the bottom of the pit, dusky and swollen. "It's Cain," she said.

They hustled from the dank room, down the hall to the entry. "Where the hell is she?" Heath growled in frustration.

Bea said, "I trust Lucy got the hell out of here before Wenter showed up. There's no sign of struggle. She'd never have gone quietly into any damn night."

"That's for sure." Heath kneeled to check out a dark blotch next to the hatch. "What's this?"

"Oh, God, not blood?" Bea shuddered.

He dipped his finger into the liquid, then sniffed it. "Motor oil."

Bea let out a groan of relief. "Maybe they have Cain's dirt bike."

Once outside, they explored the ground with their lights. Heath bent low and said, "Check this out, Bea. I think you're right."

She joined him, looking carefully at the tracks. "Yep, a small motorbike. Took off on this trail above the bunker." She nodded up the hill the bomb shelter was built into.

They followed the tracks on foot, noting that the bike turned to head back toward the barn before its traces disappeared amid the gravel and rocks of the hard ground.

Heath's voice was low and menacing. "A truck couldn't follow this trail. ATVs could. Smart of Wenter to post a bounty, one he's gonna regret, big time,"

"I have a hunch," Bea said. "Lucy's not going to make it easy for us to track her. But my guess is she'll try to get to where we parked, just beyond the barn. She and I used that spot several times before. It's not camp property. She'd figure that if we knew what was going down, we'd come in that way again to try and find her."

"Okay, let's go," Heath said.

They returned to their ATV, then slowly, carefully, drove up the trail trying to follow the route Lucy, Isabella, and her son might have taken toward the parking spot.

The hordes of ATVs continued to move closer. Heavy metal music blasted from afar. Then Bea's attention caught something else.

CHAPTER SIXTY-SEVEN

Lucy was well aware that the three of them, hiking across the open desert, would be easy prey. Isabella was slow, with a hitch in her step. Lucy wondered how that happened, but the question quickly shifted to one of survival. What they needed to do now, until the ATVers became exhausted or drank themselves into temporary oblivion, was hide. But where? The desert flora was thorny and dangerous, perfect camouflage for unfriendly reptiles, scorpions, and spiders ready to defend their territory. It was no easy challenge to conceal their little group.

Then, as their options looked bleak, they literally stumbled into what might be an opportunity. It was a small, humble cemetery. Rotting wooden crosses, gravestones with inscriptions that were sand blasted over the years to bare, rune-like indentations, and unmarked piles of rocks the size of bodies, both big and small. Ironically, here in a neglected graveyard, amongst the dead, they just might find a chance to survive.

"This must be Eden's Gate cemetery and body dumping ground," Lucy said.

Isabella nodded. "Heard it was out here somewhere. Figured this would be where I'd end up."

Amidst the long black shadows, as the moon rose, a harsh swell of sadness filled Lucy's heart. This was likely once a place of loving grief, but tonight, it was a scene of obscene tragedy. They did not want to end their days here beneath a pile of Wenter's bloody gravel.

At the gate they found a shovel leaning against the fence. A smidge of energy sparked Lucy's exhausted brain. "Good, another weapon, much better than the church key and soup can lid." She patted her pocket.

"I still have the hammer." Isabella pulled the tool from her cargo pants. "I think I accidently killed a man with it a few hours ago," she whispered and rubbed her neck. "It was him or me."

Lucy nodded. The thought of Isabella being a murderer made no sense. But all that mattered now was that they lived.

The women sat for a moment on the gritty sand. Asher, worn out, had fallen asleep. Isabella had been carrying him; her face was drawn and weary. She took off her hoodie and laid the boy on top of it.

"What are we going to do?" she asked, her soft voice anguished. "It won't take them long to find this place, and us. Mark always wins."

"Maybe not this time." Lucy rubbed her thumb across the sharp edge of the shovel. "Okay," she said, "I'm grasping at straws here, but I have an idea."

Isabella sat up a little straighter.

"We can at least dig. So, I'm going to dig a hole for you and your son to hide in."

"Bury us?" Isabella's voice was panicky. "How will we breathe?"

"Here's what we'll do—we'll put boards from some of these crosses over the pit and then I'll pile stones on top, so it looks like a grave, like the others." She pointed toward several of the rocky funeral mounds. "But you can easily push out when we have our chance to escape."

Isabella, her hand on her son, said nothing. The wail of Toby Kieth's patriotic country hymns echoed from across the harsh, rolling landscape. Firecrackers popped and Roman candles hissed and exploded.

Lucy sped up the explanation. "Okay, okay, I know it sounds crazy, but I think it could work. You won't be like, really buried; you'll just be under a little roof. Plenty of air. What do you think?"

Isabella's smile was faint but then she said, "I think it sounds pretty clever, actually. And you'll do one for yourself, too."

"Yep. Let's get to work."

Isabella struggled to her feet.

"I see you limp a bit," Lucy said, offering her a hand. Isabella hesitated, then accepted it. "Did you get hurt?"

A narrow cirrus cloud split the moon above like a knife. The woman frowned and looked away.

"I'm sorry, it's none of my business," Lucy said, regretting calling attention to it. "Let's get digging."

Isabella slowly turned back to Lucy, her face a ghostly mask. "When Mark Wenter found out I was pregnant by Cain, he had me shackled in the barn."

"Good Lord," Lucy gasped.

"I gave birth there with that ghoul, May Lou, overseeing. I almost bled to death, like Jaime. The bitch is as much of a midwife as I am, and I can barely pull out a splinter. I think they wanted both me and the baby dead. Or best case, teach me a brutal lesson. Either way, I'm lucky I survived." She rubbed her hip and abdomen. "Cain did a little service and a sacrifice in that room from hell every year, honoring the lucky birth. That's what he was doing before it all blew up."

Like a horror film, the image of the neck yoke, chains, and the bloody mattress streamed in Lucy's mind. The little square of fabric they had the CSI analyze revealed only rabbit blood, but there was obviously much, much more to the story. "Wenter is truly the devil," she said. "We're not going to let him get us."

Lucy shouldered the shovel and Isabella pulled out her hammer.

Just as they began to make headway in the hard soil, Lucy heard the sound of an engine coming close. Her heart pounding, she grabbed Isabella and ducked behind a gravestone. An ATV, its lights out, was stealthily approaching.

CHAPTER SIXTY-EIGHT

Like a wolf pack to prey, bounty hunters stalked through the low hills, totally amped to be in blood pursuit. Bea wondered how much longer she and Heath would have the stolen quad bike before being discovered.

Another half mile along in the darkness, she pointed to an area maybe twenty yards away. "Look at that. What the hell?"

Surrounded by a sagging wrought iron fence was what appeared to be an old graveyard, ashen as dried bones in the tepid moonlight.

"Should we keep going or check it out?" she asked. "We can't waste time." They were now somewhere between the bomb shelter and the barn, with no sign of Lucy. The whine of engines drew ever closer.

"We definitely need to check it out," Heath said, face grim. "They could be buried there for all we know."

Bea sucked in a fast breath. She drove up to the cemetery and stopped the quad along the decrepit fence. They climbed out. Old gravestones stuck up from the earth like drunken playing cards. "This place looks like it's been abandoned for a very long time," Bea said. "The Sheriffs will want to take a good look."

Stepping carefully through the gate, she startled as a lizard skittered into the darkness behind a grave marker. The radio in their rig blasted another encouraging and vile message from Wenter to his posse.

Scanning with a flashlight, Bea said, "Those two rock piles look fresh."

"And looks like someone recently tried to dig a hole over there," Heath added, whispering, as seemed appropriate among the dead. They moved slowly in the direction of the empty, unfinished pit.

Then, a blood-curdling shriek.

A silver slash split the air. Bea saw it coming a second before it crushed her skull. Stumbling backwards over a gravestone, she grabbed her Glock.

The shovel rose and was about to come down again, but Heath tackled the assailant before Bea could pull the trigger.

Another figure held a shadowy instrument high over Heath's head.

Bea aimed her gun and screamed, "Stop or I *will* shoot. Drop it. Now!"

A child cried out. The attacker released the tool and ran to the plaintive sound.

"Isabella?" Bea gasped, lowering her gun.

"Yes! It's me."

"And Lucy!" Heath quickly recognized the shovel-swinging maniac he had slammed to the ground. "Thank, God." The bloody tension in their bodies eased. Their arms encircled each other for a moment.

Bea holstered her firearm. "Are any of you hurt? Holy Jesus and Mary, that was a close call."

"We're okay," Lucy said, breathless. "Insanely happy to see you guys." Heath helped her up. She grabbed Bea in a grateful hug, then her eyes went back to Heath. "Where is Henry? Is he safe? Grace? And Jaime?"

"They're fine. With my parents," he said.

Lucy choked back tears. "How'd you find us?"

Before a response could be given, a half dozen ATVs, headlights bouncing over the landscape like pinballs, crested the ridge above the cemetery.

"Fuckin-ay! There they are," someone shouted.

"Let's go." Heath grabbed Lucy and Isabella, who carried Asher, now crying.

They jumped into the quad and tore out toward the barn.

Bea drove fast, but not fast enough. A bullet whizzed by her ear.

Heath pulled his weapon and leaned out, returning fire. Bea handed her Glock to Lucy, who was in the rear with Isabella and Asher.

"You two, get on the floor," Lucy ordered.

A side-by-side ATV with two passengers began to close in on them. Lucy lay on her belly across the two back seats and readied for a shot at the marauding vehicle's tire wall.

Bang, Bang!

Bea glanced back as Lucy made the hit. The tire exploded. The rig disappeared into the darkness, its passengers screaming curses.

'Oh, yeah," Lucy shouted.

Another ATV kept pace and pulled tight next to them. Sand sprayed, stinging Bea's face. In the rear view, she spotted Isabella clamber up at Lucy's side.

In an instant, the marauding ATV's wingman, a big brute dressed in a camo jumpsuit with a confederate flag headband, leaped from his seat across at Lucy, brandishing a hunting knife. Isabella threw her hammer, hitting him squarely in his leering face. The guy squealed, lost his grip and flew off. Only his rancid whiskey breath lingered.

"This is insane," Bea shouted. Her eyes scanned the terrain, they were almost to the barn. Could they make it to her car before they were picked off? A bullet shattered the windshield.

"Don't hurt the kid," someone yelled.

Sounded to Bea like they were all fair game but Asher. The threat of accidentally hitting the child might protect them, but not by much. These dudes were too wasted to know who they were shooting at.

Three quads pulled in behind them. More gunshots. Heath returned fire, hitting a driver.

Bea careened ahead toward a rocky outcropping bordering the old corral and the barn. It looked like an obsidian dragon's spine rising from the earth. Over and behind it was a deep ravine. Then, she got an idea. It was dangerous, maybe homicidal, but could be their only chance.

Rounds popped back and forth. She heard the distant staccato blast of an AK draw closer. Where did these assholes get all these guns?

Heath leaned out and returned fire again. Another ATV peeled off from the chase and crashed, headlight beams flying skyward. Two down but more joined in the chase.

Bea sped toward the rock wall ahead.

"You're gonna kill us," Heath yelled.

"I know what I'm doing," she shouted. "Hold on, everybody," "Hold the hell on! Now!"

With yet another gang of ATV's closing in, pedal to the metal, Bea bore down on the shadowy outcropping before her. It rose ahead, fast. Faster. Rock music blared. Isabella shrieked. At the last second before impact, Bea hung a hard right and skidded around the jagged formation, scraping the edge, but their quad stayed upright.

The lead ATV behind them, unable to veer away in time, crashed full force into the rock wall, flipping over onto the rig next to it. Other ATVs followed the leader, slamming into the scrambled mess, plunging over the outcropping and into the ravine. Screams rent the air.

"Holy hell," Heath yelled. "Way to go, road warrior."

Bea accelerated past the corral and up the animal trail behind the barn. Her SUV was in sight. Breaking to a screeching stop, they scrambled from the ATV and piled into the car. Lucy climbed in back with Isabella and Asher.

Bea powered up and sped down the dirt road heading toward the freeway. In the rearview mirror, a gaggle of ATVs stopped, circled, then finally their headlights turned away.

With a deep sigh of relief, Lucy leaned between the front seats.

"You two saved us. You're unbelievable." Lucy pressed her hands onto Bea and Heath's shoulders.

He winced.

Lucy's hand came back covered in blood.

CHAPTER SIXTY-NINE

Lucy stammered, "You been shot." The moment of feeling safe was obliterated.

Heath looked at his arm, as if he was aware of his blood-soaked shirt for the first time.

"Oh, shit," Bea said. She handed her phone to Lucy. "Call an ambo. We'll meet them at the camp's front gate. Pete's there. Call him, too. Let him know we got y'all and that Heath needs medical—STAT."

Face pale, Heath pulled off his shirt to examine the injury. He gritted his teeth as he probed the wound.

Lucy dialed 9-1-1 with shaky fingers, waiting an eternity for someone to answer. Struggling not to hyperventilate, she explained the situation and gave the dispatcher the rendezvous spot, along with Pete's direct line.

Next, she called the detective. He answered immediately. "Bea, where the hell are you?"

"It's Lucy."

"Luce! You okay? What's going on? Been worried shitless. Is Bea..."

"She's safe. We're safe in the car with Isabella and her son. Bea's driving. Coming in hot. Heath's been shot. Those ATVers tried to take us all out. Give Bea a steel mini-dress and she could've out-Tina'd Tina Turner in Thunderdome. Saved our butts."

Pete growled. "Lord, have mercy." She heard his name shouted in the background. "Wait, just a sec, Luce." He had a quick conversation and issued orders to someone nearby. "Okay, I'm back. Heath bad?"

"He's bleeding a lot. I'm trying not to freak out," she said, remembering what happened with Jaime. "I called an ambo—should be arriving at the camp's front gate any time. Our ETA's about ten minutes. A few of those Tennessee boys gonna need some medical attention back by the barn, too."

"We'll get to them when it's safe for the EMTs. For now, I got the warrants, backup, SWAT. We found out about the bounty, got hold of the radio and canceled it. Now we're dealing with a bunch of pissed off drunks, and some of these asswipes are even shooting here at camp."

"I heard what I swear was an assault rifle out there," Lucy said.

"Not a shocker. I found a goddamn bump stock on a Spider-Man air mattress floating in the pool. Some of these big-mouth idiots want to turn this into a bullshit confrontation. Wanna be on TV. Not gonna happen."

Lucy heard the sound of sirens through the phone.

"The bus is here," Pete said. "So fuckin' glad you're safe." Background chatter was growing louder. "Gotta boogie," he said. "Shit going down. And I have a call coming in from Heath's old man. Lemme take it." He disconnected.

Lucy wondered what a call from Old Doc could mean.

Bea pulled onto the camp's gravel drive skidding to a stop next to the ambulance. The area looked like a battle zone. The smell of gunpowder and spent fireworks floated in the unsettled air.

"This way," Bea said, hustling the emergency folks to her car where Lucy was helping Heath out of the front seat.

"I'm okay, I think it's just a through-and-through," Heath said to a young, dark-skinned man with an Army medic patch on his uniform.

"We'll assess it," the medic said.

"He was Marines Special Ops Medical," Lucy said, wanting to let them know that they had someone who knew what he was talking about.

The medic smiled. "They're the worst patients."

"I'll go with you," Lucy said to Heath.

"No, Lucy. Get the kids from the clinic. Take 'em to my place. Make sure they're okay. Please." His face was drawn and pleading

Lucy tried not to let her fear for him overwhelm her. "Yes, okay. I'll call you as soon as I pick them up."

"Great, thank you. And I'm fine. Just a scratch. Don't worry."

"Roger that." Lucy kissed his cheek, then worried like hell as they loaded him into the ambulance. She stood in the drive, watching, as it sped away, sirens wailing.

"Girl, come over here," Bea said, handing her friend an energy bar and a bottle of Gatorade. "Have something to eat. You look like you're gonna faint."

Lucy tore into the food, realizing she was shaking and starved. "Can I have another bar?" she asked. Bea gave her two.

Isabella and her son sat in the back of a cruiser, also chowing down. Pete came jogging in their direction. Locks of his dark hair hung wild, looking like Elvis at the end of a steamy performance. He gave Bea and Lucy quick hugs. Before he could say anything, his radio crackled out a message, "Six of the men, armed, have taken over a cottage. Ten women and three kids inside with them."

"Fuck." He began to pace. "Treat it as another hostage situation," he ordered. "Call the Lieut and have her set up tactics. I'm on my way."

"*Another* hostage situation?" Bea asked.

Pete took a deep breath. "I just got a call from Doctor Sinclair, senior."

"What is it, Pete?" Lucy demanded.

He took a deep breath. "Henry and Jaime are gone."

"Gone?" Whatever fear Lucy had felt before, this was worse.

"What happened? Where are they?" Bea pressed. She took Lucy's hand.

Pete said, "Old Doc and his wife were taking Jaime and Henry into the patient waiting room to use the facilities, when Mark Wenter came out of the can with a gun. Dude locked the front door to the clinic and made Doc and his wife take them out the back. Doc refused but Mark threatened to shoot his wife. That dickwad Cooter had an assault rifle. They grabbed Jaime and Henry, loaded them in a gray panel van, and took off."

"Plate number?" Bea asked.

"No plates." Pete's radio cracked with comms from the hostage negotiation team. The situation was heating up. He answered their questions then turned back to Bea and Lucy. "We have good people on it. Liaising with Ventura County PD."

Lucy nodded, strangled with terror.

"I'll join them as soon I can get this mess under control and hand it off." Pete nodded at Lucy, "We'll get Henry and Jaime, tonight, safe and sound. I promise." He hustled toward the cottage under siege.

"Where in God's name, could that monster. Wenter, have taken them? Tears rolled down Lucy's cheeks.

Isabella, who had been listening to their conversation, joined them and said, "I think if you could find the Eden's Gate lawyer, you might find Mark. I don't think the guy has an office; he's retired and works from home. At least that's what I remember Mark saying."

"You know where this lawyer lives?" Lucy asked.

"No, sorry."

Bea laughed without mirth. "I know where the sonofabitch lives." Face grim, she grabbed Lucy's hand. "Let's pay him a visit."

CHAPTER SEVENTY

B ea sped north along Highway 23 on the way to Santa Paula, a small, primarily Hispanic town with the title, "Citrus Capitol of the World." Traffic was light. "We should be there in about forty minutes," Lucy said, examining the GPS on Bea's phone. Her own was probably still on the floor back at the ranch, spattered with Jaime's blood.

"In seven miles, turn onto 126 west to Main Steet," Lucy said. "We go through town to the east side and hit *Huerto de Limones* Canyon Road and follow it to the very end. On satellite view, looks like the lawyer's place is in the middle of a huge acreage, all groves. Nothing else close by. The house is maybe a mile in from the main road. One way in and out."

"How should we approach this?" Bea asked. "Security's gotta be tight."

"Who knows. The lawyer must be in his late nineties. Likely not tech savvy. And Mark probably figures nobody knows anything about this place. If it wasn't for Heath's dad remembering a random address file from decades ago, we'd have no clue either."

Bea nodded. "We have to assume the worst-case scenario, though. Like camera's everywhere." She paused in thought. "You think the lawyer's still alive?"

Lucy shrugged. "Jaime said he made that woman Tanya Lee's passports, so he must still be around."

"We probably should wait for the Ventura P.D." Lucy said. She massaged her neck; it felt like a steel beam.

"But we won't," Bea glanced over at Lucy, her friend's face cast greenish in the glow from the dash. "Too much at stake."

"Yeah, like everything."

The dark rural countryside sped by, punctuated by yard and porch lights from passing farms and ranches. When they hit the outskirts of Santa Paula, they had little trouble finding the road they were seeking. In the middle of nowhere, and dark as crow feathers, the air was scented with orange and lemon blossoms. It was heavenly. Lucy breathed deeply to try and settle her nerves. She couldn't save her son if she was acting out of panic mode.

She double checked the GPS. "There's the turn-off."

Bea drove the narrow, pot-holed five-mile stretch through the canyon. Near the end, she pulled the car to the side of an agricultural drainage ditch and stopped. "How far ahead is the house from here?"

Lucy checked the SAT map again. "About a mile. On foot, we can walk through the orchard and stay off the main drive."

"Sounds like a plan," Bea said. She pulled farther away from the road, then turned off the ignition and doused the lights. They exited the car. Bea checked her gear and handed Lucy an extra flashlight.

Standing still for a moment, Lucy heard only crickets, cicadas, and the ticking sound of the warm engine beginning to cool. In the near silence, sharp pecks of fear ripped at her heart. She shuddered. "Bea. What if..."

"Stop," Bea whispered into the thick blanket of darkness. "We both know anything can happen in life. We do our best, we risk, we try, we love. The rest in life is a crapshoot. But tonight, our odds are decent. We're smart, resourceful, got the element of surprise, and we're motivated as hell."

Lucy nodded and gave her friend a long hug. They turned and entered the fragrant lemon grove together. The contrast between the sweet blossoms and the stench of Wenter's evil was ironic.

—

Attorney at Law, Sean Sinclair, Esquire, sat at a wide oak desk, finishing up Mark Wenter's new passport. Completely bald except for wiry gray hairs sprouting from his nose and ears, the old man wore a head gear of magnifying glasses and pin lights. He looked like a steampunk Ebeneezer Scrooge, dressed in a leather apron over a slightly threadbare white shirt and red bowtie. A row of scalpels, scissors, glue, paper, embossed covers, and an array of magnifying glasses, lined the desk. It all said 'old school' but effective.

Across from the desk, Mark Wenter sat on an antique, emerald green velvet couch, working on his laptop. Jaime, secured with duct tape, slumped next to him. The room was an oak-lined library with a classic design common in the Victorian era. In the background, *I'll Be Seeing You*, a poignant World War II standard sung by Bing Crosby, played on a Victrola turntable.

Henry was sound asleep on a loveseat near French doors, opening to rear gardens.

The yard and outbuildings were quiet.

"Thank you for bringing me a new wife," the old man croaked at Mark. "Fine payment." He winked at Jaime, his eye resembling a giant egg yolk through the magnifier. "Those blue pills are very effective, even at my advanced age." He licked his non-existent lips.

Jaime groaned beneath her duct-taped mouth. The two men snickered.

"Are you almost done, old man?" Mark asked. "My plane leaves from Burbank in three hours."

"Finito." The lawyer snapped the navy-blue passport cover shut. He handed it across to Mark. Checking the document carefully, Mark nodded. "Very nice. You're a true craftsman."

From a crystal decanter, Sinclair poured them both a finger of scotch. His hand was remarkably steady for someone well into his nineties.

"Thank you, sir," Mark said, then turned to glare at Jaime. "Cooter's taking everyone to Tennessee tomorrow, including the boy. He's mine now."

Jaime whimpered. Her mouth was sealed in duct tape.

"And you don't think the police will bother me?" The old man pulled the magnifying apparatus off his head.

"You are off the grid, as they say, living in a time warp. But if the gendarmes do show up, feign dementia," Mark said, smiling.

"Ha! Easy to do. But seriously, my young pastor, I'm sure they found my name on the Vega woman's documents."

"Yeah, but this place has never been linked to Sean Sinclair. You and my father covered every angle. You're a ghost, old man, and Citrus Canyon Ranch is a ghost ship in a sea of lemons. And I just sold it."

"What?" Sinclair rasped. His wild brows gathered into a single gash above his eyes.

Mark chuckled. "The money's already in an offshore account."

Cooter, who'd been lurking just inside the French doors, slinked toward the desk with a throw pillow in his hands. He grabbed the old man from behind and stuffed it into his pasty face. Sinclair struggled hard, flapping like a fish out of water.

Jaime shrank in horror.

Henry stirred, but didn't wake.

Cooter pressed the pillow ever tighter, smothering the lawyer. When the man stilled, Cooter finally let go and stepped back. From his desk chair, Sinclair fell sideways onto the floor.

Mark took a quick look at the man and shrugged. "Okay, Coot, well done. When somebody eventually finds him, it'll look like he died naturally."

"Easy peasy." Cooter grinned and tossed the pillow into Jaime's lap. She recoiled like she'd been bitten by one of Mark's serpents.

He laughed.

"Let's have a drink, have the whore, and then you can drop me off at the airport and head south with her and the kid." Mark pushed one of the whiskeys the old man had poured toward Cooter. "To the bounty of the Lord raining upon us." They raised their glasses and drank.

CHAPTER SEVENTY-ONE

Bea and Lucy crouched in the darkness at the edge of the tree line in sight of the house, a barn, and several smaller out buildings. All was quiet. A gray panel van was parked in front of a stunning 1920s Victorian-style house, an era Santa Paula was known for. Hot pink roses climbed on trellises against its walls and broad porch. The whole scene would have seemed idyllic if Lucy and Bea hadn't known what was likely going on inside.

The women carefully scanned the area for cameras, spotting one above the barn and another on a light post near the house.

"Like you thought might be the case, a little thin on the digital security," Bea said.

"Must think they're pretty safe out here."

"They are, or were, 'til we arrived."

A figure in dark clothing emerged from one of the smaller buildings, a dog at his heels.

Bea pressed Lucy's arm and whispered, "So, likely we have the old man, Mark, Cooter, at least one guard, and a dog. Let's circle around behind the house."

Stealthily, they retreated into the trees. The dog raised its head and sniffed the air. The women froze.

The man stopped and perused the area. An owl hooted. Satisfied the disturbance in the atmosphere was caused by the night bird, he proceeded toward the barn, a flashlight raking the ground.

When the guard and the dog disappeared inside, Lucy and Bea edged through the grove to the far side of the house.

"Always liked owls," Bea whispered in Lucy's ear. It hooted again. "Sign of good luck."

"But some say they're messengers of witches."

"We are the witches," Bea mouthed back.

Lucy smiled, drawing a bit of comfort from her friend's audacious self-confidence. They both knew it was bluster, but sometimes sounding good is good enough.

Eyes riveted on the house, they crept toward the back yard which was enclosed in a fence ringed on the inside with roses, hibiscus, and toxic oleander. Lots of it. Solar garden lanterns lined a short walk. They kneeled low. Warm illumination poured from open French doors into the cool night.

That's when Lucy spotted Henry, asleep on a small couch. She gasped. Bea immediately slid a hand over Lucy's mouth, holding tight until Lucy calmed. When she let go, Bea hissed, "You have to stay in control, or we're gonna lose him. Do you understand?"

Lucy nodded. Bea pointed to the big doors off of what appeared to be a library or study. They crawled closer to get a better view.

Along with Henry, Jaime slouched, taped up, on another couch across from a broad desk where Cooter perched on the edge, a gun stuffed in his waistband. Mark stood at the far end of the room, taking something out of a wall safe and stashing it in a canvas bag. An old man, unconscious, or maybe dead, lay on the floor between the French doors and the desk.

"Gonna text Pete," Bea mouthed. After several quick tries, she shook her head. No cell service.

As she stashed her phone, the crunch of light footsteps in dried leaves was followed by a low, menacing growl. The young Doberman crouched near a tree stump only yards away. It growled again.

"Stay still," Lucy whispered to Bea. "Don't give it any excuse to go after us. No eye contact if it gets closer."

"I hope the dog can't smell our fear," Bea muttered.

Lucy fumbled in her pocket for remnants of an energy bar Bea had given her.

The canine didn't move, body tense, it watched, carefully assessing the threat.

Lucy broke a bit of the bar and tossed it toward the dog. The pup hesitated, sniffed it, then went after the treat, chomping it down and moving in closer. Lucy threw another piece of the bar. This time the dog went for it more quickly. Lucy repeated the task two more times until there was only a small bit of the treat remaining.

The dog slinked slowly up to them. Lucy held her breath and released the last morsel, holding it in her palm. The dog took it. Lying down between Lucy and Bea, the pink-collared female dobie smacked her doggie lips.

"This isn't a guard dog," Lucy said. "This is a family pet." She gave the pup a belly rub and got a lick to the fingers in reply. "You are such a good girl," Lucy whispered to the dog.

"Paloma!" A strident, gravelly voice hollered from near the French doors. The dog's ears perked up. She rose and scurried along the fence to an open garden gate. Dressed in black, it was likely the guard who entered the barn with the dog earlier. He pulled off a dark cap revealing messy gray hair in a bun.

To Lucy and Bea's surprise, the guard was a middle-aged woman.

The dog bounded inside, went to the downed body, whined and began to pace. The woman kicked the dog away, then stepped outside and scanned the dark shrubbery. After a long moment, apparently satisfied, she went back inside, leaving the doors ajar behind her.

Bea finally let the air hiss from her lungs. "Could that be May Lou, demon midwife?"

"Kicking the dog? Same sweet, empathetic behavior as described by Jaime and Isabella. Must be her." Lucy grabbed Bea's hand and pulled her again into the shadowy lemon trees. "What now?"

They huddled in the darkness. The distant sound of a helicopter interrupted the night. "Ventura County Sheriffs?" Bea asked.

"Don't' count on it," Lucy said.

Bea tried to reach Pete again. Nothing. Minutes crawled by. Then, the lights in the library went off.

CHAPTER SEVENTY-TWO

"They're leaving," Lucy said. "We gotta move."
Abandoning the cover of the orchard, the women crept along the fence to the garden gate and ducked inside the yard. They headed for the French doors, backs pressed against the house's exterior clapboard wall. Bea steadied her Glock and bent to peek through the window. All was dark and quiet. They crept forward and stepped inside.

Then a sound. Lucy froze.

Click.

A hammer pulled and ready. Icy fear needled her skin.

The lights snapped on. Lucy's eyes dazzled for an instant.

"Drop it or I shoot your friend right here, in front of her kid," Cooter growled at Bea.

She dropped the gun.

Lucy gasped. Henry was huddled across the room on the couch with Jaime. The young woman's mouth looked red and raw where tape had recently been ripped off.

Mark and May Lou stood on the far side of the big desk. Like a black, soulless sylph, May Lou hustled forward and booted

Bea's gun away. It landed near the old man, the lawyer Sinclair, lying dead on the floor.

Whining, his Doberman had been crated.

Lucy thought she saw the man's eyes flicker beneath thatched brows. But post-mortem motion was not unusual. Ready to fly apart, Lucy took a deep breath, trying to steady herself.

"Mommy!" Henry jumped from the couch and darted across the room. He threw himself into his mother's arms. Love and terror squeezed her throat.

"Just give us Henry and Jaime," Bea said. "And you three assholes can go on your merry way." She sounded more-angry-and-impatient than afraid. Lucy knew better.

Mark sneered. "Jaime and the kid are coming with me. I want hostages."

"They're not going anywhere." Lucy took a step toward Wenter. Bea grabbed her arm.

Mark zipped closed a canvas bag bulging with cash. "Cooter, shoot the mouthy whores." He glowered at the women. "Jaime, get the brat."

Jaime remained unmoving.

"Stop fucking with me, Jaime!" Mark's voice crackled with mania as he glared at his former Chosen One. "Do it. Or you'll join her in judgement!"

Lucy squeezed Henry closer. At that same moment, she saw the lawyer's bony fingers, skin yellow and translucent, crab slowly toward Bea's gun. Barely moving, Sinclair was alive.

Jaime stumbled across the room, eyes flitting like a caged animal with nowhere to flee. Weeping, she pulled her brother, screaming, from his mother's arms. Lucy tried to offer him reassurance that wasn't there.

Bea growled. "You'll roast in hell for this." Her dark eyes spewed fire.

Cooter looked spooked for an instant as he took aim at Bea. *Bang.*

Cooter dropped. His pistol flew sideways.

Lucy gasped. The old man had managed to snatch Bea's gun. The burning, sulphureous smell of a discharged weapon choked the room.

"You've gone too far, young pastor," he croaked. "Too far." He pressed his gnarled hands to his chest. The Glock slipped away. With a last rattling breath, he went limp, his eyes still open but vacant.

Bea pounced, wresting her weapon from the man's dead fingers.

At the same instant, Mark grabbed Cooter's pistol where it lay in a growing pool of blood.

Bea framed Mark's head in her weapon's sights. May Lou shrieked and ran from the room. Mark followed, grabbing Jaime and Henry as shields.

Bea and Lucy dashed after them, but Bea couldn't get a good fix on Mark without putting Henry and Jaime at risk.

Mark dragged his two panicked captives out and into the yard. He shoved them into the gray panel van still parked in front of the house then took the wheel. May Lou crawled in beside him, carrying what was probably the basket of snakes Jaime had described. The door locks thunked.

Overhead, a chopper circled. Lucy could feel the vibration pounding like a heartbeat. A searchlight strafed the house and grounds, turning the darkness white. She waved her arms frantically.

A loudspeaker sounded. "Mark Wenter, step out of the vehicle with your hand's up."

There was no response.

The order was repeated several times. Still nothing.

A Ventura County Sheriff's armored tactical rescue vehicle pulled across the entry to the compound, disgorging a weapons team and blocking escape down the main drive. Cruisers, lights flashing, backed them up.

Lucy's anxiety hummed like hornets ready to swarm. "Why

is he just sitting there in the van? What is he doing?"

"Maybe strategizing," Bea said.

The speaker in the hovering chopper called out to Wenter one last time, then turned and sped away. Shadowy figures pulsing red and blue, the on-ground SWAT crew moved in closer. A hostage negotiator tried to coax Mark from the van, to no avail.

An hour passed.

Bea and Lucy were still hunkered outside on Sinclair's front porch, several yards behind the panel van's double rear doors.

"I got through to Pete," Bea whispered. "Texted him what happened inside the house, including the two dead bodies. They're calling crime scene and medics. I confirmed that Mark is armed and has May Lou, Jaime, and Henry."

Then Pete's voice came over a bullhorn. A flicker of hope glinted amid Lucy's dark thoughts and the two women briefly hugged.

"Looks like Pete convinced Ventura County that his familiarity with the assholes would give him an edge," Bea said.

But Wenter refused to engage.

Pete came on the loudspeaker once more, refusing to let the negotiations come to a standstill. "So, Mark, one of the witnesses just told me there are two dead victims inside the house. Sounds like your man Cooter and the lawyer took each other out. You won't be charged with their murder. You can be glad of that, right?"

Pete let that sink in for a couple minutes, then continued.

"And if you let Jaime and Henry go, right now, you may live to see your Eden's Gate Community thrive again. And May Lou, I know you were just trying to do your best to support the young pastor, your brother, just like Jaime is trying to do with little Henry. Right?"

Lucy looked at Bea. "Confirms they're related, but I think Mark's her son."

Pete's voice grew more patient. "You're family. I get it. But this is a losing situation, May Lou. If you go along with Mark and don't turn yourself in, you'll be charged with aiding and abetting, at least. Think about it, ma'am. You've made some bad choices, but it's not too late. What do you want? Life in prison without parole? Or a chance at redemption?"

Bea texted Pete with something he might be able to use.

He came back on the loudspeaker, voice affable. "May Lou, you're a God-fearing woman and I'm sure you know John 1:9. It says, *If we confess our sins, he is faithful and just to forgive us and to cleanse us from all unrighteousness.* Isn't that what you really want?"

Lucy heard raised voices from within the panel van. Arguing. She and Bea's eyes met. Was something about to happen? Adrenalin rose in her veins.

The van's ignition roared. The vehicle lurched backwards, almost running them over. Then it turned, accelerating into the grove.

"No!" Lucy shrieked. She sprinted after the vehicle. As it veered through the narrow, bumpy lanes between lemon trees, the van hit a pothole. The back door kicked open. May Lou and Jaime tumbled out, crashing against a tree trunk, stunned. The police were all over them in seconds.

Lucy raced ahead, heart pounding. This could be her only chance at saving her son. She caught up with the van as it skidded through piles of crates and harvesting ladders.

In a split second, she grabbed one of the open, swinging rear doors and clambered into the van. Crawling to the front of the jerking vehicle, she snatched Henry by the shirt. He was limp, maybe drugged.

Mark accelerated, weaving between the trees. Branches raked the vehicle like nails on steel. He pointed Cooter's gun over his shoulder and fired at Lucy, missing by an inch.

Screaming, Lucy ducked low, sheltering Henry. Abject rage took over. On the floor behind the driver's seat, inches from her face, was retribution.

The basket. Grabbing it, she wrenched off the lid and hurled it onto Mark's lap. Cursing, he slammed on the brakes. Lucy crashed forward, then rebounded backward, colliding painfully against the edge of a metal rack.

Wenter accelerated again. Grabbing Henry, Lucy stumbled the length of the van and leaped out the back door. Her last vision of Pastor Mark Wenter was of snakes writhing in his hair like Medusa.

Protecting her son from the impact, Lucy hit the ground hard. She gasped for air.

Seconds after they landed, Bea was at their side. "You okay?"

Lucy nodded, panting. "Let them cops know there are rattlers loose inside the van. A bunch of them."

Bea texted Pete with the information. Then, grabbing Lucy's hand, she said, "Let's get you both to the medics. Come on!"

The SWAT team stampeded after the zig-zagging van. The chopper's hot beam lit up the grove. Lemons glowed silver like Christmas ornaments on the gnarly limbs. Mark finally lost control of the vehicle, smashing full into a police cruiser in his path. The tactical unit swarmed the van, Pete was in their midst.

Bea helped Lucy stand. They staggered through the grove, Henry, eyes blinking open, was in Lucy's arms. At the ambo, Jaime lay wrapped in a blanket, as May Lou was loaded into the back of a cruiser.

A paramedic immediately took Henry and checked his vitals. Lucy refused to let go of his sweet, cold hand.

"Heartbeat's strong," the tech said.

Lucy cried with relief as they administered oxygen.

Lucy heard Mark Wenter shrieking in pain and calling to God for mercy he didn't deserve. She watched the monster as he was hauled into another ambulance and cufffed to a gurney.

What else did she see in the chaotic din? "Am I hallucinating or is Heath's truck really parked between the ambos?" Lucy asked Bea who stood next to her.

Bea smiled. "It's definitely that vet you seem to be so hot for. He's got your back, kiddo."

"Yes, he does." Relief, gratitude, and yes, love, flooded her heart. Arm bandaged, and in a sling, Heath was being helped by a med tech to load up a syringe of anti-venom to save Mark Wenter's horrid life.

AFTERWORD

The Bea Middleton and Lucy Vega Series
Book 6

As the series draws to an end, the following provides a bit more information on what has come about with Beatrice Middleton, Lucia Vega, their friends, and family. The theme of family and the many forms that can take is always in the forefront.

When the series began with the book *Deadly Focus*, Bea had just lost her job as an on-camera reporter at a major Los Angeles television station due to a buyout. From there she moved to cable network news. But she has had enough of the corporate world and is putting her energies into her own personal passion—an online indy news venture. This journalist-founded nonprofit outlet won a major national award for the Eden's Gate story along with a 1.4 million-dollar grant from the Foundation for Independent Regional Journalism.

As of this final book, Bea has also largely accepted that she has raised children who are much like her—irritatingly independent and smart with hearts of gold, who will live their lives often coloring outside the lines. Alyssa is back from dance camp with a girlfriend lover. Dexter has taken a freelance reporting gig in the Ukraine with his Iraqi-American NGO administrator girlfriend. Rio, Bea's brother/crush, and his wife have divorced. Michael Burleson and Rio's ex are a couple, living the exciting, dangerous lives of correspondents in the volatile Middle East.

Homicide Detective Pete Anthony is always worried about what peril his investigative journalist wife, Beatrice, (yup, they got hitched—Bea hopes the third time's the charm) will get herself into. She worries the same thing right back at him. He's been promoted to lieutenant and doesn't like the paperwork. Might be regretting the advancement. His happy place is nailing criminals, cooking up a tasty remoulade, enjoying his kids, and making love to his wife. What more could a man want?

Lucy and Heath are living together at Lucy's *Rancho de la Vega* in the Santa Moncia Mountains above Malibu. Heath's ex-wife temporarily called off her child custody suit because she landed a prestigious job in Paris. But the issue will likely raise its nasty head again.

For now, and now is all anyone really has, life is good with Lucy, Henry, Heath, his daughter Grace, and all their beloved critters. The lawyer Sinclair's Dobie, Paloma, is now a beloved part of the canine pack at the ranch.

Lucy, orphaned from early on, is no longer wracked with survivor's guilt that plagued her in earlier books in the series, but has accepted that she lived for a reason. She's going to always honor her wonderfully quirky Mexican-Norwegian heritage by living her best life. She reprinted all of the portraits what were ruined in the gallery show break-in and delivered them to The Getty Center for Photography.

Bea has asked Lucy to work with her as photog on her next

major indy news project—hazing on an elite firefighting squad. Clearly, the two women are not slowing down.

Elsa, in her 80s, who helped raise Lucy, returned to her home country of Norway for the summer and was not featured in Book 6. She has decided to remain in Scandinavia due to many friends and family, plus the excellent free healthcare and senior support programs. Lucy and Henry will be visiting her next summer in Oslo.

Jaime is living at the ranch in the apartment over the barn where her father once stayed. Communication with her family has opened up significantly. She has committed to therapy and to finishing her degree—she's thinking Criminal Justice, at nearby Cal State Channel Islands. She was a key witness in the Eden's Gate trial and narrowly avoided being charged with obstruction.

Cody is back from one of several film shoots he booked as the equestrian stuntman over the last year. He and Jaime often go horseback riding in the mountains with Odin and Cody's new chestnut mare, Traverse. Now in the money with several other gigs lined up, he's renting Heath Sinclair's house in Old Agoura.

Mark and May Lou were charged with fraud, kidnapping, child endangerment, sexual assault, and murder. Mark barely survived the multiple snake bites.

Isabella and her son Asher are working with social services to start a new life. Lucy and Bea are helping to support the two.

Tanya Lee Riggs is in the wind.

At Folsom prison, Mark watched an award-winning Middle Eastern pornie and recognized a familiar face and body parts...

And life goes on.

ACKNOWLEDGMENTS

Deep appreciation to the Rocky Mountain Fiction Writers and my amazing Littleton, Colorado critique group including Mindy McIntyre, Rick Duffy, Susan Schooleman, Kathy Reynolds, Cathy Clark, Dallas Jomes, Tom Farrell, Marla Bell, Bill Brinn, Jim Morris and other smart, kind, wonderful folks over the years. All amazing writers, mentors, and colleagues. I am so blessed.

Always thanks to my dear Sonja Massey, aka G.A. McKevett, https://www.gamckevett.com/, Sigrid Orlet at https://sigridorletstudio.weebly.com, and Gaye Lucas for getting me started way back when.

Kudos to my amazing beta readers on this one: musician/composer Peter Tavalin, master gardener/editor/bookophile Carolyn B. Olson Adams, and political agitator/writer and college administrator Det. Marlene Simon.

Sincere gratitude to Susie Brooks, publisher and Editor-in-Chief at Literary Wanderlust. It's a privilege to be part of this great indie team.

Props to my husband, Alan Klein, who's been patiently watching me disappear into reading and writing for years. Thank you for the love and support from my daughter Lacey, her husband Michael, and my four-year-old granddaughters, Lillian and Paige who already love a good book.

To my readers, I love you all and am grateful for the time you have spent with the characters in this series. Hopefully, more new characters and adventures to come!

Be well,

Sue

www.suehinkin.com

ABOUT THE AUTHOR

Sue Hinkin is the author of the award-winning thriller series, The Vega & Middleton Novels, featuring the investigative team of Los Angeles TV news journalist Bea Jackson and best friend, photojournalist Lucy Vega. BestThrillers.com called Lucy and Bea one of the top 10 female detectives of 2023. A former Cinematography Fellow at the American Film Institute, Hinkin has worked in higher education and as one of the earliest female TV news photographers. Now living in Colorado, she was voted Rocky Mountain Fiction Writer's Writer of the Year. She is active in that organization as well as Sisters in Crime, and the Rocky Mountain Chapter of Mystery Writers of America. She loves her friends and family, growing things, and long walks with her puffy white rescue dog, Harley.

www.ingramcontent.com/pod-product-compliance
Lightning Source LLC
Chambersburg PA
CBHW061632190726
48289CB00006B/1580